BURN, DO NOT READ!

A NOVEL BY

KEVIN FLANDERS

KEVIN FLANDERS

BURN, DO NOT READ!

ACKNOWLEDGEMENTS

Every character in every book is born in darkness. Far too many of our would-be literary heroes live forever that way, unknown and searching for a light to shine upon their stories.

Thanks to the tremendous efforts and assistance of the following individuals, as well as the constant support of readers, I am blessed to know that my characters have found the light.

Brian Allenberg
Michael Flanders
Susana Flanders
Ed Londergan
Cheryl Malandrinos
Brandi McCann
Kimmy Palmucci
Olivia Richman

ALSO FROM KEVIN FLANDERS

Please check out the following novels to be released by the author in 2016.

WELCOME TO HARROW HALL
Jan. 2016

INSIDE THE ORANGE GLOW
Feb. 2016

LASER TAG
Feb. 2016

THE INHABITANTS (trilogy)
Mar.-Apr. 2016

GRIDLOCKED
Apr. 2016

For more information about upcoming works, visit
www.kmflanders.wordpress.com.

BURN, DO NOT READ!

Part I: Unwelcome Morning

Chapter I

What a terrible day.

It hasn't contained more minutes than any other day, yet it seems to have stretched on for a week, protracted by every shock and subtlety. How did it even begin?

The fog, that's right.

The fog was thick and rebuking this morning, spreading its gloomy cloak over Grandpa Jack's funeral but also casting a pall of criticism over many of the attendees, myself included. Knowing what we'd done - or, more accurately, what we hadn't done - the weather seemed undeniably fitting, a somber morning for a family that let its patriarch fade into obscurity, only the sharp black and gray of guilt and grief to knife at our hearts as the people from Grandpa's new life spoke highly of him, each of them dressed in black and nearly swallowed in gray.

Their praises were to be expected. Grandpa was an honest, hard-working man who once told me the wealthiest folks are those enriched by family and friendship. But some of Grandpa's friends mentioned strange things to us at the reception this afternoon. They hadn't seen him around town in over a week. He'd missed his last three chess club meetings. He hadn't brought his dog Night in for a veterinary appointment. A few people had dropped by the house to make sure he was all right, but he'd turned them away, promising he was fine. *Just feeling a little under the weather lately, that's all*, he'd said, and shooed them off, his voice barely exceeding a strained whisper beyond the curtains. His friends had suspected a deeper burden, though, especially Mr. Howard, Grandpa's veterinarian.

"There was something about his voice I didn't like," the snowy-haired Howard told my parents earlier at the reception. We were seated at an austere, candlelit dining room table at a country club owned by one of Grandpa's other friends, fog swirling about the raised deck out back and trailing fingers of moisture down the windows, the distant mountains swallowed from view.

"Did it seem like he was drinking?" my father asked Howard, a question I'd known was coming yet still wasn't fully prepared for. "He's been sober for over thirty years, but I'm convinced something weird was going on with him, not only because of what people here have told me but also how he acted lately. I talked to him almost every day on the phone since he moved here, but these last few weeks he was unusually quiet. He almost seemed depressed, and he kept getting confused about

the simplest things. I offered to fly out and see him, but he refused, told me he wanted to be left alone. He didn't return anyone else's calls, not even my two brothers."

Ponderingly, Howard lifted a hand to his chin. "Now that you mention it, I do believe I smelled alcohol on him a few of those nights at chess club. His play dramatically declined, too - I even thought he let me win one game, gave up a queen like that," and he snapped his finger. "Then he just stopped showing up altogether this past week. Tell you what, you folks oughta talk to Oscar Montoya - he and Jack were very close. He's in Boston this week for his granddaughter's wedding, and he was absolutely devastated by the news. I'll get you his number."

Later, along with my parents and most of the family, I saw Grandpa's house for the first time. Forming a procession of three rental cars, we turned off the serpentine road and cut through the fog-lorded woods, following a series of bumpy dirt roads until one of them eventually became the driveway and the slowly abating fog gave way to a house in the distance.

A brown one-story house far out in the forest, with worn wooden siding and white-framed windows.

A bleak house.

Affixed to the porch railings are empty, cracked flower boxes, the plants nothing more than forgotten skeletons. Battered wind chimes hang twisted and tired, in no hurry to welcome the next storm. The front door displays a withered wreath, but there is no doormat, no additional decorations, no reminders beyond the chimes of Grandma, who died five years ago, shortly before Grandpa moved out here.

The house is dark and dreary, but worst of all is its heaviness, which I felt like a burst of air upon first stepping through the door. The place is stifling, musty, but there's something more, pulsing, charged with hostility, warning us that we don't belong here. It echoes our thoughts - we don't belong, not in Grandpa's house, which we never troubled ourselves to visit when he was alive, only after he died of a heart attack. Maybe the others felt the strange exudation from the house as well, or maybe their initial collective silence was simply an externalization of guilt and grief...or, even likelier, a reaction to what lay before them.

It was hard, almost physically painful, to walk around Grandpa's house and see the way he lived his final days, none of us knowing how bad it got because we weren't there for him. He moved here almost five years ago to finish his life in a new place, a place without haunting memories, and we allowed him to go with little protest, mostly because it was easier for everyone to let him move across the country, thousands of miles separating his problems and our lives. We can deny it, but we'd only be lying to ourselves.

Two colors present at the funeral this morning, black and gray.

"He went nuts, absolutely nuts," my father said shortly after we entered the house and spotted Grandpa's mattress in the middle of the living room, a decrepit looking thing penned in by two sofas, a rocking chair, a coffee table, and the television cabinet. Sheets and blankets were sprawled messily across the yellowed mattress, partially covering two bare, rumpled pillows unfit for a prisoner.

Was this where they found him?

Immediately surrounding the worn edges of the mattress were framed photos of Grandma and Grandpa together, many of them lying flat, as well as dozens of Grandma's old crucifixes and

9

religious knickknacks. There were two flashlights and a candle present as well. Apparently this had been Grandpa's sleeping place for some time, a thing none of us could understand. It was as if another man had resided here, not Grandpa, who'd always been easygoing and light of spirit - at least before Grandma's death and the accident - but instead a lunatic burdened by unknowable maladies.

At the reception, the police chief, who was also one of Grandpa's chess club members, told us to be prepared for what we'd find, but no one could have prepared for *this*. It was all too much, the heaviness of the house seeming to wrap around my neck and choke me.

Guilt and grief, only black and gray at that funeral.

It wasn't long before someone pulled aside the curtains and drew our attention to the living room windows, newspapers taped to every inch of glass, misty light seeping through. "What is all of this?" Uncle Paul said. "Why did he block the windows?"

Touring the lonely house - heavy and cheerless - we saw further evidence that suggested a disturbed mind. In addition to the concealment of each window with newspapers, every aperture of every door was sealed by duct tape. And the mirrors were covered with scrap papers and notebook pages, in some cases with envelopes and financial statements and torn pages from the phone book, Grandpa's supply of local newspapers apparently having dried up. And when the gray duct tape had run out as well, its black and transparent counterparts had served as dutiful substitutes for the doors, pinning chess group pamphlets and take-out menus and old calendar tear-outs to the gaps and slits (even the finest beginnings of cracks in the wood). These ubiquitous tapings that held everything in place, jagged and varying in size, indicated a hasty, almost careless endeavor, as though a child had been instructed to plaster anything at his disposal to points of entry and reflective or transparent surfaces, a prize to be had if he could accomplish the task in under ten minutes.

But there was more. The analog clocks were all dead, frozen at precisely the same time, even the big grandfather clock, its pensive sounds of childhood silent. The digital clocks were dark, unplugged. In fact, most of the electrical appliances were unplugged.

The house was quiet. Heavy. Watchful. Colder than the raw, drizzly, foggy afternoon. And darkness would be an early guest.

"Jesus Christ," my father murmured, taking it all in with dismay.

Quiet. Heavy. Watchful. Cold.

I had to get out, but the heaviness was outside as well. The woods seemed to be closing in on me from all sides, the pine trees imposingly, oppressively tall, the eldritch fog creeping across a front yard pond I hadn't noticed before. I lit a cigarette and tried to relax, but with the house at my back that feeling of being watched quickly sharpened. I turned, stared at

the front door, wondered what had possessed Grandpa to do all of these crazy things. Grandma's death? The accident a year before that? I struggled in search of a reason, couldn't come up with anything. I just wanted to go home, to fly to the opposite coast and forget this place.

But the guilt kept nagging. Keeps nagging. The guilt and grief may never relent. Two colors at the funeral.

I never visited Grandpa here in five years. And now Grandpa is dead, his place left in confusion. The kitchen and dining room were strangely neat - dishes washed and stacked in cabinets, floors devoid of clutter, countertops recently wiped clean - though the windows and doors were of course covered. Yet the rest of the house was a disaster, especially the living room, Grandpa's pitiful mattress surrounded by furniture, religious items, and light sources.

Why?

We spent an hour picking at tape and ripping down newspapers as night neared, the repetitiveness of the tasks oddly peaceful, the sort of monotonous work that preoccupies and sometimes soothes the mind in times of distress or uncertainty. When my father tore off the tape sealing Grandpa's bedroom, he found a mess of papers scattered about the room, a scene to be replicated behind almost every taped door. Drawers had been flung open, closets torn apart, shelves ransacked. It looked like thieves had gone through the house, though the police hadn't bothered to investigate any of these rooms because most of Grandpa's valuables remained in plain sight in the central corridors of the house, including his cash-stocked wallet, and there'd been no signs of forced entry.

So what was Grandpa searching for so fiercely? Did he die trying to find it, or obsessing about it?

After a full examination of the main floor of the house, then a quick trip into the cobwebby basement (which was sealed as well), we all looked at each other for a moment of miserable, perplexed silence, and I could tell the others feel the same guilt that ravages me. We are each, everyone seems to realize, partially responsible for Grandpa's decline. Whatever wracked him in his final weeks/months, our failure to visit him and break his solitude undoubtedly contributed to it.

He was seventy-five, still so many years to live.

Chapter II

The boy's death that sunny morning was both a cruel end and a dire beginning. Dressed in a small, snug black suit, held in his father's arms, his young life bled swiftly onto the pavement. This was the end for little Peter Elliott, the final chapter of a story that had contained only six – but for Jack Gibson, the driver, the sudden conclusion of one story was also the beginning of a new one, a nightmarish tale as grim as the fatal gash on Peter's head.

So much blood.

Staring numbly, disbelievingly, at the sobbing father's repeated attempts at CPR on his son, vaguely aware of the gathering crowd, Jack was shredded by horror and disgust when the numbness began to subside. Here was a boy whose eyes were vacant, his white shirt splotched almost the precise color of his narrow tie, church bells ringing off to the right, police sirens whooping in discordant rivalry.

And Jack Gibson, growing nauseous with suffocating realization that a fragile little life had been shattered because of him, covered his mouth with shaking hands as he fell to his knees on the double-yellow line, the hot May sun blaring down on him from a cloudless sky.

So much blood.

Consumed by an extreme agony beyond the reach of words, beyond the darkest depths of description, Jack forced his eyes shut and felt a convulsing rage take over, at first directed inwardly but later to shine like a sweeping beacon upon the day itself, reaching senselessly for someone or something to blame. Jack had never believed in God or a supreme creator of life, but surely something of great power had been responsible for this. All of those oddities along the way – undeniable aberrations in a normally mundane crosstown Sunday morning trip from the diner to his office – couldn't possibly have been coincidences.

Jack cracked open his tear-blurred eyes, dreading what he'd see, feeling cold and sick and helpless. If only the boy would move, just a little twitch of the hand or a flutter of the eyelids to keep hope alive. Jack searched desperately for movement, panicking, willing the boy to come back from that irreparable, final place.

Just blink, please, just open your eyes…this isn't happening…no, it can't be happening. Please wake up, just wake up, just move your hand, Jack thought as he stared into the ruined face of the blond-haired boy who'd darted in front of his pickup truck, appearing between two parked vehicles, no time for Jack to stop, only the purest fear for him to witness in the boy's eyes. A dreadful recognition had also risen in those blue eyes, wide with resignation that there was no way to outrun death, Jack's brakes screeching, the Stone Temple Pilots jamming "Interstate Love Song" over his radio…Breathing is the hardest thing to do…

"I'm so sorry." It was all Jack could say, three choked, virtually soundless words. He stood shakily, tears falling to the pavement. Rendered breathless by terror, an old man whose morning had been off to a fine start, Jack could now only lay a hand upon the father's shoulder when the man lurched away from his son and relinquished the futile bids for resuscitation to a cop.

"Ohhhh God, please don't take him, please please no!!! Not my PETER!!!" the father wailed, throwing his hands skyward, his chest hitching and heaving in the throes of grief as sharp and black as a raven gliding past the moon.

Never before had Jack witnessed a man assailed by such suffering, but this was well past suffering, an unimaginable, ineffable torment that burrowed its way deep into every soul surrounding the six-year-old boy splayed out on Main Street in his Sunday best, his tiny hands scraped and bloody, his black sock visible in the absence of a shoe torn violently away, so much blood on such a little face. Jack had skidded and slowed but had still hit Peter Elliott with a sickening jolt, the sounds of impact scarcely more substantial than those of a collision

BURN, DO NOT READ!

with a pothole but resounding in their implications, fear screaming in his heart as he scrambled out of the truck – and then the disbelief.

How could it be real?

"Sir? Sir?" The voice came into focus like a beach sound heard only when the wind calms and the waves whisper back to sea. "Sir, were you the driver?"

"Yes, me, I hit him, it was me," and the words nearly made Jack vomit. He allowed a pair of officers to lead him away, a dull throbbing ring in his head and little else from an auditory standpoint, insane thoughts and memories clapping together like thunderclouds…and now the caustic need for blame was burgeoning.

The truck. If it hadn't been for the truck he'd be alive. Barfield and Brickley, you caused this, a damn furniture delivery truck!

They pushed through the throng of aghast onlookers, many of them in suits and dresses, some of them just children like the boy lying dead in the road. The police were ordering everyone back to make room for the ambulance. "Get back, get out of here, get out of here now!"

Jack took one last backward glance beyond the dispersing crowd at the boy, half-expecting him to be moving, but still with death he remained in his father's arms. It was then Jack Gibson's breakfast rose and spilled, realization reaching a new height. His heart felt as if it had come loose from the ferocity of its palpitations, his throat dry and achy.

Barfield and Brickley – a *little boy is dead because of you.*

17

Chapter III

When senatorial candidate Stephen Gibson learned that his father had struck and killed a child crossing the road that morning, his first few questions were of an almost journalistic nature. (*Where did it happen? How? Was Mom with him?*) In time he stumbled into asking how Dad was doing.

"He's fine, physically," Stephen's wife Claire assured. "But he's shaken up bad, Steve. Give him a call, let him know you're there for him. I can't even imagine what he's going through. It wasn't his fault – I guess the kid just ran out in front of him, but he's going through Hell."

"Okay, I'll call him, but I gotta run right now. Call you later," Steve said, and ended the call, taking a few moments to rub his temples and absorb this mess. *Jesus*, he thought with a cold, dismal awareness that fell heavily and unceremoniously on him like a downpour. *This could cost me the election.*

The polls had narrowed significantly in recent weeks, Steve's lead on Michael Mason for the upcoming special election slimming to uncomfortable levels. They were vying for the Senate seat of the late Norman McElhinney, the second debate scheduled for Thursday, and bad publicity for the family at a time like this could do serious damage. Any other family could easily withstand it, but other families didn't have a past like the Gibsons.

Steve's head ached dully. His muscles were tight. He texted an important backer and told him he'd need to delay their meeting an hour. Then he made a call to his campaign manager and rattled frantically through the story.

"I've gotta get out ahead of this thing, Jim, gotta meet it head on or it'll eat me alive. Schedule a press conference. Prepare a statement. I need to play this up, make a speech on how my heart goes out to the family, blah-blah-blah – you know what to do. If they dig into Dad's past, we're looking at a major damage control situation."

"What's the legal status?" Jim asked. "Could your father face charges?"

Steve slammed a fist against his hotel room desk and swiped the little notepad halfway across the room. "How should I know? It happened this morning, damn it, I just found out about it! They say it wasn't his fault, but who knows what'll go down. The goddamn DA out there's a Republican, I think – they'll probably put the squeeze on him just for bad press."

Pacing the room, Steve said. "I should have taken his license away. I should have known he could be a liability. This is a disaster, an absolute nightmare. They'll dredge up the past, say he fell off the wagon. Even if he was stone-sober, there'll be accusations no matter what, and you know what that means, Jim. Everyone will wonder if I'm an alcoholic, too – guilt by fucking association."

***

Jack didn't get a call from his youngest son Steve until after dark.

"Dad, so sorry I didn't call sooner. I've been buried with campaign stuff all day and thought you could use some time to rest. How are you holding up?"

Seated at the head of the dining room table, his wife and best friend Mary glancing worriedly at him from the kitchen, Jack focused on the bowl of cooling chicken noodle soup before him, a package of crackers and a salt shaker off to the side. The soup smelled good, but the thought of sipping it summoned nausea to his stomach. He hadn't eaten anything all day; he'd tried to sleep after arriving home from the police station, but he'd wound up lying in bed for hours, his mind replaying the violence of the morning, over and over and over. Blue eyes; red tie; double-yellow line; pale, innocent, beautiful face of that boy…blood everywhere; sunny morning; sickly hot; "Interstate Love Song" easing

19

over the radio. And the police were probably still examining Jack's F-150 at the station, determined to identify a reason for why he hadn't been able to stop in time.

"I don't know, Stevie," Jack said, tears in his eyes, feeling strained and hollow and isolated. *Who kills a little kid? No one, no one but me.* "It all feels like a bad dream, I guess, like I'm gonna wake up and realize I didn't kill that little…" He set the portable phone down, rubbed his eyes, returned the receiver to his ear. "It's been a bad day, a real bad day."

"Dad, I know you don't want to hear this right now, but there's gonna be reporters coming to the house. I've already told Mom to ignore them, and you have to–"

"Would you stop thinking about the damn election for one second?" Jack shouted, pushing forcefully back from the table and standing, the spoon clinking in its bowl, Mary wincing in the kitchen. "A kid is dead and it's my fault!"

Much later, after many hours of lying still and quiet in bed with Mary, her frail hands massaging his shoulders, Jack finally stood and stared out the partially opened bedroom window, the scent of rain creeping through, their dog Night watching him from the end of the bed and nervously wagging her tail, always leery of wind and rain, among a few hundred other things.

Jack's body ached as though he'd come down with the flu. He didn't want to move, didn't want to think, desiring only to stare into the darkness until his body shut itself down. He wished he were dead, wished it down to his bones, wished it until he was shaking and clenching his fists – if only he could switch places with little Peter Elliott. Mary had reluctantly told him the boy's name and age that night after watching the news, her hazel eyes soft and desperate, searching for a way to help him.

But in her heart she knew what Jack did. This could destroy him.

Unable to drive Peter's broken, bloody face from his mind, more tears pooling in his beleaguered eyes, Jack pulled the blankets up to his sleeping wife's chest and clicked off the bedside lamp. There he

lingered for a long while, listening to Mary's soft breaths and Night's occasional sighs, and then he forced himself downstairs. The rain was starting to patter against the roof now, and still Peter's face was painted in Jack's mind like a vicious mural, the rich red and pale white indelible, a face to haunt him forever.

Dropping to his knees in the dark living room, Jack sobbed again and gritted his teeth and cursed the powers that be for stopping him at the damn railroad crossing, then planting the Barfield and Brickley truck in front of him. As if the truck hadn't delayed him enough by driving so slowly, the heedless driver had stopped incomprehensibly in the middle of the road, then proceeded to make an absurd series of advancements and reversals, taking up the entire road and eventually backing into a driveway on the other side to get himself turned around, traffic stopped in both directions.

The stupid driver, it's his fault. If he hadn't done that I never would have hit Peter. And the damn train, if it had been a few cars shorter Peter would be alive, poor Peter, just a boy coming out of church. And he's dead…but why couldn't I stop soon enough?

Jack's lips spread into a cracked, maddened rictus, his mouth dry, his throat burning.

Barfield and Brickley. I hope those people enjoy their precious furniture. Then came the urge, the strongest urge in decades, one Jack knew he needed to fight with the entirety of his strength.

But the urge made promises to him, promises of taking the pain away, promises of eradicating that vivid image from his head. So quickly one image could multiply into two, four, eight – little Peter, his bloody face, his shirt stained, his black sock, his shoe all alone in the road, the song on the radio – and the urge steadily built, built, built, until it had him moving toward the front door, desperate and unseeing, ravaged by the evil day, harried by the rainy night and its thoughts, and now he was outside, his soul the night's to claim, the driveway slick with cold, insistent rain, stepping toward Mary's car, sliding into it, a trembling hand on the steering wheel. The day was over, the police interview seeming as if it had occurred two weeks ago – and now this.

This is what it will be like every night, unless...

He couldn't do it. No, he mustn't. "Get back in the house," he whispered, as afraid of himself as he'd been in thirty years. He felt out of control, a vessel unmoored and set adrift, helpless to bring himself back.

But he had to. "Get back in the house," he said, this time with greater urgency, but he remained in Mary's car, watching the relentless rain upon the windshield with tortured eyes that galloped back and forth, straining to glimpse every detail and freeze it in his mind. If he concentrated hard enough on the rain and shut other thoughts out, he told himself, then he couldn't be haunted by the memories. If he kept a close enough watch, he'd have no need for urges and promises.

"Get back in the damn house! What are you waiting for?"

The hoarse, cracking, desperate fragility of his shouts sent him lurching out of the car, back into the cold rain. It felt oddly, punishingly pleasant against his skin, as though this was precisely where he belonged. And so he stood in the middle of the driveway and looked up into the darkness, the strengthening rain pounding mercilessly down on him. Soon he was drenched and shivering, but he kept reminding himself this was nothing compared to little Peter's last morning, memories of a son's blood and a father's screams glowing hot in his mind. Nothing could compare to such horrors. If Jack stayed out here all night and caught pneumonia, if he was hospitalized for weeks, if he declined to the point of immobility – to the point of moribundity – none of it could replicate the exponential terror Peter knew upon time's betrayal. He'd been just a boy, so small and delicate, dashing cluelessly into the road, probably eager to get home and put away his Sunday suit so he could play ball with his friends, the lush diamond at Peavey Field theirs to

enjoy until the sun arched orange and dusky shadows crept across the infield.

But the day hadn't unfolded for Peter. He was gone – gone forever. No one could bring him back to his dad, no way to undo the tragedy of a hot, sunny morning. And now it was night.

Damn you, Barfield and Brickley. And the train, too!

Indifferent to the pain in his knees, Jack lowered himself to the asphalt and stayed there, shoulders sagging, rain weighing down his clothes. Kneeling, his eyes fell level with the fender of his rusted 1974 Ford pickup truck, which sat forgotten about twenty feet away by the shed, a restoration project that hadn't graduated from ambition to actualization. The fender shined dimly in the rain, barely reached by the ambit of the motion sensor light mounted to the garage. Staring at that fender, the truck seeming as massive as a locomotive from Jack's low perspective, he imagined what the final seconds must have been like for Peter Elliott, an inexplicable realization of approaching death brimming in the fresh blue eyes of a six-year-old.

Eyes that had flashed with helpless defeat, one moment the eyes of a happy, oblivious little kid...and did Peter die instantly or was there suffering?

Jack ran back to Mary's car, his legs aching sharply in protest. Once inside, again watching the night rain hammer down against the windshield, choking back the sobs, he shot a hand over to the passenger seat and fumbled for the keys, found them, brought the car to life. Then the car was moving, headlights cutting through the sodden dark, the driveway opening to the lonely road.

Turn around. You have to turn around NOW! You promised Mary you'd never touch the stuff again. You can't throw it all away now, but control was eluding him, rising up and away like a little boy's lost balloon.

Following mostly empty streets to the package store, splashing through puddles that glowed orange beneath streetlamps, Jack felt as if he were the only person in the world. It wasn't very late but hardly anyone was out here, the streets virtually deserted. After such a cruel day, Jack figured, surely no one would want to witness how the night planned to match it. And who in their self-preserving mind would want to navigate the same streets as Jack Gibson, child killer? Undoubtedly, therein lied the reason for these desolate streets.

Jack pulled off the road often during his short trip with thoughts of returning home, but that urge kept calling to him. Mute the pain, take the memories away, it promised. Mute the pain, take the memories away. Whenever Jack came close to changing the car's direction, he would think of little Peter lying dead, his father wailing and shredded, a sunny morning gone fatal.

Almost to the package store, Jack turned into a gas station and got the car pointing toward home, but once again Peter's face stormed into his head, bloody and savaged, his eyes faraway and still, so very still. Jack shook his head. No, this wouldn't work. He couldn't do this. He simply wouldn't be able to free himself of Peter's face without a few drinks, and it was with that despairing reality rooted firmly in his heart that he completed the trip to the little package store at the corner of Elm and Broadridge. It would still be open for a few more minutes, enough time for him to decide if he absolutely wanted to go through with this.

Still time. Damn you to Hell, Barfield and Brickley!

Parked outside the store, lightning sidling in the distance, Jack thought of Mary and all she'd endured during his drunken days. Jack's father had been a drunk. His grandfather had been a drunk – and a mean old drunk at that, beating his kids with whatever he could find when they got in his way. For all Jack knew, his great-grandfather had been a drunk, too, the Gibson men filled nearly equally with nitrogen and alcohol.

Mary had threatened to leave him thirty years ago if he didn't dry up. And Jack, who'd just been fired from his own uncle's auto repair shop for drinking on the job, might have let her walk away if it hadn't been

for their three kids. He'd loved Mary since the day he met her, but his relationship with the bottle traced all the way back to his early teenage years. Alcohol had always been there for Jack, helping him through the

tough times and offering its tireless companionship and support during the good ones. No matter what had been hurled his way, the bottle had been there to assist him in sorting it all out, an old friend that had promised to never leave, a constant relief that had taken the edge off when life got sharp, and a freely flowing cascade when life had been smooth. Alcohol had bookended countless days, had put an end to troubling nights, had settled him amidst the storms – it had been his friend and sustained his friendships, particularly those with his high school friends, the ones who'd stayed in town or returned after their service like Jack to run their daddies' shops or work their daddies' farms or charge into burning buildings because their daddies had done so. *It's easy, Jack, just quit. Don't take another drink,* Mary had said, but she hadn't understood how inextricable alcohol had become for him, entwined so tightly with his identity over the years that it had practically become part of his DNA double helix. He hadn't been able to imagine his life without sneaking a few nips at work and greeting Jackie Daniels after a hard day on the job.

But even if Jack had been willing to risk his marriage, he never would have risked losing his three boys, and so he'd quit thirty years back, disentangling himself from the intricate knots that had defined his adult life. It hadn't been easy. It hadn't been without several sleepless nights of shivering and shaking and nausea and pulling at his hair and wondering when the headaches would stop. It hadn't been without days of fearing he wasn't strong enough to hold out, that he would give in

25

and return to what he'd always known. Quite simply, it had been the hardest thing Jack had ever done, but he'd done it for his kids.

Lightning flickered off the windows of the package store, the bald, large-headed clerk bobbing in and out of view behind the counter, busy with his closing chores.

"Can't go home," Jack whispered, but it was the whisper of a dehydrating man in the middle of the ocean, the ruthless sun filling him with urges. Deep down, beneath the searing pain, beyond the bloody face of Peter Elliott framed in his head, Jack knew this urge was only a drooping red carpet stretched across a massive chasm, not a single beam underneath to support it, but the notion of somehow walking across it to the other side imbued him with desperate, delusional appeal. Just a sip of the salt water, the dehydrating man might say, and for Jack it would be a sip of whiskey, then another.

It'll get better, echoed Mary's voice. *Take it one day at a time, and it will get better.*

But Peter's face would never be any less bloody in his head. Peter's fear-riven eyes, damn it, they'd never change, and the bottle was calling again, an old friend on the phone, reminding him that *life has gotten awfully sharp, Jack, how about I help you take the edge off? The clerk will be closing soon, Jack, do you want to be all alone with Peter in your head? The dark, rainy night will be very long, Jack, and Peter's parents are staring at his empty bed and crying right now, his mother clutching his teddy bear, his father cursing you, Jack. He's cursing you, because it's all your fault their son is gone. All your fault. All your fault. And he's cursing the God they worshipped this morning, Peter in his little suit and tie, worshipping a God that let him die on the road after church, a God that let church bells ring, ring, ring, ring after he was gone...What God? What God would do that? Why did Peter have to die? His body is cold and dead now – and he's gone, long gone. His eyes will never open again. Why didn't his dad just hold his little hand????*

26

Jack yanked open the door, staggered out into the driving rain, his head feeling like it would explode with memories of Peter's eyes, which had expanded and transmogrified to black, hateful voids as the hours had passed and the sun had given way to clouds, eyes that had glared at the man whose truck provided their final, terrified vision.

"Barfield and Brickley," Jack muttered absently, glancing through the window as he approached the store.

The clerk, still occupied with closing tasks behind the counter, nodded at Jack as he stepped inside, greeted by the smells of cardboard and stale beer. "Made it just in time," he mumbled, and for a moment it seemed as though he'd been waiting only for Jack's arrival.

The aisles of merchandise called excitedly to Jack, each touting a different style but making the same promise. Yet Mary's voice in his head reminded him of another promise, the one he'd made to her thirty years ago.

I'm so sorry, Mary. I love you. I'll always love you.

Plucking a bottle of Jack Daniels from the shelf, Jack Gibson stared at the old friend within and dwelled on his decision, Mary's words and Peter's face inundating him with ambivalent upheaval.

This could ruin my marriage, he thought, but then: *There's no other way to take away the pain.*

A few sips, just to get through the night, he decided, feeling resolute and capable, a man back in control. If he could get through one night, it would all be better in the morning, he assumed. He'd go into work late and get on with the day, then come home and have dinner with Mary, little Peter's face sure to fade, right? Wouldn't it? Perhaps Mary would cook pasta with homemade garlic bread, his favorite, and they'd watch Jeopardy together, and there'd be no further need for old friends.

I'm only taking the edge off, and Jack paid the clerk just before closing, the last customer on a stormy night.

Chapter IV

Lightning strobed across Main Street as Jack neared the church, rain bursting down and limiting his vision. There was no need for him to be out this way. The bottle of whiskey tucked into a paper bag in the passenger seat, he should have been heading home to reunite with a very old friend, but something had impelled him to return to the scene of the tragedy, just past the church, where Peter Elliott had come springing out between parked cars.

Those cars were gone now, the curb empty. The church stood dark and silent to Jack's right, the police station to his left, and up ahead, in the road, he thought he saw Peter lying dead on the double-yellow line, drenched and forgotten, his father no longer there to hold him. Jack pulled over and lowered his window, staring at the cursed spot until lightning played across the pavement and confirmed Peter was gone.

Just an empty, rainy road tonight. And tomorrow the Monday morning traffic would come again, and Peter would begin to fade from memory.

I've never been stopped at that railroad crossing before on a Sunday morning, Jack thought, still staring at the spot where Peter had died and remembering the awful thud, remembering the final fear in the boy's eyes, remembering his father's sobs. *Should have just gone through the crossing. There's no gates, and the train was going slow.*

Jack reached for the bottle, clutched its neck with an empty smile. The train had been seven locomotives and at least one hundred cars long, he recalled, though the short line railroad that operated those tracks usually ran trains consisting of no more than a few dozen cars. Jack crossed the tracks every Sunday morning on his way from breakfast with Mary at the diner to his office, where he caught up on spillover work until noon, and he'd never so much as seen a locomotive's headlight in the distance on a Sunday. But earlier that morning the huge train had held him up. Then there'd been a slow-moving van in his way, two old ladies tottering through a crosswalk to slow him further, and finally the ridiculousness from the Barfield and Brickley truck, all of it so random and strange, almost as if something had intentionally

delayed him so that his truck would ultimately pass through a certain stretch of Main Street precisely when little Peter Elliott was trying to cross.

A divine, evil hand.

Exhaling deeply, Jack twisted off the bottle cap and took a long sniff of the stuff, its smell extending a warm greeting.

Just taking the edge off.

He brought the bottle to his lips, closed his eyes, Peter's face bright in his head, but then he lowered the bottle to his thigh, recapped it, set it on the passenger seat. *I can't. Mary will never forgive me.*

But you have to. It's the only way.

I made a promise.

It's the only way to get through the night.

No! I promised her.

She'll never know, Jackie. Just have a few sips. It'll help you sleep.

Jack nodded, his eyes roaming back to the road, thunder rumbling in the distance. His turn signal flashes reflected dimly against a puddle. The wind was picking up now, the rain keeping its pace. For an ephemerally clear moment – his mind briefly free of Peter's face – Jack knew the only way through the darkness was to throw away the bottle and head home. But then Peter drifted back to the forefront and he couldn't see beyond the rain, couldn't imagine a conceivable way through the pain and the darkness, feeling suffocated and stifled and sick. He clenched his fists, bit his lip hard, wished himself dead.

The urge. An old friend in the passenger seat.
Take the edge off, Jackie.

Jack Gibson returned home, the bottle remaining in his possession, the heart of the storm closing in.

Chapter V

We organized Grandpa's house as best we could for the rest of the day, packing things up and throwing things out, the fog yielding to a cold, steady rain. Grandpa's lawyer came this evening and read his will, which dictated that the house and all of its contents be bequeathed to my father, his eldest son. As we went through the house following the lawyer's departure, I wondered if this decision would stir at least a little friction between my father and the rest of our family, especially Uncle Steve, who, according to my dad, has always been the most spoiled and demanding of the three Gibson boys.

No one showed any bitterness, though. We were all too saddened and shocked by what we'd found here.

Later, just after dark, Night was returned to her home, Grandpa's lonely house in the woods...but you never would have known it was her home by the way she cemented her legs and had to be carried in whimpering and flailing by Mr. Howard, the veterinarian. Having looked after Night since Grandpa's death, Howard said the dog had been whining and barking almost nonstop. "She misses her daddy, barely touched her food," he murmured, and that wrung even more tears from a house of bleary eyes.

The sight of the miserable dog, an eight-year-old black lab mix, almost made me cry. I can still remember her as a playful, energetic pup, but after Howard set her down and unleashed her, she trudged over to Grandpa's mattress and curled up on his pillow, letting out a long sigh and studying each of us warily. Whenever someone tried to pet her, she slinked behind one of the sofas and hid.

"Just leave her alone," my mother said. "It'll take time for her to heal, just like the rest of us."

"This house is creepy," chimed my youngest cousin, a girl who has never been shy about speaking her mind. "It's almost like Grandpa was trying to keep something out."

Glancing dolefully about the house, my father kept shaking his head. "If I'd known it was this bad, I would have come out here and gotten him some help. I just...I thought he'd get through it." Tears fell down his cheeks. "God, if only I'd known."

Chapter VI

Remaining in Mary's car in the driveway, the wind and lightning and thunder clouting all around him, Jack sat for many minutes with the bottle in hand. Uncapped, the tantalizing scent of whiskey rose up to him with promises of dulling the pain.

Just a few sips. Mary will never know. You've been wronged by the universe, and now you need to find a way through it.

Peter's face still dominating his mind, Jack raised the bottle to his lips. Tilted it. Brought it forth – it, yes, *it* – an old friend. Swirled the whiskey around his mouth, indecisive, scared, stung with familiarity, dwelling on the promise he'd made to Mary. There were claws of rain upon the roof, scratching and ticking, the lightning a wild, lashing menace.

Jack very nearly spat the whiskey out.

You've been wronged, Jack. Just take the edge off.

A bolt of lightning straight ahead, raking the night, and Jack swallowed a touch of whiskey involuntarily, felt the stuff forging its once inveterate path, warming him on a stormy night.

From there, the rest was an easy swallow, effortless, falling into the arms of his old friend.

A crack of thunder, the wind buffeting the car.

That's it, Jackie. See, nothing to it, buddy.

Jack took a long swig, then another, feeling better already, Peter's image seeming to fade, just as his friend had promised. Before long, little shafts of light were corroding his darkness, and he smiled at the thought of feeling better, of being free of his grief.

34

BURN, DO NOT READ!

It wasn't your fault. Barfield and Brickley – and the stupid train. It was their fault. And what about the father? He should have been holding his hand, should have been watching his kid. And where was the mother? Was she even there?

The indefatigable rain. A short time ago Jack had desperately tried to focus on it, an effort to banish Peter from his head, but now its sound was relaxing as Jack drifted off, guiding him one swig at a time closer to sleep. Gradually the laces of lightning and shuddering rolls of thunder became less frequent, the storm trundling away, a slow, deliberate process, like the lifting of a pulley.

Mechanical and soothing, and surely the sun would rise again.

You'll feel better soon, he thought, leaning his head against the cold driver's window and settling in. *Time for a little nap, then you'll go inside. She doesn't have to know.*

Chapter VII

Minutes after Stephen Gibson concluded his brief statement on the Peter Elliott tragedy the next morning – extending his sincerest condolences to the family and announcing that the Elliotts would be in his prayers – he received a call from his mother.

"How's Dad doing?" Steve's cell phone was tucked between his chin and shoulder, an open suitcase on the hotel bed before him. He had to be in the next city by noon, an afternoon of campaign stops awaiting him. Frankly, he didn't have time for the dead kid debacle right now, even if he knew reporters would inevitably dig into Dad's past and learn about his alcoholism. And if they dug far enough and found out about his family history…no, Steve wouldn't allow himself to think about the disaster that could result from such investigations. People would assume that he, too, was a heavy drinker, if not a full-blown alcoholic, a senator who'd kick up his feet in D.C. and down shots all day on the taxpayers' watch. But he'd worked too damn hard to be brought down by family history, way too hard.

If only Dad would just move away to a remote island – then I wouldn't have to worry about him causing problems.

"Your father's not well, Stevie. I found him sleeping in my car last night with a bottle of whiskey," Mom said. "This has really torn him up – I don't even know if I can blame him for drinking. That poor little boy–"

"Jesus Christ," Steve muttered, slamming a fist against the bed. "This is a mess, a total mess. Of all the times for him to fall off the wagon."

"Cut him some slack, Stevie. If I killed a child I'd be in pieces, too, we all would be. Your father will get it together – he's strong. He did it before."

Steve pointed a shaking finger at the wall, a portrait of a flowery field substituting for his mother and enduring Steve's rant with as little interruption or opposition as his mother would have mustered had they been face-to-face. "He better get it together!" Steve shouted. "It wasn't his fault, right? The kid popped out in front of him – it was an accident. Accidents happen all the time."

"You need to keep him away from the reporters," Steve continued. "Ignore them when they come to the house, and if they call, just say no comment. I spoke with Jim this morning – he'll be in touch with you to set up a meeting on all the do's and don'ts. This is a critical time right now, and I just know Mason will use this thing to his advantage. He'll try to bury me with bad press about our family."

"That's got nothing to do with you, Stevie. You'll be–"

"It won't matter to voters, Mom. They see a family of alcoholics – they only assume one thing about the next guy in line."

***

Jack woke shivery and afraid following another version of essentially the same nightmare – one that had ravaged him last night in Mary's car and again now, Monday morning. He'd been chased through the woods by an amorphous creature, nothing about its physical characteristics memorable other than the color: black. The thing had been vicious and hating and fast, snapping at Jack as he sprinted through the trees with a quickness he could never hope to achieve in the waking world. Strangely, even though the beast could have easily caught Jack and torn him to bits, it had seemed to relish the hunt and the inevitability of its capture.

The two nightmares had been vastly different in one regard – one culminating with a small, obscure house, and the other finishing at the edge of a cliff – but in both cases Jack had woken with seven vivid words bristling in his head.

Morning does not welcome those who die.

It was almost as if someone had whispered these words in Jack's ear just before he'd stirred. Last night, Mary had been standing in the drizzling rain and tapping on the window when he'd jolted awake, and now, lying in their bed and staring at the muted television, with its cheerful national morning program and smiling hosts, Jack pondered the line yet again. Had he heard it on the radio recently? Read it in the newspaper? Perhaps overheard it during one of Mary's TV movies, the ones she selected with alacrity each night after dinner, her yarn and needles at the ready and later a bowl of fruit or sometimes popcorn?

Morning does not welcome those who die.

It seemed like such an odd thing to twice jar him from sleep, especially considering its symbolism. Peter Elliott would never be welcomed by another morning, would never see another sunrise. He wouldn't graduate or get married or have children. He was dead, gone, deprived of a chance to find his place in the world, and Jack kept brooding about whether another driver would have reacted quicker and saved his life, possibly by swerving or spotting the boy through the parked vehicles and managing to stop. Jack had been a few ticks over the 30-MPH speed limit, and maybe another person would have gone slower down Main Street, enough to spare little Peter's life.

It was all your fault.

No, no, it was the father's fault. He should have held his hand.

All your fault.

But what about the Barfield and Brickley truck? The driver has to shoulder at least some of the blame.

Jack rubbed his eyes, a mild ache lingering in his head – his old friend's dirty laundry. But the incessant thoughts wouldn't depart, Jack's need to assign blame overwhelming. If it was someone else's fault – even an unknown cosmic force responsible for yesterday's delays – then little Peter's death wouldn't be entirely on him; and if it wasn't squarely on him, maybe he could find a way to move on. Maybe. But now, supine in his bed and wondering what they were saying about him, wondering how the police investigation was proceeding, wondering how often his name had been called over the local news reports, a hopeless dread seemed to add fifty pounds to the blankets pulled up to his chin. He felt constricted, helpless, completely at the mercy of the public. Some people would undoubtedly say he was senile. Others would cite him as yet another example of why elderly drivers lack the reflexes and quick judgment needed to drive safely. A few might even remember him as the drunk who'd gotten fired from three jobs in a year – including his own uncle's auto body – for drinking at work. Those individuals would surely question whether he'd crawled back to his old haunts, but Jack had been as sober as a Mormon for thirty years until last night.

Throwing aside the blankets, Jack slid into his worn slippers and padded down the hall, Night hopping off the bed and trailing after him, eager to see if Jack might fix himself a big breakfast. He wasn't very hungry, though, not after last night.

At the top of the stairs, Jack could hear Mary on the first floor, speaking quietly to someone on the phone, bits and pieces of her conversation floating brokenly through the house. Jack heard enough to know she was talking about him. Of course she was talking about him – who else would she possibly be talking about? Jack, who'd called in sick earlier that morning before loading up on water and returning to bed, knew it was only a matter of time before his coworkers learned about the incident. Then they'd be talking, too.

Maybe I'll just retire, he thought. *How can I face them? How can I face anyone?*

Before nodding off in bed last night once his wife had gotten him inside, Jack had expressed to Mary his wishes to attend Peter's funeral, but she'd shaken her head solemnly and placed a cold, damp cloth over his forehead, telling him, "That's probably not such a good idea, Jackie, but you're very kind for wanting to be there." Then she'd kissed him and he'd fallen into merciful oblivion, forgetting the strange words in his head until hours later.

Morning does not welcome those who die.

Strange, indeed.

Slumping into the dining room, Jack waved to Mary in the kitchen before taking a seat at the head of the table. Her face brightened when she saw him, and she came hurrying in with a smile. "Jack, it's Stevie on the phone. Would you like to talk to him?"

"Sure," he said, though he didn't really want to talk to anyone.

Mary's smile faded. Nodding repeatedly, she said, "Stevie actually needs to finish packing for his trip. He said he'll call back on the way."

Jack waved a hand. He supposed he couldn't blame Steve for wanting to distance himself – he had the election to focus on, and here Jack was complicating things for him (complicating things for everyone). His eldest son, Robert, had called yesterday and expressed his support, even offering to fly home for a few days to be with him, but Jack had told him to stay put and focus on his heavy caseload with the law firm. Jack's middle son, Paul, an Alaska state trooper, had called late last night and left a message asking if there was anything he could do to help, maybe a connection or two he could reach from his law enforcement days in the Lower 48, but Jack still hadn't returned his call, reluctant to describe how he was doing yet again. His family didn't need this burden, especially not Mary, who he'd hurt even worse last night by breaking his promise. But she hadn't uttered a scolding word when she'd found the bottle, desiring only to help him back inside and get him up to bed. Now, he feared, the wrath would come.

Mary told their son to drive safely and then set the portable phone on the table. There was a momentary uncomfortable silence between them,

Mary taking a seat to Jack's right and reaching diagonally across the table for his hand. The scent of coffee rose up from the kitchen, appealing mildly to him.

"Talk to me, Jackie," Mary said, squeezing his hand.
Jack's gaze drifted to the edge of the room, where Night took a break from drinking water to glance interestedly – perhaps even a little suspiciously – at them. Jack wished he could trade places with his dog. Life sure would be a lot simpler then, but there was no magic wand that could get him out of this one. He didn't know what to say, didn't know if he should apologize again for leaping off the wagon or just keep his mouth shut.

"I'm so sorry," he finally said. "I just couldn't get Peter out of my head. I see him, Mary, see him dead in the street, laying there in his dad's arms. Every minute."

"Shh, shh, shh," she said. "There's no need for sorries right now. After what you went through, I'd be shocked if you weren't traumatized. It's going to take time, but you will get through this, Jackie, I promise."

The understanding and sympathy in Mary's eyes made Jack feel like something was melting inside him. For a moment he thought he would break down and cry again, his eyes heavy with the need to spill more tears. Instead he blinked them back and stood, walking the length of the table and turning back to his wife from the other end. "I love you so much, Mary. So damn much."

She came to him with arms outstretched, pulled him into her embrace, and Jack clung to her as if he hadn't seen her in years, as if she'd returned from the dead, a revenant with a final message for him. He hated feeling so weak and vulnerable and needy, but he resignedly accepted that he couldn't get through this alone. He needed the support of friends and family, but most of all, he needed Mary's support.

I'll get through this, he thought, still hugging her, immeasurably stronger in Mary's presence. *I'll get through this without alcohol.*

41

Just like quitting the stuff thirty years ago, Jack knew it would be hard, but going through that struggle had shown him he could persist through extreme adversity. Moving past Peter's death might be even harder than defeating addiction, but Jack vowed in that moment to try as hard as he could, sooner scratching his fingernails bloody than taking another sip. He owed it to his wife.

BURN, DO NOT READ!

Chapter VIII

No one wanted to stay at Grandpa's house tonight. We were depleted by a depressing, confounding day, and the house only added to our weariness. We would all stay at a motel in the center of town, my father initially decided, then come back and continue packing things up tomorrow. The most valuable of Grandpa's possessions will be immediately shipped back home; everything else will be given away, sold, or thrown out.

The inanimate objects, it seems, will be fairly easy to deal with. But Night is another matter.

"Do you think the motel will let us bring her?" my father said.

"Maybe that vet will take her back," Uncle Steve suggested.

My mother shook her head. "No, he said he's heading out of town in a few days."

We all looked at the dog. She'd returned to Grandpa's mattress in the middle of the living room. Now she was lying on the blanket, looking toward the front door. Waiting.

The sight tugged violently at my heart. "I'll stay here and watch her tonight, and we'll figure out what to do with her tomorrow," I said. "She should at least spend the night at her home." One of my teenage cousins said he would stay as well, Uncle Steve's eldest son. Watching him stare at Night, cross-armed and blinking, it looked like he would cry.

"Are you guys sure?" my father said. "We could probably sneak her into the motel if she doesn't make too much noise."

"No, we'll stay," I insisted, but I knew this decision was much deeper than a simple offer to care for Grandpa's dog. This was guilt and grief manifesting yet again - two colors at the funeral. I stayed away for five years when Grandpa desperately could have used a few visits from family, and now I need to spend a night in this house, a thing I should have done a long time ago. It's too late for apologies, too late for excuses. But if I stay over and take care of Night, I keep thinking, maybe Grandpa can see me and know how terrible we feel about how it all played out. Even though no one from the family ever came out here to visit, we never stopped loving him. We thought our phone conversations with Grandpa had sufficed. They hadn't.

When the others were gone, the taillights of their rental cars sliding into the darkness, my cousin Stevie and I were left in

heavy silence. Night, who'd only nibbled the food my mother had prepared in her bowl, was lying on Grandpa's pillow, not

looking sad or sleepy but alert, her ears perked up and eyes darting to the ceiling.

"Place is pretty scary, huh?" Stevie said. Having given up on trying to get reception for his cell phone, he'd plopped onto his back on one of the sofas.

I took the opposite sofa, Grandpa's fortified mattress between us. "It's really weird how there's no service tonight. I always reached Grandpa on his cell out here."

"I know, right? Me, too."

"Can you feel the heaviness?" I asked in a little while. "It's almost hard to breathe sometimes."

"Yeah, like there's no oxygen in here." He scooped up the remote control from the sofa and tried to turn on the TV, not realizing how grateful I was to hear him say that - to know I wasn't alone with my impressions.

"Unplugged," I reminded Stevie, and when he plugged in the TV and tried again, there was nothing but fuzz.

The sound made me uneasy.

Stevie switched off the TV, and silence ruled once more. Now that everyone had cleared out, I sensed that watchful presence again, redoubled, as if the house itself were alive. I told myself to cut it out, that it was only a house. Grandpa's old house. A place in which he'd covered all the windows and taped the doors shut. Why?

The idea of it kept drawing my eyes to the windows, searching, half-expecting...something out there in the night. Surely Grandpa wouldn't have done all this for nothing, would he?

It was a thought that couldn't be denied words.

"So what do you think drove Grandpa to do such crazy stuff?" I eventually asked, studying the room and its oddities, trying not to obsess on the fact that Grandpa died somewhere in this house a few nights ago.

Stevie shrugged. "I don't know, but it's really weird. Like they said before, it's like he was trying to keep something out." He sighed, shook his head. "He was never the same after he killed that kid."

"No, he wasn't," I agreed. "And without Grandma he just seemed lost."

Pointing to the grandfather clock in the far corner, Stevie asked, "Why do you think he stopped the clocks at the same time?"

I glanced at the three clocks in the room. The hour hands were frozen just before twelve, the minute hands stuck almost equidistantly between eleven and twelve. Like everything else, we couldn't make sense of why Grandpa did it.

And it seemed we never would, Grandpa's final days to be forever shrouded in mystery.

Later, around eight o'clock, Stevie found a take-out menu for a restaurant in town called Antonio's Pizza. WE DELIVER! it proclaimed, and after plugging in the landline, Stevie ordered us a large pepperoni pizza. The driver arrived forty minutes later, claiming he'd never been out this way before and had gotten lost in the fog. He looked oddly nervous, and he kept glancing past me into the house. After I paid him, he jogged back to his car and gunned it down the driveway, fog creeping in from the woods now that the first batch of rain was gone. It lapped at the driveway like an incoming tide.

In the dining room, Stevie had torn open a bag of potato chips and set it on the table along with two cans of beer.

Grandpa's chips.

Grandpa's beer.

But Grandpa was an alcoholic.

"Where did you find that beer?" I said.

Stevie, still dressed in his suit from the funeral, his tie loosened, took a sip from the can. "In the fridge - they were in the drawer. Looks like Grandpa might have fallen off the wagon. I can't believe nobody noticed these."

I frowned, setting the pizza box on the table. "This might explain why he acted so weird. But why would he start drinking again after so many years?"

Stevie offered his trademark shrug. "Take your pick - depression about Grandma, guilt over the kid he killed, living alone in the woods. With all of that, I'd be surprised if he wasn't drinking. I'd sure as shit be drinking. Heavily."

I rubbed my chin. Alcohol would also explain why Grandpa hadn't returned any of my calls in the last few weeks and had

dramatically shortened his daily conversations with my father. Yet still there seemed to be something more, much more, alcohol only scratching the surface.

After a few bites of pizza, I told Stevie, "Last time I checked you weren't even eighteen, never mind twenty-one. Are you sure you should be going to town on Grandpa's stash?"

He waved a hand. "This isn't a night for soda, dude. I might need two or three."

"Good point. Maybe after two you'll finally take that tie off."

He tugged self-consciously at his tie, and then came another shrug. Chuckling at him, I looked into the living room and noticed for the first time that every light in the house was on. It hadn't been as obvious during the gray afternoon, but now

49

the house was burning brighter than an airstrip. Grandpa's mattress looked painfully lonely in the middle of the room, Night finally settling into sleep atop the pillow, the little white spot on her chest showing as she lied there all curled up, never to be stroked behind the ears again by Grandpa.

Munching our pizza, we talked some more about Grandpa and the strangeness of his house. What would drive a man to cover his windows and seal his doors? Drunkenness appeared to be the easy answer, but what if alcohol had played only a minor role? Stevie presented a strong point when he noted the meticulousness Grandpa had shown in taping each door at the apertures; every single crack had been covered. Grandpa had even blocked the highest windows, way up in the arches, requiring a ladder and a high degree of persistence one wouldn't think achievable for a drunken old man.

Earlier, my mother had suggested that Grandpa might have grown sensitive to sunlight and cold. Therefore, he'd covered the windows to keep the sun out and taped the doors to reduce the drafts. The theory made partial sense, but it still didn't explain why Grandpa had assiduously covered every single window, even the sliders in the basement, not a centimeter of glass exposed.

"It's not that," Stevie said, referencing my mother's theory. "It's something...else. We'll probably never know."

Stevie was right. It's likely we won't learn what tormented Grandpa to such lengths. We can only go forward, away from this house and its heaviness and the things left behind.

Grandpa would want it that way.

Chapter IX

Taking it one day at a time, just as he'd done in his quest to overcome addiction, Jack Gibson found his way through the darkest tunnels, navigating persistently until he came to a place glowing with the faintest traces of light. He didn't have to do it alone, Mary at his side every step of the way, assuring him each night that Peter Elliott's death hadn't been his fault.

Five days after the accident the police announced that no charges would be filed against Jack, which further helped his healing process. Peter had darted between two parked cars along the curb and dashed into Main Street, officers had confirmed through witness reports, allowing Jack no time to stop. A breathalyzer test performed after the collision proved that Jack's blood hadn't contained a drop of alcohol. It had been an accident, a horribly tragic accident and nothing more, yet still Jack struggled to get Peter out of his head. He was slowly healing, but the gruesome memories burned into his thoughts countless times a day. It happened when he was eating, instant appetite killers. It happened when he was watching TV. It happened when he was at work, Peter's face flashing at him, but most often it happened when he drove his Ford F-150, the same vehicle that had ended the boy's life, a vehicle that now brought anguish with each mile. It also brought fear.

"Driving that truck is just too much. How can I possibly drive when I keep expecting another kid to run out in the road?" Jack told Mary one night in bed, the room shadowy and moonlit and disquieting, Jack immensely grateful for his wife lying beside him.

She traced a hand across his cheek. "How about I drive you for a little while?"

"No, no," he hastened. "I couldn't ask that of you. I just have to figure out–"

She was shushing him, her finger upon his lips. "I'll be your chauffeur as long as you need me, Jackie. It'll be good for me. What else is a retired old lady gonna do with herself?"

Mary wound up chauffeuring him for nearly three months, until finally Jack's pride made it intolerable to let his wife drive him everywhere as if he were an invalid. Gradually the clarity of his memories had faded and their frequency had decreased, which enabled him to drive relatively comfortably again, though never as comfortable as he'd once been behind the wheel.

And he always drove with the radio off.

Almost four months after the accident, with help from Rob, Mary reached out to the Elliott family and arranged for a meeting between Jack and Peter's parents. It would help both sides move forward, she said, but Jack, though he'd agreed, still wasn't sure about it. He feared that seeing the devastated parents would tear open his healing wounds and revictimize the Elliotts, but he knew he couldn't ignore this opportunity, especially if the parents were willing to meet the man who'd killed their son.

Driving to the Elliott house across town, Jack took solace in knowing that Rob and Mary had partnered with Peter's parents to set up a benefit foundation in their child's memory. Annual fundraisers of all kinds would be held to support the Peter Elliott Foundation, the first one slated for next month, a 5K run. Having been elected senator, Steve said he'd pull a few strings to ensure the events were well promoted.

At least they know we care, Jack thought. He was almost to the Elliott house now, driving considerably slower than usual. It was a bright, nearly cloudless day, not unlike the morning Peter had lied dead in his father's arms. Jack tried to dispatch the memories, tried to think of something else. Anything else. The house was just ahead to his right, Jack confirming the address with a look at the mailbox. He was here – but now what would he do, knock on the door and say, Hi, I'm the guy who killed your kid, so nice to finally meet you?

Jack pulled cautiously into the driveway. He'd decided to take Mary's car; it would be hard enough for Peter's parents to stomach the sight of Jack, never mind the awful truck. He wondered if they'd greet him with shotguns, a thought that kept him momentarily glued to the driver's seat, glancing out at the recently mown lawn. The house seemed to be in top shape as well – a porch flag fluttering in the slightest breeze, flower boxes adding vigor and color, the front gardens neatly mulched – nothing falling apart or caving in, no outward signs of the grief and trauma that resided within those walls. No one could have guessed by looking at the house that the Elliotts had lost their only child in May, but Jack shuddered with memories, so much blood on that little boy's face.

Jack thought about turning around – maybe they wouldn't even know he'd come.

But Mary wanted him to do this. She said it would be good for him, and so far everything she'd advised had helped him, even talking to a shrink once a week for two months, an idea Jack had at first adamantly resisted. Mary always knew best, it seemed.

Morning does not welcome those who die, Jack thought upon stepping out of the car, the words clattering into his head with sudden and discomforting randomness. He hadn't been exposed to that line since those two nightmares immediately following Peter's death, but now it had sprung back into his head.

"I shouldn't be here," he murmured, feeling cold, but he forced himself to keep going, up the flower-lined front walkway to the door, the house seeming to hulk over him like a forbidding fortress.

Jack hesitated before ringing the doorbell, still questioning whether this was a good idea. *Do it for Mary*, he thought, and thrust a finger toward the doorbell, pressing swiftly and firmly before he could change his mind, the crisp sound met by a prolonged silence. Jack checked his watch – just after ten o'clock. Mary had said they'd agreed to meet him at ten, but maybe they'd decided it was too much, that they couldn't

54

endure a single moment with him, not that Jack could blame them. Since the wreck he'd often wondered how he would have handled the death of one of his own children at Peter's age, but on each occasion he'd retreated into a defensive, blaming mindset, assuring himself that he and Mary never would have let a six-year-old run free near a roadway. Searching for culpability had been an inevitable component of his emotional response, a natural tendency to divest himself of guilt, but Mary kept saying the only way to completely heal was to accept that accidents are no one's fault. God needed that little boy with Him in Heaven, she'd said, but she was a spiritual woman, her faith helping her through hard times. Jack, conversely – an agnostic turned atheist – could see no place in a fictional afterlife paradise for Peter Elliott, only the black nothingness that exists before you come into this world and after you leave it. Peter wasn't sitting on a cloud way up in those blue skies, dressed in an elegant white robe and playing the harp alongside a haloed angel – he was in the ground, decomposing.

Just as Jack was about to leave, the door was pulled partly open, Peter's father squinting into the sunlight from a tenebrous interior. His face was haggard and heavily stubbled, appearing to have aged ten years in a few months. For a moment the two men stared at each other in haunted silence, the same chilling current running between them, the same sunny morning connecting them inextricably.

"I'm so sorry," Jack said, his voice an unfamiliar rasp. "I just want you to know that, if I could trade places with your son, I wouldn't think twice."

The man nodded, his face twisting and darkening so inscrutably that Jack couldn't tell if he would burst into tears or shout at him. "Come in, please," he said in a small voice, opening the door and exposing the gloomy foyer to the sunlight. Jack reckoned he'd never seen a home this dark in the daytime, as if there were no windows to receive any light.

Morning does not welcome those who die, he thought again, following Peter's father into a dim, cheerless living room sealed by maroon blinds.

"I'm David," the man said, flipping on the light and settling into a rocking chair. "I appreciate everything you and your family have done. My wife, she wants to meet you, but it's still too soon for her. I hope you understand."

"Of course, absolutely," Jack said, straining to find the right words. "If I were in her shoes, I wouldn't want to see me either."

The man pointed at the sofa opposite his rocking chair, and Jack took a reluctant seat, his eyes roaming up to the mantel and the line of photos above it, almost all of them including Peter. "A very nice home," he said, feeling as though he were wobbling along the edge of a steep escarpment…and a stiff, evil wind insisted on giving him free tickets aboard a doomed flight.

David sighed, glancing about the room with tormented eyes. "This place is so quiet now – that's one of the hardest parts. We just can't get used to the quiet. We'll probably end up moving soon; I think that'd be best, a fresh start." He rubbed his eyes, sighed again, injected a little energy into his voice. "Would you like something to drink? Coffee? Water?"

"No, thanks, I'm all set," Jack said.

There was another lingering silence, broken when David said, "We don't blame you for what happened, you know. If anyone's to blame, it's me." Tears glistened in his eyes, the weight of a million agonies pressing on his sagging shoulders. "My wife was at her parents' place that weekend, and I…I was supposed…"

He took a long time to compose himself, Jack waiting patiently on the sofa and studying the photos – in every one Peter was not merely smiling but brimming with joy, even as a toddler. He'd been a very happy kid, with two loving parents and a great life, all of it stripped away on a sunny Sunday morning.

Morning does not welcome those who die.
Jack shifted, scratched his chin, his eyes returning to David, who was now rocking back and forth and staring at his shoes. Jack wondered if he should leave. He'd never been overly socially adept, preferring to talk to the vehicles he'd repaired in one garage or another for much of his life – and this was beyond anything he'd ever experienced, beyond anything he'd imagined he would experience. At times, as now, he felt like none of it was real, like the whole thing was just an elaborate nightmare that would eventually end with a brand new day and a swell of relief, perhaps, too, with a whispered line in his head.

Morning does not welcome those who die.

Watching a broken father attempt to recover himself, Jack grappled with an odd thought that they were both being drawn toward some inexorable happening. Certain people might call it destiny, others fate. Jack had never believed in all of that stuff, but the force of whatever "it" was poked uncomfortably into his ribs, an invisible burden that demanded his attention. The Barfield and Brickley truck, the aberrantly long train, those two shuffling old ladies in the crosswalk – all of it had caused him to hit little Peter, but that hadn't been the end of it, he sensed. No, not the end but instead the beginning. This had all happened for a definitive, undeniable reason, a creeping thought insisted. Jack remembered his reactions in the hours and days following the accident, the ones that had filled him with rage at some perceived greater power, the same force that was quite possibly drawing him toward…toward what?

You're making too much out of this. It was just a horrible accident. There's no grand scheme, no magnet pulling you toward–

"He's here," David said in a ragged, whispery voice, glancing at Jack with moist eyes that gleamed with revelation. "Peter, I feel like he's still here. When it's quiet and I'm alone in here, I hear his footsteps on the stairs. Sometimes I even hear him laughing. I know he's in a better place, but he's here with us, too, I just know it." He inhaled deeply, regarding the room with crushing despair. "He would have been seven now. We'd already bought a few of his presents – didn't know what to do with them afterward. Come to think of it, I'm not even sure who ended up taking them."

Jack nodded repeatedly, debating what he should say, feeling oddly hot in spite of the cool house, like he just might be sick. Mary would surely say something moving about Peter living on in his parents' hearts or watching over them from Heaven, but those words would bring nothing but emptiness and sorrow coming from Jack's lips. No matter what other people said, he just couldn't bring himself to embrace spirituality. Life would be so much easier if he could, especially the process of healing from Peter's death, but the idea of God felt like a great big crock, a fantasy people filled their children's heads with to make the cruelties of life a little more manageable. For people who truly believed their loved ones were thriving in Heaven, there'd be a reason to force themselves out of bed on cold, dreary mornings and hurry off to work, another day closer to meeting their deceased family members in paradise.

But for Jack there had never been a blind faith in some great beyond, no guarantee of life after death. There was only the here and now, he believed, the clothes on his back and the people in this life – and once they were gone, once that final sun went down, there was nothing but darkness, so you might as well enjoy each day to the absolute fullest. Mary had always said that must be a horribly lonely way to go through life, often trying to convert Jack to a churchgoing, crucifix-wearing Christian, but as much as he'd wanted to believe for Mary's sake, changing his mindset had been about as easy as changing his eye color.

"How have you been doing?" David said after a while, clasping his hands together. "Your wife told me you took Peter's death really hard. That means a lot to me."

"It does?"

"Of course. You could've driven off and just left him there. You could've chosen to avoid us, but you cared, Jack. You cared about our son. He stayed with you."

Jack straightened, his back growing stiff. "He was a kid, just a little kid. That day…it'll haunt me forever."

"One thing we'll always have in common," David said. "It all happened so quickly. We were getting out of church, walking toward the road. It was our neighbor's kid's Confirmation that day, everyone excited for the party afterward, the kids moving a lot quicker than they usually do after church. A few of the other boys were ahead of us and" – his eyes went dark and grim, falling to the carpet – "one of them collapsed. Tanner Crawford. He was having a bad allergic reaction, but his mother was still inside. People were panicking. *He was stung by a bee, get help, find his mom*, they were shouting. I tried to help the kid until his mom got there with the EpiPen, but Peter…next thing I knew he was running away, toward the road."

David shook his head, tears streaming down his cheeks, his eyes seeming to shrink inward with the horrors of memory. "The police station's right across the street. Everyone was yelling to get help, and that's all Peter wanted to do, to get help for his friend. I couldn't catch him, Jack, just couldn't get there in time." He wiped his eyes. With a few deep breaths he managed to bring himself back from the edge. "He was a good boy," he whispered. "Such a good boy."

Jack's jaw hung open as he heard more, his thoughts drifting to the Barfield and Brickley truck and the lengthy train and those two old ladies. But there'd indeed been influences on Peter's side as well, drawing him to the road – an anaphylaxis crisis and the cruel lure of the police station, multiple cruisers parked out front, little Peter wanting only to help his friend – and yet again Jack wondered if some greater power had been responsible, not necessarily a god but something else.

Jack left the Elliott house a few minutes later feeling cold and achy, a dead boy and seven words clinging stubbornly in his mind.

Morning does not welcome those who die.

BURN, DO NOT READ!

Part II: The Book

Chapter I

Stevie decided to sleep on one of the sofas tonight, but sofas and sleeping bags aren't for me. Having injured and reinjured myself playing college football, my back always gets sore when I don't sleep on a firm mattress (man, was last year's camping trip a disaster). And so I chose to sleep in the guest bedroom, even after Stevie gave me the *DON'T GO* frown, blue eyes swelling with nervousness perhaps spawned from thoughts about whatever had been on Grandpa's mind when the newspapers and the duct tape came out.

But I went anyway.

Now, moments after leaving Stevie behind in the living room, tired but not sleepy, I add fresh sheets to the thin guest bed and change into my pajamas. I reach for my paperback in the travel bag, but reading doesn't appeal to me. I'm too edgy to read. Instead, overtaken by an urge to investigate, I pull open the cluttered desk drawers and then the nightstand drawers, thinking maybe, just maybe I'll go to Grandpa's room next and have a look in there.

Night watches me from the end of the bed as I remove forgotten books and magazines from the drawers, many of them about chess and automotives. For some reason the dog followed me when I decided to come in here, and suddenly she's alert again, ears straight up as she glances into the closet.

The closet. Piss-scented and dingy, there are several boxes in there, carefully stacked on dust-layered suitcases that once traveled atop Grandpa's old station wagon. The first few boxes yield nothing of interest - mostly just archives of financial statements, some dating back decades - but at the bottom of the third box I scour through is a book. On the front cover of rough, worn brown leather, it announces READ! in black marker, the penmanship very closely resembling that of my grandfather. Above that capitalized word appear three others etched jaggedly into the leather and stained in fresh, thick, insistent red:

BURN, DO NOT

These upper components of the title seem like they were torn into the cover using a knife or a box cutter, then carefully finessed with red paint or ink to complete the presentation of,

BURN, DO NOT
READ!

BURN, DO NOT READ!

An incurably curious journalist, I of course feel compelled to open the book and read. But something swift and baleful tells me I shouldn't read it; no, I definitely shouldn't pull open the cover and find upon the first page...

I have forced it back, nailed the door shut, and now I wait. Now I wait.

These words are the only contents of the book's first yellowing page. Written in unfamiliar cursive, their author using blue ink that had dulled with time, the words - without the guidance of margins - undulate gently across the center of the page. The consistency of the paper itself closely resembles that of construction paper, thick and unpleasant to the touch.

There is nothing on the backside of page one, which would ordinarily be considered page two, but on the next page (labeled as the second page), in the same faded blue handwriting, a single cursive line at the top...

It can never be let out.

"What?" I ask Night, who has hopped off the bed to join me.

The dog sniffs the book appraisingly as I keep flipping. Pages three and four are empty, but on page five are Grandpa's words, put down in the small choppy penmanship I've seen scribbled on countless birthday cards. But these words are even messier than usual, jotted by a hurried hand.

I saw it and it saw me, and things will only get worse from here. Don't panic, not now. Don't even look around. Just keep reading. You can't let it know that you know. If you draw its attention, it might kill you. It won't let me leave. I let it out, and I fear it will eventually kill me. If it does, YOU must lock it up again. Here is how you must do it.

I hesitate before turning the page, a cold shudder gliding through me, warning me to put the book away. What the hell is all of this?

A moaning wind buffets the house, the first significant gust in a while, its breath seeping through the bedroom window and chilling my arms. I place the book on the nightstand and settle into bed, comfortable in the cool sheets but uncomfortable in the room, searching the layered shadows beyond the lamplight, expecting... something, feeling watched and a little childish, a startled pang in my gut when Night jumps on the bed again and curls up at the end.

Curiosity prevailing over reluctance, I grab the book and move on to page six, which, in keeping with the theme of previous pages, only displays writing on one side.

It lives in the dark. First, you must always keep the lights on. Never let the house go completely dark. Always have a flashlight and candles nearby. When I first saw it, it was in the darkness. I never should have opened that door, never should have torn out the nails, but Mary was screaming for help and I had to open it. I had to, but Mary wasn't in there. It was in there. I saw something moving, distinguished from the darkness.

I can't believe I opened the door.

Below Grandpa's words, at the bottom of the page, a large red message is painted in drippy streaks, dry yet fresh, so fresh I can smell the paint.

MORNING DOES NOT WELCOME THOSE WHO DIE!

I shut the book with an awful, dust-dashing clap, my neck clenching, the hairs on my neck and arms standing. Another burst of wind outside...and a creak of a floorboard at the edge of the room, near the closed door. Glancing beneath the door, I wonder if I've just seen a shadow sliding past in the hallway. I leap from the bed, open the door. Nothing there, of course. No, this is just me scaring my stupid self. I never should have opened the damn book. Never. But now I'm captured, no more advanced than a fish on a hook. I stand in the guest room doorway for a while, listening to the spattering of water in the bathroom. Stevie is taking a shower, unaware of the turmoil into which I've immersed myself.

It is 9:40. Standing there in the doorway, I listen to the house - the splashing in the bathroom, the intermittent wind spiriting the chimes on the porch, each sough spreading the cool, drizzly night through the walls.

Grandpa's dog has come to my side and is looking down the hallway toward the living room, ears perked, head tilted slightly, almost as if she can detect something invisible to me. The intensity of her gaze is unnerving.

"Come back in, girl," and I shut the door behind us. I'm glad Night is with me tonight, to be honest, and Stevie, too. If I were alone, I definitely would have driven to the motel and shown the book to the rest of my family.

The book.

It waits amidst the sheets, the blankets flipped open by my hurried departure. Night is regarding it from the floor, or maybe

66

she's looking at the window beyond, the curtains trembling almost imperceptibly. The wind lashes at the house again,

drizzles blossoming to a tick-tick-tick of rain against the roof. The wall clock, Coca-Cola themed, stands dormant at 11:57, yet another clock stopped at that time.

I take a deep breath, return to bed, and set the book on the nightstand, Grandpa's trusty black lab jumping on the bed and reclaiming her place at its end. Time for some fiction, I decide, anything to distract me from Grandpa's bizarre (perhaps drunken) ramblings. But I can't concentrate. The lines all jumble together. With each new paragraph of fiction, my mind shifts to contemplations of It and what It is supposed to symbolize and why Grandpa wrote about It.

Specifically, why did Grandpa say he feared It would kill him and then proceed to offer abstruse instructions to an unnamed reader? It was as if he'd been writing directly to the next owner of his home, providing a warning that it is inhabited by...by what? What is it?

What is It?

I scoop up the leather-bound book, fiction and madness trading places. But as I do so, Night looks at me and whines, then leaps off the bed and scratches the door.

"You want to go outside again?" But the dog just went out twenty minutes ago.
Night continues to scratch, this time more adamantly. I open the door and follow her down the hallway, through the living room, and into the dining room, gasping violently when Stevie pops out of the kitchen. He's wrapped in a towel, dripping, a dispenser of liquid soap in hand.

"I don't think Gramps smelled too good in his last days," he says on his way back to the bathroom, flip-flops making a squishing squeak. "There's no soaps, no shampoos, nothing in the shower."

I can't stifle a laugh, even in my disturbed state, thoughts of BURN, DO NOT READ! overflowing.

I let Grandpa's dog out into the rainy night, but she only sits on the back deck, watching me with glittering eyes and gently shaking her tail, indifferent to the rain.

"Come on, girl, do your business," I encourage, wondering what Grandpa would say. Night looks so lost and forlorn, like a ship without its captain, utterly directionless. She might stay out here all night, I fear, or disappear into the woods in search of her master. At least there is a fence surrounding the back yard to

protect her, but it goes back a long way, deep into the woods, and there's no way of knowing if Grandpa maintained it.

Worried, I call Night in and she obediently returns inside, trailing me back down the hall and into the guest bedroom, where Stevie is waiting for me, half-dressed and shivery, a towel draped over his shoulders.

"You have deodorant? I forgot mine." He dries Night off with his towel and scratches her beneath the collar, standing a few feet from the book, oblivious to the silent storm it caused.

I toss him my deodorant from the travel bag. "Thanks, dude," he says, then shivers his way back to the living room.

I contemplate joining Stevie and taking the other sofa. Maybe we can read this thing together and talk about it. A part of me badly wants to share the book with him, but something tells me to keep going on my own. After all, the damn thing's title is: BURN. DO. NOT. READ!

I have no idea what to do. Night watches me intently from the end of the bed, stationed there like a sentry, ready to defend if necessary. It's almost ten o'clock now, and the rain is pouring down on the dark house in the middle of the woods, where ours are the only lights around.

I slide beneath the covers again and clutch the book, tracing my fingers over the etched words, debating whether to open it. What will I possibly gain from reading more? Grandpa is gone - nothing can bring him back. Maybe this was just a late-life fiction project. Many decades ago, before he became a mechanic, Grandpa had wanted to be a writer, my father once told me. Perhaps, in retirement, he lived out his early dream.

Instinct tells me different. A better possibility is Grandpa's writing was an alcohol-driven attempt to counteract the guilt he'd endured after killing that boy six years ago, guilt that might have resurged in the wake of Grandma's death.

Curiosity winning out again, I open the book, flip through the first few pages, stare at *MORNING DOES NOT WELCOME THOSE WHO DIE!* for a fearful moment, and steel myself for more, expecting to find Peter Elliott's name lurking somewhere in the next pages.

Chapter II

Mary died almost a year after Jack struck and killed Peter Elliott, just two days shy of the grim anniversary, in fact.

May was not a good month.

Unlike Peter's death, Mary went out with the quiet grace for which she'd always been known, no blood or suffering or agony, just a silent fade in the night, death creeping in to take her. Jack knew something was wrong when he woke to find Mary lying beside him. She always rose early on spring and summer mornings, sometimes beating the sun to get a start on her gardening, Jack usually waking around nine on Saturdays and finding her out back with her straw hat and floral-patterned gloves, busy watering the plants or trimming the bushes or cleaning one of her many garden ornaments, a collection that had grown every birthday and Mother's Day over the years. Upon seeing Jack each morning, Mary would take recess from whatever she was doing and hurry over to him, never failing to ask how he'd slept. Then she would make him breakfast and update him on household tasks that needed to be accomplished.

But on that cloudy Saturday morning Jack called his wife's name with a chill of dread in his heart, hoping it was only sickness that kept her in bed. But an awful, half-lucid instinct had ravaged him upon first seeing her, and soon, panicked by her continued stillness and silence, darkness suffused his soul like a black, rolling fog.

He checked her pulse. Nothing. Checked again. Nothing.

There was a moment of breathless inaction, terror briefly stopping Jack's heart. "Mary, Mary, wake up, please!" He shook her shoulders, Night jumping on the bed and whimpering, worried brown eyes locked on Mary, tail wiggling with uncertainty, right paw scratching gently at Mary's blanketed leg.

When tear-hazed CPR attempts failed, Jack scrambled to retrieve his cell phone, but even as he dialed 9-1-1 he knew it would be too late. The operator asked a few questions Jack would later forget, and then, as if by a severe malfunction in time's mechanical progression, Jack was letting the paramedics inside. He'd secured Night on a leash, and soon he was pacing the back yard, following his dog's every tug. Later – a minute? an hour? – one of the paramedics told him she'd passed on, his words hollow and unreal, like the words in a dream.

Disbelieving tears streamed down Jack's face, his thoughts going quiet. There was a weird pressurized ringing in his head, the world suddenly distorted and deranged, blurring and slowing. He could hardly breathe.

Falling to his knees, letting the leash slide free of his grip, seven words dominated Jack, sneaking up on him as they'd done before.

Morning does not welcome those who die.

Rob and Steve flew in that evening, arriving in time to help Jack prepare dinner – dinner without Mary, though Jack felt like she'd step through the door any second, smiling and cheerful, Night dashing over to greet her.

Is she really gone? Is it all over, so many years, just like that? But what about breakfast tomorrow? We have to have our Sunday breakfast.

Paul, on duty at the time of his mother's death, had called from Alaska and promised to catch the first flight out of Anchorage tomorrow morning. It comforted Jack to have his sons with him, and for a few surreal moments it was like they were boys again, tramping through the house to help their father with tasks that suddenly seemed unimportant.

Jack, seated on the sofa beside Night, watched dazedly as they bustled about the house, the aroma of pasta floating in from the kitchen. It reminded Jack of Mary; she'd always made a delicious pasta dinner, layering slices of cheese upon each steaming plate and letting them conform meltingly to the meat and noodles, then completing the meal with homemade garlic bread. Closing his eyes, Jack could envision her watching Wheel of Fortune or Jeopardy on the little kitchen television

as she prepared a salad or readied the dishes. So many memories. So much time together.

And now it was over.

Jack rubbed his reddened, streaky eyes, another dart of reality breaking through the insulating fabric of denial. Those darts were especially painful in his raw state. He liked to think that Mary was out buying groceries, or running a little behind after helping the senior center folks with another project. It wasn't even that late – there was still time.

But Jack's sons were here, both of them, and that could only mean bad news. He couldn't recall the last time Rob and Steve had both been in the same room, the Gibson brothers always pulled in opposite directions at the holidays by family commitments. Steve's wife was the daughter of an Indiana millionaire CEO who hosted lavish Thanksgiving and Christmas parties, insisting that everyone in his family attend each event with the demanding force of a captious bride-to-be. And Rob's wife, always kind and shy, was the daughter of two religious radicals who loved nothing more than a good old-fashioned family protest outside an abortion clinic to celebrate the holidays, often inviting Rob to take part or at least look after the cats while they were away, such strange people.

"Strange people," Jack muttered. He was staring absently at Night, his fingers finding their way beneath her collar for a scratch. He wasn't hungry – just the thought of eating made his stomach clench. He'd only begun preparing dinner because it was almost dinnertime and Mary wasn't home.

"Dinner's almost ready, Dad," Rob called, appearing in the living room doorway.

"That's okay, son, you guys go ahead," he mumbled. "I think I'll just rest for a while longer."

Rob frowned. "You should at least try to eat a little."

"Okay, okay," and he was up, following his eldest son into the dining room, where Mary had just yesterday changed the tablecloth to match the patriotic theme of the season. In anticipation of Memorial Day and the Fourth, she'd decorated the house in red, white, and blue as she always did, asking Jack last week to hang the fireworks flag from the porch, a thing he'd grumbled about because he never enjoyed going through bags filled with dozens of flags every two to three weeks and finding Mary's latest choice. *Do you have to change them so damn often?* he'd complained, but now that memory brought moisture to his eyes.

A craving for whiskey shot through him.

No, no, you can't. Mary would never allow it.

Just take the edge off, Jackie, no big deal. Morning, it only welcomes the living, you know.

At dinner there was mostly silence, save for the clinking of silverware and the clicking of Night's toenails on the hardwood floor as she roamed the dining room, circling the table in search of the person most likely to feed her scraps. That had always been Mary's job, Jack snapping at her whenever she tossed Night a piece of meat or set down an empty bowl for her to lick clean. *If she gets up all night, you're taking her out*, he'd often warned, but Mary had only smiled and reminded him that Night had a stomach of steel. *Stop being such a Grouch-o Marx* had been one of her go-to lines, but never again would Jack hear it.

Mary was gone.

Forever.

Not just grocery shopping gone, not this time. Forever gone.

Night assumed Mary was coming back, glancing often to the door.

But she wasn't coming back.

Another dart.

Morning does not welcome those who die.

Take the edge off, Jackie. Just a few sips.

Jack, suddenly nauseous, pushed away from the table. "I need some air, guys." His sons both stood as if to follow him, but he waved for them to stay. "Keep eating. I'll just be a few minutes on the porch. Need some fresh air."

The night was cool and starry. Rounding the house to the back yard with small, indiscriminate steps, Jack gazed up to the glittering firmament and remembered Mary's many talks about her loved ones looking down on her from Heaven. She had always spoken so confidently – almost knowingly – a peaceful trace of a smile on her lips sometimes as she stared skyward.

Is Mary really up there somewhere, watching?

It was a quick, uplifting thought that poured in and then burst like bubbles cavorting out from a child's wand.

"No," Jack murmured softly, new tears in his eyes, his lips trembling violently. "Nothing up there but stars and space. Just emptiness, is all."

Soon Jack found himself among the rows of flowers in the back yard gardens, his attention drawn specifically to a large rosebush that had recently been in bloom. Just last weekend Mary had summoned Jack from the garage to take a moment to appreciate the flowers, two glasses of lemonade in hand as she spoke excitedly about the white roses. Jack, irritated that morning by the challenges of repairing his lawnmower, had complained about always being asked to look at the gardens. *I've already seen the flowers*, he'd cranked, Mary, with a sigh, leaving behind his glass of lemonade on a shelf and returning to the garden.

But now, only a week later, Mary was gone and her white roses had wilted, their fallen petals like melting snow beneath the dim exterior lights, soon to vanish altogether. Mary's solar-lighted lawn ornaments, meanwhile, glowed in lambent greens and blues throughout the yard, leaving Jack feeling cold and regretful.

It's too late to see the flowers now. Too late for Mary. Way too late for Peter.

Too late.

But there were so many words unspoken, actions unfulfilled, promises not kept, only the chirring crickets for Jack to converse with out here tonight. Watching Mary walk down the aisle to him so many years ago, it had seemed like they would last forever, like eternity was theirs, like it would never end, the way you feel at the beginning of a ball game, when the sun stretches goldenly across the outfield seats and the light towers aren't needed just yet.

The wedding, *their* wedding. That had been the radiant sunrise, but darkness had fallen and the roses had died, only the petals remaining – and even they would disperse and disappear.

It was over, really over.

Mary was wrong. You only get one go-round, and once it's over, it's gone forever.

Above, twinkling in the sea of nothingness, the stars were bright and foreboding.

***

Rob started after Dad, but Steve told him to stay. "Just give him some time alone," Steve said.

There was a moment of hesitation before Rob returned to his seat. When Dad closed the front door behind him, Rob said, "I'm worried

about him, Steve. He's already so fragile – what's this gonna do to him?"

Steve looked up from his cell phone. He'd just received a text message from one of his most powerful backers asking if he would miss the cancer fundraiser dinner Monday night. The man and his wife had contributed significantly to Steve's successful campaign, and now it was time for Steve to pay down the debt.

Nothing is ever free in politics, and it was a very bad time for Steve to be away from Washington.

"He'll be all right. It's gonna take a while, but he'll pull through," Steve said, distrait, finishing his text message. When he glanced up and saw Dad's dog scratching at the front door, eager to join her master on the porch, he said, "But what about the damn dog? I get the feeling Mom kept track of it all day – with Dad watching it, the thing'll probably run off and get lost within a week."

Rob shook his head miserably. "She was so healthy, never smoked, hardly even drank. How can she be gone, Steve? She was only seventy-five."

"Way too soon," Steve mumbled, his attention already drawn to the next message on his phone. "So how are things with the firm? I could use a change of subject."

"Good, busy but good. What about you? D.C. treating you okay?"

Steve shrugged. "Can't complain, playing the game a day at a time. Only one way up the ladder, you know?"

Rob took a few bites and sipped from a glass of soda as Steve completed his response.

"What are we gonna do about Dad?" Rob said after a while, looking earnestly at Steve. The uncertainty in his eyes was sharp and direct, an unnerving thing to see in the eyes of a man who'd always been so confident and resolute. Rob was the leader of the Gibson boys, but now he seemed desperate, no longer making definitive decisions but reaching out for advice on how to proceed.

Steve sent his message, then set his phone on the table. Before him a plate of pasta was cooling off. "We let Dad grieve, that's what we need to do," he said. "After a while he'll come through it. Time heals all wounds, right?"

"But this house, what if it's too much for him to handle all by himself? He doesn't cook or do laundry or buy groceries – Mom always did all of that stuff. This place'll be a mess without her, and none of us are close enough to help him out." He spoke in a virtual whisper, glancing often to the front door to make sure Dad was still outside.

Steve rubbed his chin, a few ideas coming to him along with a dim smile at the thought of solving a problem that baffled Rob. "We'll pay for home care. Those people do everything for you – he'd never have to lift a finger. Or we could put him in a senior living community, a nice place where they buy your groceries for you and do your laundry. And if they don't offer something, I'll pay someone to provide the service. How does that sound?"

Rob shook his head. "Come on, this is *Dad* we're talking about. He'll never go for either of those things."

"Well, we can't have him driving around distraught and killing another kid, can we?" The problem was coming more clearly into view, like rounding a bend and seeing a downed tree in the road. Steve took a long sip of soda, his irritation settling. In a calmer voice he said, "You're the one who said he won't be able to live alone. This place" – he raised a hand to regard the house – "is just too much for him."

Rob sighed. "Good luck asking him to let people in here to help him out. And getting him into a senior community – I sure as hell am not mentioning that one."

"Fine, I'll do it," Steve said, bringing a forkful of pasta to his lips. "It's what needs to be done. After the funeral I'll let him know, but you need to back me up on this, and Paul too."

Rob mulled over the possibilities as Steve ate. "It would be a lot easier," he eventually said, "knowing Dad's in a safe place where he won't get overwhelmed with chores. No more mowing the lawn, no more snowblowing the driveway – the thought of him out there all alone on the icy driveway always makes me nervous."

"Me too," Steve blurted through a mouthful of food, pointing adamantly at his brother. He blotted his lips with a napkin. "We're all very busy people, Rob. We have busy lives and commitments – we don't have time to fly back here all the time to help Dad out. At first he won't like a big change, but in the long run it'll make life easier for all of us. I can even pay a guy to drive him to and from work. That way we don't have to worry about any more driving debacles."

Rob nodded repeatedly. "Yes, that would definitely be a major convenience if we can just get Dad to agree to it. Those senior communities aren't so bad, are they? We'd just have to find one that allows pets."

"Damn right we will. Let's face it, we can't afford to have Dad living alone. He's a liability, and I don't need any liabilities right now."

Chapter III

Jack wasn't exactly sure when he'd decided concretely to move across the country. The idea had at first struck him as impossible on the night of Mary's death, a fantasy that could never be transformed into a practicable plan. But then there'd been the sleepless nights, his first consecutive nights without Mary beside him in over forty years, and the thought of spending the rest of his life in this house without her had seemed torturous.

Then the wake had come and gone on a humid night, thunder rolling in the distance, Jack forcing himself to look upon Mary's lifeless face and give her one final kiss – and later the idea of moving far away had appealed with greater strength, drawing him into the logistical equations and presenting a promising offer. A new place free of memories.

I can do this, he'd thought. *I can make it happen.*

Perhaps the funeral had clinched it for him. The sun had been bright that day and the smell of freshly cut grass had drifted in along a warm breeze. Seven words had pestered Jack on occasion – Morning does not welcome those who die – and memories of Peter Elliott had galloped cruelly across his beleaguered mind. He'd tried to put all of that to the periphery and concentrate on the good times, so many good times with Mary, but the fear of a dismal future had overshadowed the warmth of a cherished past. The single worst part was the crushing weight of knowing he would never see the love of his life again, a force strong enough to suck the air from him.

Well beyond the cemetery, on the town common, workers had decorated the gazebo with red, white, and blue flag banners for Memorial Day, the world moving forward as it always did. And Jack had known with frigid sorrow that he would never again watch the parade with Mary, time having run out for his wife, just as it had expired for little Peter last year.

Later, when the service was over and Jack was home, he'd again entertained the notion of traveling across the country and establishing a new home for himself. Online research of locations and real estate listings had led to fresh thoughts, and those thoughts had blossomed into an aching desire to leave this town behind. When his sons had asked him the next day if he would be interested in moving into a senior living community, he'd felt an even greater urgency to set the wheels of change into motion.

Now, almost two weeks after the funeral, Jack Gibson called Rob with the news. "Son, I've decided to move out."

"That's great, Dad! So you talked to the woman from Valleyview? I knew you'd like that place."

"No, Rob, I'm not talking about the damn retirement home. I'll be moving across the country, to a little town in..."

By the time Jack finished describing his next town of residence, Rob could only groan helplessly on the other end. "Jesus, Dad, are you sure about this? What if you need help with something? What if you get sick? You won't know anyone. Tell me you haven't made any permanent arrangements. Please tell me you haven't bought the place!"

Seated on the sofa beside Night, Jack scratched his dog behind the ears, a shadow of a relieved smile upon his lips. Mostly he was straight scared about setting out on his own.

"I'm seventy years old, Rob, not ninety. The way you boys talk makes it seem like I'm an invalid shuffling around with an oxygen tank. I can do this – I *will* do this," he said with proud conviction, again taking a moment to remind himself that he was more than capable of making this most needed move. "I can't stand living in this house another second. And a retirement home? Give me a break – what would I do all day, play checkers and watch paint dry?"

"Dad, it's not a retirement home. It's a *senior living community*," Rob corrected, emphasizing these last three words as if Jack were hard of hearing. His three boys had done exceedingly well for themselves and therefore always thought they knew best, but Jack wouldn't buy what they were selling this time. No, sir, he wouldn't be put away in some stuffy home like a pants-soiling, drooling, doddering, cane-bumbling old codger, nor would he go for his sons' other idea and welcome a parade of strangers into his house to do all the chores and then steal his valuables. He still had several good years left, and Mary would want him to move on and find a new place, he kept telling himself, a place far away from all the darkness. She'd want him to be happy and independent, and damn it, he was going to enjoy life again…or at least try. The world had put him down, had licked him good, but he would spring back up swinging. He hadn't even touched a single drink following Mary's death, resisting the strongest urges, sometimes sobbing until he fell asleep, but with a new home he knew he could be better again.

"What about your job?" Rob said.

"I'll quit, find a new job. Or maybe I'll just retire. With the money your mother and I saved up, I don't have to work another day in my life."

"But what about your friends?"

"Screw 'em. Can always make new friends." Jack was smiling broadly now, pleased with his terse, bold replies. If these boys intended to put him in a home, they'd need to drug him, tie him up, and stuff him in the trunk.

Rob sighed. "Are you sure you want to move all the way across the country? I can understand wanting to get away, but what about somewhere closer, maybe a house up my way a little? Or closer to Steve in D.C.?"

"Nah, I don't want to be a burden to you boys. You've all got lives to live, families to raise. I can get on just fine by myself – don't need people checking in on me all the time and asking if I remember my

damn name. We'll talk on the phone as much as you want, how about that?"

"But what will you eat, sandwiches and fast food? Can you even cook?" Rob's voice had risen with frustration.

"I can grill, and maybe I'll learn to cook. It'll be an adventure, like that book Paul got me for Christmas after he moved to Alaska. I'll be an independent contractor, son."

"Are you talking about *Into the Wild*?"

"Yeah, I think that's the one."

"Dad, the guy in that book died alone in an abandoned school bus in the middle of the woods."

"Then it wasn't that book. Another one. The guy was an adventurer, figured everything out for himself. That's gonna be me – I don't need anyone to hold my hand. It'll be just me and Night, a couple-a pioneers, you hear?"

* * *

Steve got the call from Rob around eight o'clock. He was on his way home after a long day of handshakes and posturing – another day of playing the game – and what he wanted most was a cold beer and a hot meal. What he received instead was a massive annoyance.

"We've got a big problem," Rob said. "Not only does Dad hate the idea of moving to a senior living community, but he's bent on moving across the goddamn country!"

84

"What? Christ, you've gotta be kidding!"

"I wish. I just got off the phone with him. He's done all kinds of research online – he even picked out a few houses he wants to tour. He's obsessed with this town out in…"

"That's absolutely insane."

"What are we gonna do, Steve?"

Steve bit his lip hard. "This is a total disaster. Again. Why does everything with Dad have to be a problem? It's like he searches for ways to complicate our lives." Steve picked up speed and began zigzagging across the Beltway, drawing the ire and horns of several motorists. "You and Paul need to handle this. If I talk to him, I'll only make it worse. You know that."

"But there's nothing more I can say to change his mind."

"You're a goddamn lawyer, come up with something! Scare him, threaten him, tell him he's on his own if something goes wrong. I don't care what you say, but let him know he's making his bed. When things go south, he's gonna lay in it!"

Steve forced himself to breathe, knowing he probably sounded to Rob like a lunatic.

"I shouldn't have moved up here," Rob said, his voice turning sad and regretful. "Things would be manageable if we still lived close to Dad."

Steve shook a finger at the windshield. "You made a career move, man. Don't ever feel guilty for that. He's obviously playing a game here – he wants one of us to move back so he won't be on his own, but that's just not how it works. We're all grown men, Robbie. We've got commitments – we can't be responsible for babysitting him. I made him a perfectly reasonable offer. I'm even willing to pay someone to drive him around, but no, that's not good enough. Nothing's ever good enough for Dad. He insists on making things difficult."

"Maybe I could work something out where I fly down there twice a month. I feel like I need to do this, Steve. For everything he did for us, I feel like I need to be there."

"Well, if that's your decision, then go for it. You're a better guy than me, but if he's serious about moving across the country, you don't owe him a damn thing."

"He sure sounded serious," Rob said quietly. "I'll tell him I want to fly down twice a month. Maybe that'll get him to change his mind."

"Let's hope so. I'm getting awfully tired of his nonsense. He could have cost me the election if I didn't play my cards right – I'll be damned if he messes anything else up."

Chapter IV

Jack knew the perils of purchasing a house without seeing it in person, but that's precisely what he did three weeks after Mary's funeral. The realtor seemed like a pretty straightforward guy, and the online photos of the house were comprehensive. Plus, with the boys continuing to hound him, he knew he needed to get away fast. There was no time for deliberation, not with his sons eager to lock him in some place where they drooled and knitted and watched TV all day.

The one-story home was surrounded by a nine-acre property, the majority of it comprised of wilderness, with a few rolling fields and a little pond and stream mixed in to remind potential buyers this was the wild, sprawling west, where you didn't have to worry about the guy next door waking you up with his loud music or his early morning lawnmower. The nearest house was more than two miles south, and though worn and rustic, Jack's new place had an undeniable charm, squat and quiet and unassuming, a little home in the big woods.

"It's a great place for hunting, fishing, hiking – whatever outdoor stuff suits your fancy," the realtor had said. "If you're looking for quiet, mister, then this is certainly the place for you. A great town, too. People here are real friendly, nobody in much of a hurry, everyone just enjoying the slower pace of life."

Slow. That was good. Slow and quiet. Jack imagined himself on a porch rocking chair at his new home, easing back and forth one early morning and watching a pair of deer at the edge of the woods. Night would probably chase them off, bounding after deer and rabbits and squirrels until she tired herself out. And Jack would build a fence to keep her safe, wide enough to allow Night a good chunk of running room. She'd never gotten that before, having to settle for evening walks with Mary, but now she and Jack would enjoy all the benefits their new home had to offer.

On cold evenings they would keep warm with roaring fires, and on hot days they'd take dips in the nearby lake (even though Night sometimes got a little skittish around water). Jack could buy a few classic cars and

spend a summer restoring them, or perhaps he'd get another motorcycle and take in the scenery, cruising unfamiliar roads and savoring the thrill of the ride. Of course, on his very first night at his new place he would have to celebrate with a grilled steak, but he hoped to eventually learn to cook – how hard could it be? He would never come close to matching the deliciousness of Mary's meals, but who besides a decorated chef could hope to do that? Simply preparing edible, unburned food would be an accomplishment, and at his new home he would get it done, finally breaking free of sandwiches and microwave meals.

A new home, quiet and remote and cozy, a house in the middle of the woods, with nothing to disturb it and no bad memories to infect it. Perfect.

The perfect place, Jack thought excitedly as he finalized the transaction.

BURN, DO NOT READ!

Chapter V

Page seven of the strange book is steered by consternation, all of it courtesy of Grandpa.

You must get it back to its room in the basement. Don't go there now. Don't even look up. Just keep reading, stay with my words. You mustn't attract it. If it feels threatened, it may try to kill you even quicker. But with a little luck, you might be able to trick it back into that room. I never should have taken out those damn nails, but I thought Mary was calling. She was calling me from the other side. But it wasn't her. It was scratching and slamming and screaming. Somehow it took Mary's voice.

In a few minutes, go to the basement. Pretend you're checking on the furnace or something. Don't look around, and don't let on you're afraid. Bring a flashlight and turn on every light. Know that it's always watching you. It is every noise, every shadow, every footstep. It comes in the darkness, but it's always there. Night can sense it far better than me. If she starts growling at something you can't see, you know it's close, real close. That's when you need to get out, even if the lights are on. I think it's getting stronger. Who knows? Before long, maybe it will live in the light too. This is why I can't sleep at night anymore. It turns out the lights. I hear it going from room to room every night. Even in the day I can't get out. It's keeping me here.

So why, Grandpa, I wonder, did you cover all of the windows with newspapers if you wanted light in the house? Again my mind wanders back to the idea of fiction. If this is a scary short story, then it has sufficiently done its job in scaring me. But if Grandpa was enslaved by the bottle in his final months, how could he have composed a fiction work of such creative depth, paralleling his environment to that of a fabricated setting wherein a narrator educates his reader on how to defeat the monster in his home? And what would have inspired him to produce such a piece, the writer and narrator one and the same?

A long, shrieking gust of wind.

I look up. Night is curled up at the end of the bed, but she's watching the closed door, alert and expectant, not tired in the least.

Neither am I.

I can't put the book down. On page eight Grandpa wrote...

BURN, DO NOT READ!

So now you know what to do if you can get it back to where it came from. You must do it. Not right now. Do something else first. Then do it.

Confused, I glance to the edge of the page and notice the rough remains of a page torn out between seven and eight. This means the real page eight was stripped for some reason, a page that - according to Grandpa - would have offered instructions on what to do when "It" was back in its room.

I am reading page nine, not eight, yet the page is labeled as eight.

A loud thump elsewhere in the house. Teeth bared, hackles raised, Night leaps from the bed and growls at the door, looking not like Grandpa's black lab but a snarling coyote. She barks once, then twice, followed by a fury of barks that sends me racing through the door and into the hallway, Night preceding me.

I hurry into the dark living room, mind-bent with fears about Burn, Do Not Read! Too dark in here. *It lives in the dark*, Grandpa had written, and without thinking I react, flipping all three switches on the nearest wall and lighting up the room.

Night, having already circled the house, is growling and scratching at the basement door behind me in the hallway.

Blanketed on the sofa, Stevie sits up and squints at me like I'm insane. "What the hell?"

"Did you hear that noise?"

"What noise?"

Night falls silent, stepping back from the basement door but regarding it with suspicion, head tilted.

"You didn't hear anything? It was really loud."

Stevie shakes his head. "I fell asleep for a few minutes." Now he looks a little wary, glancing about the room as if he, too, had heard something.

I feel like an idiot. "Never mind."

I call Night, who reluctantly turns from the basement door.

"Good night, cuz," Stevie says, and I tell him good night, turning off two of the lights, fighting an urge to ask him to keep the final light on overnight. This book is really getting to me. Combined with Night's odd behavior, its words seem even more threatening, enough to fuel an urge to call my father and show it to him.

But it's just fiction, I tell myself, a story not necessarily about *this* house but any house. If it's fiction, though, why did Grandpa use Grandma's name? He wrote that Mary had called to him from the basement room, but would a man as private as him have really written a dark fictional work with Grandma as a character? It makes no sense. Absolutely none. Grandpa told us he'd moved out here to live in a place without memories of Grandma, so why would he write a first-person work of fiction containing such personal material? Why not choose the third-person perspective and change Mary's name to Denise?

I return to the guest bedroom, this time leaving the door open and turning on the hallway light, chilly shudders of fear creeping through me. Night finds her place at the end of the bed, lowering her head to her forepaws and watching the doorway. I try not to look at her. Every time I do she freaks me out even more, wearing on me like a dull knife against a thin rope.

For a while I eye the book. I don't want to read any more. I just want to sleep, but I'm not tired, especially not now. And the book keeps calling me.

I read on, skipping page after page of stories about Grandpa and Grandma. Happy stories. I begin to relax. Maybe writing this book was a cathartic process for Grandpa, a way to drive out his grief and embrace the positive memories. Perhaps he

initially planned to ask his family to read the book, then decided against it.

Yet the title seems far too intense for such thoughts. Something tells me this was beyond catharsis, beyond cleansing, beyond all understanding.

Night barks, a shrill, yelpy, alarming sound that rings in my ears and shoots currents of dread up my chest. She is peering into the hallway, ears perked again, eyes locked on something unseen.

I snap the book shut, shifting my focus from anecdotes of Grandpa's wedding in Florida to the dog he left behind. I try to convince myself that she is only acting weird because she's lonely and shaken by her master's sudden disappearance. There have been strangers in her house all week, and she was forced to spend a few days living at that veterinarian's house. If I were a dog, I would be growling and snarling and scratching as well.

But cold instinct hints that there's more. Way more. More to all of this. Drunk or not, Grandpa wouldn't have endeavored on such an epically odd writing project without a definitive reason. And his writing sure doesn't seem to be a sample of a maddened mind. The fact remains that he used Mary's name and the pronoun I, writing in this very house, perhaps feeling the same heaviness that has cloaked me since I arrived this morning, his doors taped shut and his windows covered with newspaper, candles and flashlights and religious pieces surrounding his mattress in the center of the house. And now I'm hearing bumps and thumps, and Night, always known for her friendliness - even as a puppy back in Grandpa's old house - is jittery and irascible.

All coincidences? Or is this house...can it really be...? I recall my trip to the basement with my family this afternoon - there was no room down there that could have been used to lock something up. Or maybe we didn't look closely enough?

The wind brushes against the house. Night jumps off the bed and looks up to the ceiling in the corner of the room near the closet. She barks once, then makes a little circle and continues her staredown with the ceiling.

If she starts growling at something you can't see, you know it's close, real close.

Frustrated by the dog's increasing strangeness, especially my reactions to it, I slide the book beneath the bed. Enough of this! I switch off the lamp and turn onto my side, but as soon as the room is dark Night begins growling menacingly, louder,

louder, so loud I fear she might be growling at me. I yell at her to shut up, feeling immediately bad about it, but she vaults up to the bed, still growling. Afraid she'll bite me, I turn on the lamp and she goes instantly quiet, wagging her tail and alighting from the bed once more.

It comes in the darkness.

Footsteps. Creaking floorboards. A shadow in the hallway, pressing closer.

I've never been so relieved to see a person's face. "Why is Night freaking out so much?" Stevie says, patting the dog on the back when she comes to him in the doorway. He's wearing a sweatshirt and boxers and long black socks, looking tired and not quite right, a little queasy maybe.

"It's a major culture shock." I shake my head. "Grandpa loved this dog more than any pet he ever had."

Stevie nods understandingly, trying to put things together in his head. Mostly, he's straining to reconcile the deranged owner of this house with the grandfather he once knew. He's never been as close to Grandpa as me, his relationship with Grandma and Grandpa limited mostly to Thanksgiving and Christmas family get-togethers that usually hadn't included his father. It was different for me. My parents and I used to live thirty minutes from my grandparents' house. I remember playing chess with him, going for weekend rides on his Harley, and hiking with him on day trips. He and Grandma used to love taking their last dog, Harmony, for walks and letting her chase down the Frisbee. They watched old movies almost every night, and they loved to dance, too, always smiling and laughing and picking the positives from even the most gloomy days.

The Grandpa I knew wouldn't have written the things in that book, not unless he felt forced into it.

I saw it and it saw me, and things will only get worse from here.

Stevie is hugging himself and shivering, his hooded sweatshirt failing to warm him. "It's so cold in here. Should we turn up the heat?"

"Good idea." I walk with him to the thermostat, turning it up to seventy, the old heaters clanking to life moments later.

Outside, the wind howls and the rain strengthens.

Then complete darkness, a power outage, submerging the house in black and sending Night into frenetic ferocity.

BURN, DO NOT READ!

Chapter VI

Jack awoke very early on a hot July morning to get a head start on what would surely be an exhaustive day. The movers would arrive later to load all of Jack's messily packed boxes and furniture on the truck, and by this time tomorrow morning he hoped to be on his way west, away from the darkness that had haunted him, toward the future and his new little house in the woods.

In the dining room, surrounded by stacks of boxes, Night kept glancing nervously at Jack, taking a few bites of her breakfast and then surveying the room with bug-eyed suspicion. She'd never cared for changes of any sort in the house – even minor projects, never mind the harbingers brought on by the emergence of suitcases – and Jack couldn't imagine what troubles were dashing through her head this time around, especially with Mary gone. Those two had been inseparable, and every day since Mary's death Night had hopped up on the sofa and stared through the living room window at the porch, patiently waiting for her "Mommy" to return.

This was one of many reasons why Jack needed to get away, far away. The sadness and the longing were like ocean depths, utterly consuming. His sons were outraged, of course, taking turns calling him day and night with futile attempts to persuade him to stay. Rob had even promised to visit every month, but he just didn't seem to understand that Jack wasn't seeking companionship. He didn't need his sons to fill up the house with laughter and conversation. He needed a new place to live – a house whose every room didn't fill him with memories, a bed in which he didn't expect to see his wife, and a vehicle that hadn't killed a little boy.

Rob and Steve had suggested of late that, if he insisted on moving, he decide on somewhere closer to them. But Jack didn't want to be a burden or lose his freedoms. If he lived close to one of them, he might find himself watching as his lawn got mowed and his rugs got vacuumed and his meals got fixed, the leash growing increasingly shorter until finally someone asked if he'd like his teeth brushed or his hair combed. Plus, Rob or his wife would likely come over every day and mess around in his house, constantly rearranging things and cleaning things. And living near Steve would inevitably result in Jack being locked up in a retirement home and losing his license. The youngest of Jack's children, Steve had seemed to get his way most of the time, and now, as a U.S. senator, the guy simply didn't take no for an answer.

Jack watched as Night studied the room. Even though most of her neurotic tendencies surrounding household changes were silly, this time Jack couldn't blame his dog for being unsettled. The walls stripped bare, their contents boxed, the dining room looked completely foreign, no longer the room where Jack and Mary had enjoyed countless meals but a strange, almost foreboding place. He could still remember the excitement in her eyes when they'd first glimpsed this house seventeen years ago, an aging couple in need of a smaller house since the kids had started families and moved away. Mary had liked this place from the start, but now her gardens out back sat untended, painted rocks reading *Mary's Garden* and *Welcome to My Garden* left for the next owner. The kitchen, meanwhile – Mary's kitchen – was all cleared out, the many things that had made a house a home now sealed in boxes. The items Jack hadn't felt he'd need at his new house had already been given away to Goodwill or sold at tag sales, a process that had at times been fraught with sorrow but had usually brought him a smile or a quiet laugh. Mary's things had been the worst, and so he'd tried to scramble quickly through them, his neighbor Mrs. Hiller helping to pack up all the clothes and get them off to Goodwill. There had been a few tearful incidents, once at a tag sale as several of Mary's favorite garden ornaments were carried off by a little waddling fat man in a dress shirt and jeans shorts, barefoot beneath his loafers, his teeth yellow and crooked; strange, the memories that remained of such a painful moment.

Jack had also been reduced to tears at the pawn shop the afternoon he'd intended to sell a few items of Mary's jewelry collection. The bald man behind the counter had offered him more than five hundred dollars, but

Jack hadn't felt right selling her necklaces and rings and bracelets, pieces she'd selected with joy and worn with pride, many of them gifts

from Jack over the years, first appearing to her in tiny square boxes after the wrapping paper had been torn away.

No, Jack hadn't been able to pawn Mary's jewelry, and so he'd wound up giving most of it away to his sons, instructing them to have something to remember their mother by. Additionally, Jack had chosen to keep all of the little knickknacks that had piled up throughout the course of a long marriage, the ones that said, I LOVE YOU IN BIG WAYS, I LOVE YOU IN SMALL WAYS – I LOVE YOU THIS MINUTE, AND I'LL LOVE YOU ALWAYS and I LIKE BEING WITH YOU and A FRIEND IS A PRESENT YOU GIVE YOURSELF. He'd also kept all of Mary's photo albums spanning decades, even though he knew he'd rarely look at them. They were all tucked away in the boxes now, next to appear in Jack's new house and gather dust on a shelf somewhere.

He'd been fortunate enough to sell his current home, learning of the news just days ago, and now there was nothing left to tie him here. Next he would sell the truck, the one that had ended little Peter Elliott's life, perhaps trading it in for a sedan, something fuel efficient and trusty that would guide him and Night through the next chapters of their lives. He'd already sold his old Harley, very reluctantly, receiving eight thousand bucks and adding to his financial cushion. Maybe he would use some of it to buy a high-tech metal detector; then he could scour the lands of his new property in search of buried valuables from another time, or take it to the shores of the lake and dig up beer cans. He'd always wanted to try metal detecting, and there'd be nothing but time once he reached his new home.

A little house in the middle of the woods. The thought of it called to Jack like the lyrics of a fresh and exciting song. A new house. A new life. A new opportunity.

Watching Night finally finish up her meal, Jack considered the immensity of the relief he'd feel upon leaving this place. He could start over again out west, and maybe – hopefully – he could leave his darkness behind forever.

Chapter VII

"I can't believe he's really going through with this."

Stephen Gibson set his cell phone on speaker and placed it atop his desk, then leaned back and clasped his hands behind his head. He swiveled his leather cushioned chair and stared out the window, taking in the sprawls of buildings and snarls of traffic. Even the morning sky was alive with activity – clouds scudding along like great white-sailed ships, birds soaring way up high, an airplane lifting off from Dulles in the distance – and Steve longed for a slower pace of life. The stress of the game had been getting to him lately, compounded by his father's asinine behavior. He'd actually gone through with it, selling his house and purchasing a new one thousands of miles away, a house he'd never even seen before – utterly ludicrous.

"He said the movers are coming today, and he's planning to leave tomorrow," Rob said. "I wish I could fly down there and talk some sense into him, but I'm up to my eyes with cases right now. I just don't have the time, not after taking so many days off when Mom died."

"Who does have the time?" Still facing the window, Steve bit down hard on his lip. "There's nothing we can do, man. We've tried getting through to him, but he's gotta make his own decisions and live with the consequences. Who knows, maybe this will be a blessing in disguise. He'll spend two weeks on his own and realize he can't handle it, then come crawling back east."

Rob expelled a long, miserable sigh. "I'm worried about him, Steve. These decisions he's making – they're irrational, grief-driven mistakes. Everything's happening so fast, and he's not giving himself any time to think things through. What if he decides halfway there he wants to live from the road, or he joins a motorcycle gang, or he stops in Vegas to get remarried? At this point he's liable to do just about anything."

"And there's nothing we can do about it," Steve repeated. "I'm more worried about the drive than anything. He couldn't even get across town without killing a kid last year – now he wants to go across the

country? It's a debacle waiting to happen, but as long as he doesn't get himself killed, maybe this will be the wake-up call he needs. Living on his own will show him he has to have help at his age." Steve swiveled to face his desk again and sipped his cooling coffee. "I give him one month, tops, then he'll drag himself back. He's just going through a crisis right now. He's pissed at the world – pissed that Mom died, pissed he killed that kid, pissed we don't live closer, pissed about everything. He's lashing out, and we have to let him do it. Don't fall for his games anymore – if he says he's gonna do something that seems nuts, just tell him to go for it. Once he sees how hard it is on his own, he'll be forced to come back."

"I don't know, Steve. I feel like we might be losing him for good on this one. Paul fears he might hole himself up in this new place and turn into a hermit. What if he ditches his cell phone and we've got no way to reach him? He promised to stay in constant contact, but I don't trust him."

"No one trusts him," Steve said, "but we have to let him go. It's what he wants – and there's simply no way to stop him."

Chapter VIII

It took Jack just over four days to span the majority of the nation. He drove slowly and comfortably, taking in the scenery and the cities, Night spending much of the trip with her head out the passenger window, her gums flapping in the wind, though she became bored after a while with endless stretches of farmland and billboards for fireworks stores.

Jack enjoyed the monotony. There was a cadence of realization to the journey that set him at peace, a knowledge that every mile brought him that much closer to his new life, the darkness and despair soon to be exchanged for renewal. And at the thought of a more simplistic yet no less meaningful truth – the notion of a man and his dog covering the U.S. in a pickup truck – Jack's lips stretched into a smile.

He was almost there now, just over an hour left before he reached his little house in the woods, according to the GPS device Mary had given him for their penultimate Christmas. It was a few minutes shy of noon, Pacific Standard Time, and Night was growing restless in the passenger seat, whimpering and scratching the door.

Jack decided to stop at the next diner for lunch and a walk of the dog – and then it would be due northwest until he reached home. Per telephone agreement, he would call the realtor when he was thirty minutes out, and together they would go through the house and finalize the requisite obligations. The movers had already arrived, calling Jack a few hours ago to let him know the truck was ready to be unloaded. So far everything was going smoothly, no "disasters" striking as Steve had predicted. His sons assumed things would go wrong, that Jack was too old or fragile or emotionally frayed for such an undertaking, but this was the right move for him. Jack knew it definitively and soon his sons would, too. The thought of him describing to them his new house and, later, all of the projects he had planned, sent a frisson flashing into his gut.

They'll see. I'll show them all.

A new home. A new chapter.

With a thick hamburger and fries and a milkshake still settling in his gut, Jack crossed the town line in happy spirits and followed the GPS directions down increasingly narrow dirt roads that cut through the forest. The clouds had thickened and the heavy wilderness dappled the road with shadows, the trees as tall as towers, rising imposingly toward the mottled sky.

"Calculating route," the GPS said after a while, and Jack brought his truck to a stop in the middle of the shadowed road, rolling down the window and taking a moment to embrace the solitude. There was absolutely no one out here, no one around to bother him – he couldn't even recall the last vehicle he'd seen.

Suddenly that wasn't such a pleasant thought. For a few anxious moments Jack didn't like being out here on his own. Night, meanwhile, head out the window, glanced alertly into the woods, where birds chirped and squawked their afternoon conversations, sounds that accentuated the isolation, a thought popping into Jack's head about that ubiquitous line: If a tree falls in a forest...

Just as disquietude was beginning to creep further into Jack's heart, the GPS said, "Right turn in 0.4 miles," and the fleeting unease lifted up and away, replaced by the excitement that had carried him west.

Jack barely saw the next road peeking out from the forest, a little dirt path scarcely wide enough to have accommodated the moving truck (Jack could see the muddy grooves where it had swung wide to make the turn). Even the F-150 scraped against branches and joggled over muddy potholes, the turbulent movement enough to cause Night to withdraw into the truck. She glanced at Jack with a worried expression that seemed to say, *Are you sure you made the right turn? I think we might be lost.*

"Destination on the left in 0.5 miles," the GPS said, a welcome instruction that made Jack feel like he was still on the grid, the satellites tracking him deep into the woods. Technology hadn't forsaken him, at least not yet.

Gradually the potholes expanded, the road thinning even further around a bend, and up ahead there was a rusty, slanted mailbox on the left side. "Approaching destination on the left," the GPS called, Jack's chest fluttering with anticipation.

He scratched Night's neck. "This is it, girl. We finally made it. Our new home."

Fueled by a burst of alacrity, Jack made a left into the dirt driveway, which was in better condition than many of the roads leading to it, the potholes mere dimples rather than craters. For a quarter of a mile the driveway snaked through the wilderness, eventually concluding with a sharp curve that brought Jack face to face with the little one-story house in the woods, a sight that at first filled him with utter, indefinable revulsion. All he could think was, *It's so different from what I expected,* yet the sources of these differences eluded him. This was the same house from the photographs with the same little pond out front beyond the driveway, but no longer did the place look cozy and inviting. Something about the house's squat posture – looming inconspicuously beneath the monolithic trees – made it seem spurious and untrustworthy, a house with an agenda, a house that hid in the forest like a spider in a web, waiting to ensnare someone.

Looking straight ahead at the house, Night growled, a low, angry sound Jack had rarely heard. His blood went momentarily cold, and then there was movement, stealing his attention, people walking around the driveway, the moving truck parked off to the right at the edge of the woods, just beyond a two-bay detached garage Jack had also seen in plenty of online photographs. Another car was parked up ahead, a little red sedan. And the movers were approaching Jack's truck now, joined by a sixtyish man in a suit who could only be the realtor. The other people ambling about the driveway – which looped into a horseshoe surrounding the front lawn – were probably members of a regional crew employed by the moving company to assist with the offload, Jack assumed.

"Pleasure to meet you, Jack. I'm Randy Thomas with Talbot Realty," the suited man said, shaking Jack's hand when he stepped out of the truck. Night, left behind, barked wildly and scratched at the glass with both forepaws.

"Easy, girl, easy," said Jack, who'd rolled up the windows and set the air conditioner on high to ensure Night was comfortable. "I'll be right back, okay?"

After talking briefly with the movers and providing instructions, Jack followed Thomas toward the house, his initial bad reactions to the place wearing off. *It's gotta be the weather, that's all,* he assumed. *It's gotten cloudy and all of the photos were taken in the sunlight. A few fixer-uppers and this place'll be just like new.*

"I'll make the tour as quick as I can," Thomas said, propping the front door open with a stone so the movers could begin delivering items inside. "Don't want to leave your dog waiting too long. What breed?"

"She's a mix. Part lab, part foxhound. Can run as fast as lightning."

"Oh, I'll bet," Thomas said with a congenial smile, but Jack was looking past him, his eyes adjusting to a dark house that had greeted him with a wave of cool, dank, disagreeable air when Thomas opened the door.

The realtor immediately began flicking on lights and pulling open curtains to bring a little light into the house, which consisted of a large living room at the center, a kitchen and a dining room at the rear, and a mudroom on the left side. A short hall to the right offered access to rooms on both sides, including a master bedroom and adjoining bathroom, an opposing guest bedroom with a wide window facing the

front yard, the basement, a storage room, and a little square of a room beside the master bedroom Thomas referred to as "the study."
Though Jack had already viewed these rooms online, they, too, seemed different in person, though it wasn't as dramatic a difference as the exterior had exuded.

"The place is strangely cold for July," Jack noted.

Thomas's bushy white eyebrows furrowed contemplatively. "The nights are cool here, sometimes downright cold." His eyes shifted anxiously about the living room, as if searching for the source of the dank air. "You'll get used to it after a while, I suppose. It's always foggy in the mornings out this way – rolls right in off the lake. But the nights are clear and crisp – perfect for camping."

Thomas caught himself before elaborating further and chuckled. Later, when they were finished looking through the house, he said, "Well, that's the tour for you." He handed Jack two sets of keys, then said, "Not that you'll need these. No one locks their doors in this town. You've come to a good place, Mr. Gibson."

Chapter IX

It was getting dark by the time the movers unloaded the truck and lugged everything into the house. In a committed effort to establishing his new home as a fresh chapter, Jack hadn't taken all of his old furniture, selling many items at tag sales and giving others away to neighbors. Sweet old Mrs. Hiller had become the proud new owner of several items – chairs, tables, desks – her sons hauling it all away in their pickup trucks one evening. Mrs. Hiller had promised to put everything to good use, and Jack had allowed himself a smile when she'd invited him over for tea and proudly shown him where each piece would go, shuffling in her little blue shoes like a wraith. Her husband had died of a heart attack ten years earlier, and Jack had enjoyed her company following Mary's death because he'd been able to identify with her. He'd understood the ravaging loneliness that plagued Mrs. Hiller's days, sometimes burning bright and other times glowing lambently, waiting to flare up again. She was a good woman, Mrs. Hiller, and Jack would dearly miss her and the old neighborhood, but he wouldn't miss the negativity that had harassed him there. Peter's death had cast a permanent shadow over his former life, and Mary's death a year later had brought a cold, ceaseless darkness, even in times of perfect sunlight, everything seeming dim and dismal.

But now he was in a new place, his little house in the woods. When the movers were finally gone, their truck nearly jackknifing as it followed the horseshoe loop of the driveway, the back wheels of the trailer trundling an angled path across the front lawn, Jack was able to appreciate for the first time the breadth of the silence that ruled this place, a thing as complete as a full moon. For a moment it stunned him, amazed him, left him wondering if he'd ever experienced such a silence, Night standing in the living room beside him and staring at the front door, perhaps as stupefied as her master. Together they took in the stillness and silence – and after a while Jack got the sense that this wasn't merely an absence of sound but a complete suppression, as if the walls and windows were soundproof, stifling even the crickets and

birds, not a single sound to penetrate the house, only the weakening
dusky light.
This must be what it's like to be deaf, Jack thought, briefly unsettled,
longing for the comforts of his old home…Mary humming in the
kitchen; Jeopardy on the TV; the grandfather clock disrupting the
otherwise dominant quiet of a dreary afternoon.

*The clock. It's not working! Did the movers break it? Did the batteries
finally die?*

Jack started toward the immense grandfather clock in the corner of the
living room, its hands stuck between eleven and twelve. Then Night
barked, a shrill sound that might have been a blaring siren in such
conditions, shattering the heavy silence, and at once the whole house
seemed to exhale, a cool draft fluttering the curtains and bringing the
hairs on Jack's arms to attention. Night was still eyeing the front door,
but she quickly darted into hectic, jittering motion, sniffing at every
door again and eventually stopping outside the basement door (the first
door on the right along the hallway).

Night scratched the door, barked once, and warily nudged a paw
against the frame, reminding Jack of a summer morning a few years
back when she'd come across a hunkering turtle in the park.

"What is it, girl?"

Night's tail wagged with nervous curiosity. Soon she began pacing the
width of the door, sizing it up like a boxer preparing for a bout.

"You want to go back down there?" Jack asked. He'd already taken her
through the basement and garage, wanting to familiarize her with their
new home, but apparently a second appraisal would be required.

Night scratched more adamantly at the basement door, beseeching Jack
with those soft brown eyes. "Okay, you win, girl. You win." He opened
the door and flipped on the light, his dog charging down the thin
staircase into the cool, musty basement.

But there was another smell this time, one Jack hadn't noticed half an hour ago, a rotten odor that fluctuated in strength as he wandered the basement, its source unknown. Night, meanwhile, zagged indiscriminately for a few minutes, but soon she locked onto a scent and followed it to the dusty workbench situated against the far wall. A low growl erupted to fierce barking, Night looking directly at something behind the bench, tracking it, her tail flicking back and forth. A squirrel? A mouse?

But she's usually a silent hunter.

Jack wished he'd brought his flashlight, for it was shadowy and cobwebby behind the bench, which ran the length of the wall. The basement was lit only by two bulbs at the moment, leaving the walls and corners largely in obscurity, but Night had surely seen something beneath that bench.

The dog backed away and ceased barking when Jack took an achy knee and looked beneath the lowest shelf of the bench, expecting to see a little rodent scuttling along the wall.

There were no visible intruders.

"He's gone now," Jack assured, patting Night on the back, but she tilted her head confusedly at the workbench and let out a little chirping *bwoof,* followed swiftly by a menacing, completely un-Nightlike growl.

"Come on, lady, what's gotten into you?" Jack had to take Night by the collar to get her out of the basement, the dog frequently looking back toward the workbench. "Basement's off limits for a while," he chuckled when they were back upstairs, the silence restored, though not to its previous fullness, disrupted by…the clock?

In the living room corner, it was ticking again, Jack adjusting the hands to the correct time, his eyebrows lifted. For a while he stared at the clock, hands at his hips.

BURN, DO NOT READ!

Strange. Very strange.

Eventually he glanced down at Night. "What do you say we unpack some more and get this place looking like home?"

Jack enjoyed being kept busy by his first night chores. Busying himself meant there was less time to brood about the darkness in his old life, each room that gradually came to life with his unpacked possessions a promise of better days ahead. He couldn't wait for tomorrow, when a handyman he'd spoken to on the phone (Randy Thomas's friend) would help him fix up the interior of the garage; later, Jack would head into town and purchase several new appliances and pieces of furniture. Then the handyman would be back to work the next day, all of this negotiated in advance over the phone, the guy offering to do everything for just two hundred bucks.

Jack had thrown a restaurant gift card into the deal, insisting that such hard work be rewarded with a good meal. Of course, Jack could have bought furniture online and had his purchases delivered without charge if he'd secured an internet provider, but one of his goals for his new home was to keep it free of distractions. That meant no TV, no internet, no complications and nuisances – he wanted to live simply and savor the peace of an early morning or the calm of a cool autumn night, to indulge in the land, basic pleasures that would balance him and, hopefully, return him to a happier state. If it weren't for his sons, he would have ditched the cell phone as well, but they'd drag him kicking and flailing back east if he divested himself completely of technology. The house also had a landline, Randy Thomas had informed, and Jack supposed he could tolerate the rate the phone company out here offered (it wasn't nearly as high as his bill back east).

Night watched Jack carefully as he went through the house, unpacking things and putting them in cabinets and drawers or simply setting them on countertops until he could figure out what to do with them. Occasionally he listened for the grandfather clock, half-expecting it to be frozen again, but with each auditory confirmation that it was still working, Jack nodded and returned to his tasks.

113

Everything has a place, Mary would say, and Jack smiled at memories of them furnishing their former homes.

This time around it was all up to him, though, and he still had a lot of work ahead. The movers had done a good job of arranging the heavy furniture how he wanted it, sparing him the exhaustion of dragging and hefting things around. Now it was just a matter of finding places for all of his belongings, a job he told himself he could take his time with.

You're a retired old man – nothing but time.

A while later, Jack stopped working when he realized darkness had fallen over the little house in the woods. His anxious dog had climbed to the height of the sofa and was looking out the window, the curtains trembling with the gentle insistences of a night wind. If it weren't for the rumbling pleas made by his stomach, Jack surely would have forgotten to eat.

"We were supposed to have grilled steak on the first night," he told his faithful friend, remembering his initial plan. But to accomplish that he'd need to visit the supermarket for steak and grilling charcoal, a trip he was averse to make at this hour, when the store might already be closed for the night.

Instead he found the phone book Thomas had given him and ordered a small hamburger and onion pizza, a freckled, greasy-haired teenager arriving at the front door half an hour later. The kid seemed strangely edgy, twice peering over his shoulder during the exchange of pizza and cash. When he was gone Jack stood with the hot cardboard box in hand, taking in the moonlit front yard and gaining a better understanding of the delivery boy's unease.

The place was secluded and spooky, no denying that, the surrounding trees so tall they blocked out the sky in every direction except directly overhead, as if Jack were at the bottom of a deep well. Though he found it difficult to believe, the mammoth trees actually triggered a momentary swell of claustrophobia in his chest, an absurd feeling that the forest was encroaching on his house from all sides. Staring up at the trees a while longer made him want to return inside, where he wouldn't see splashes of moonlight falling about the yard and crawling into the forest hollows.

Jack tried not to search those hollows at length, for a handful of times he'd stared at the shadows within and thought he discerned movement.

Ridiculous, he thought, heading back inside. *I moved out here for space and freedom, and here I am getting all riled up over the woods. The woods!*

Jack ate his dinner somewhat broodingly at the dining room table – the same table at which he'd eaten countless meals with Mary – agitated not by the usual elements but an advancing worry that his new home wasn't the sanctuary he'd hoped it would be but instead something entirely different. The phrases **BAD VIBE** and **BAD FEELING** kept creeping into his head, among others, his discomfort worsened with each round of Night's barking. Usually an ardent beggar, the dog had ignored the food and returned to the basement door, where Jack could now hear her scratching and growling.

"What's gotten into her?" Jack asked the empty chair across the table, visualizing Mary's face and practically hearing her reply.

You know what to do, Jackie. Entice her with food.

"Yes, of course," he blurted. Then: "Come on, girl. I've got some pizza crusts for you. Don't you want junk food, lady? You love pizza crusts."

Moments later Night slinked into the dining room, stopping almost to the table to growl once more. She was looking behind her but to an angle, toward the basement door, Jack thought, and after a few moments she was off barking again.

Thinking his dog must be upset by the smell of wild animals nearby, Jack retrieved his leash after dinner and took Night for a moonlit walk around the driveway. Oddly, she didn't bark or growl once outside, sniffing eagerly at the edge of the woods and occasionally squatting to

mark various venues of interest. But when Jack guided her back to the porch, Night resisted to the point of dragging, then barked so furiously at the house that Jack briefly wondered if someone had snuck inside.

Of course not. She's just upset by the change. She'll get used to it.

But at bedtime Night didn't curl up on the end of Jack's bed per ritual. Instead she sat by the door, outlined by the bright moonlight, and again Jack wondered if this place would be a good fit or a major regret.

Chapter X

Jack awoke very early the next morning, torn from sleep again by Night's seemingly incessant barking and growling and scratching at the bedroom door. He'd tried walking her again, tried petting her, tried singing to her as Mary had sometimes done, but none of it had provided the dog any relief.

The strangest part was that Night had never been much of a noisemaker. She'd usually only barked adamantly when the doorbell rang or when one of the neighborhood dogs went on a rant, mostly just studying her surroundings with silent contemplation and, occasionally, dashing after squirrels and rabbits. Whenever Jack and Mary had stayed at their sons' houses and brought Night along for the trips, she'd been on her absolute best behavior. Hotels had never been a problem for her, either, and when she *had* barked, the outbursts had usually been isolated and short-lived. Even in the weeks following Mary's death, Night had often seemed disconsolate and lonely but had never resorted to excessive barking.

So what the hell was going on? Night hadn't gone ten quiet minutes last night, it seemed, driving Jack to stuff toilet paper in his ears, although his endeavor had done little to reduce the noise. At times Night had sounded infuriated, scraping and rattling the bedroom door.

Presently, she was expelling intermittent, halfhearted growls, her concentration still fixed on the door. Outside, the cobalt sky was lightening, though darkness ruled the surrounding woods. An hour ago, during Night's latest fit, Jack had gone out to the porch for a few minutes, listening to the songs of the early birds and trying to figure out how to get Night acclimated to the place.

Nothing had come to him.

Now he was dragging himself out of bed and staring worriedly at his dog. Was she sick? Maybe just homesick? No, these answers didn't explain the intensity she'd maintained throughout the night. It had almost been like she'd barked at someone *inside* the house, so fiercely

resolute that the person might as well have been standing on the other side of the bedroom door, Night's rage occasionally alternating with protracted sighs at Jack's failure to acknowledge the unseen problem.

Jack let out a frustrated breath of his own. This wasn't going as planned. First, the house hadn't appeared as he'd pictured it based on the online photographs; then he'd felt unsettled by its silence and verging on disturbed by the massive trees surrounding it; and capping it all off had been Night's behavior. But this was supposed to be his little house in the middle of the woods, a place all to himself where he could restore old cars and explore the woods with his dog and sit blanketed before a fire on winter evenings, a cup of hot chocolate in hand and orange shadows flashing against the living room walls. There was supposed to be peace and tranquility here – and only good thoughts, never any trouble.

But there was trouble, all right. Early trouble, like the bases loaded with nobody out in the first damn inning kind of trouble. Night apparently didn't like the place, and didn't someone once say to always trust your dog's instincts?

Still a little groggy, Jack fed Night breakfast (she only ate a quarter of the meal) and walked her around the driveway and front lawn. To the east, streaks of pink and orange had begun to splash into the barely visible patches of sky beyond the woods. The birds were becoming louder and more abundant, a fine morning for a walk.

The house started to fade into the wilderness as Jack and Night rounded the driveway's curve near the glassy pond and proceeded toward the unseen road. It was such a small and unobtrusive little house that Jack imagined he'd return and find it gone as if it had never been there, receded fully into the woods like beach rocks beneath an approaching tide, or perhaps angled in a slightly different direction, just enough to make him second guess himself. There was something shifty about

118

such a house, he thought, feeling dewy moisture seep through his worn sneakers while he waited for Night to do her business in the tall grass, a train horn echoing in the distance.

They were just off the driveway now, Night once again seeming to prefer life outdoors, and Jack realized a fence was no longer a Later but a Sooner. Although he'd initially thought he could erect the fence himself as a summer project, he decided calling a professional would be the most efficient route. Clearly Night needed a place to run off her excess energy right away; plus, if she was tired after a long day of chasing squirrels, maybe she wouldn't bark all night. Maybe.

Back inside, Jack continued the long process of unpacking and organizing. The sun having risen and brightened the house, Night decided it was finally permissible to relieve herself of guard duty and get some sleep, curling up contentedly on the sofa as Jack puttered through each room. He hoped last night had been an anomaly not to repeat itself, a first-night storm followed by smooth, easy sailing. But something told him the debacle had only been a starting point for more trouble.

A time later, Jack decided after much mulling to leave Night home alone for a few hours. She'd never had a problem staying home before, not even after Mary's death, but this was a new house and an important step. This was their home, and Night had to get used to sleeping in a new room and staying alone, even if it scared her. Sometimes Jack wished she was more like their last dog, Harmony, a golden retriever who wouldn't have barked if a masked gunman had broken down the door and attacked them. But it was Night's zest and quirkiness and exceeding intelligence that made her irresistible, a dog who, though neurotic at times, possessed inimitable charm.

Too smart for her own good, Mary had often said.

"I'll be back in a few hours, girl. Gotta grab some breakfast and meet this handyman. Sure hope he's not a slouch," Jack said, throwing Night a handful of kibble as he always did before departing, confident that if he kept up the same rituals and routines, she would eventually accept the new house.

Yawning, Night jumped off the sofa and stretched out, then gobbled up the kibble with a wagging tail. She didn't even chase Jack to the door, a

good sign, and there was no barking as he listened from the driveway for a few minutes before climbing into his truck.

Good girl, very good girl. This might just work out, after all.

Jack's first stop was a little diner in the center of town, where he'd agreed to meet Randy Thomas and the handyman for breakfast. Hidden down by the railroad tracks, at the bottom of a hill falling steeply away from the town hub, Jack wouldn't have even seen Grimley's Diner if he didn't first note the cluster of vehicles headed down that way. Taking a quick left off Main Street, he found the only unoccupied parking space along a dilapidated wrought iron fence separating the lot from the tracks.

This place must have great food. Either that, or it's the only breakfast spot in town.

There was a creeping sadness as Jack opened the door and took in the familiar scents, Sunday morning memories coming back to him. Every Sunday he and Mary had eaten breakfast at Chestnut Ridge Diner before going their separate ways, Jack to catch up on work at the office and Mary to head home and get started on her gardening, a tradition that had seemed like it would last forever, an endless supply of eggs and toast and pancakes and coffee for them to enjoy, continuing on year after year after year. But that time was gone now, departed like a ship on the horizon, and Jack was at first stunned by the strangeness of being in this new diner across the country, half-paralyzed by a surreal, longing sorrow.

BURN, DO NOT READ!

Mary isn't here. She'd probably love this place, but she'll never get to try it. My wife is dead. I can't believe she's actually...dead.

A sharp, brief ache panged in his chest, and then he was mostly through it, almost back to normal – both physically and emotionally – observing the quaint red-cushioned booths and a bar full of diners, with their steaming plates and mugs of coffee and outspread newspapers. One of them stared at the screen of a laptop, an annoyingly postmodern wrinkle in a scene that otherwise could have played out in another decade. Jack yearned for a return to the seventies or the eighties or even the nineties, to be brought back to one of those Sunday morning breakfasts at Chestnut Ridge, long before little Peter's blood pooled on the road and Mary died in her sleep.

"Seat yourself," a passing waitress said with a smile, and Jack realized he was standing stiffly, barely inside the diner, watching the patrons like a viewer of a movie, as if he weren't really in this town or even this state, his heart still back east with Mary.

Jack slid into one of the booths, forgetting completely about who he was supposed to meet, lost in tired reveries. He'd hardly read the menu for thirty seconds when a voice called to him from behind. "Hey, Jack. Welcome to the best breakfast joint this side of the Rockies."

Jack glanced to his left and saw Randy Thomas coming up beside him, a coffee mug in hand. "Morning, Randy. Thanks again for your help with the house. You made it a heck of a lot easier for me."

"No problem at all – that's what they pay me the big bucks for, right?" They shook hands and Thomas eased in opposite Jack. He wore a gray suit and gold tie, another day of showings and small talk awaiting him. "Say, I hate to bring bad news first thing in the morning," he added, "but Derek's feeling a little under the weather today. Just finished up a huge demo job out on the Coleridge farm," – he pointed north as if it mattered to Jack where the Coleridge farm was – "and, to be honest, I think it wore that poor kid out. Should be ready to roll in a few days, though."

Jack waved a hand. "No big deal. Any time is fine. Just have him give me a call when he's ready."

"Morning, Wendy." Thomas smiled at a passing waitress, then asked Jack, "So how do you like the new place?"

The sound of Night's barking flared up in Jack's head. "Great. It's so quiet out here. A guy could get used to that."

Thomas chuckled, his eyes glinting amicably. "I'll say. How's your dog taking to the house? Sometimes moves are tougher on our four-legged friends than us."

"Yeah, tell me about it. She barked quite a bit last night, but she'll get adjusted soon enough. No choice, right?"

Nodding, Thomas said, "Probably heard the coyotes – they're real active this time of year. I wouldn't let her run off too far in those woods. Poor little pup could get herself turned around real easy."

"No, I haven't let her off the leash yet. I'm gonna call a fence contractor this afternoon, and hopefully they'll get a fence put up soon around the back yard. Night'll love that – plenty of space to run."

"Absolutely!" Thomas said in a strangely cheerful tone. "You've got nothing but space out there."

After a delicious yet wistfully enjoyed breakfast of pancakes and an omelet – with a side of hash browns – Jack found his way to the small, family-run grocery store, loading up on meats he could grill throughout the week. Then he crossed the street to drop a few hundred dollars at the hardware store; now he could get a head start on the garage while the handyman came through his malaise.

Unlike Jack's previous location, everything he needed in this town was concentrated within a mile of the town center, one main route cutting

122

through the heart of it. The people were friendly, the air was fresh, and the traffic was light – and Jack thought he could die a happy man in this place if Night would just find some peace and his sons would stop pestering him about moving back home.

Only once during his errands did Jack think of Peter Elliott, a quick but wrenching memory when he saw a woman with a stroller up ahead in a crosswalk. Bringing his truck to a stop to let her pass, there was a near-nauseous rising feeling in Jack's chest, inspired by a chilling thought that this young mother was walking directly in front of the very truck that had ended a child's life just over a year earlier, oblivious to the horrors its driver had caused, but not today, no, not this morning. This woman and her baby would live because this was a different town and a different time. There were no Barfield and Brickley trucks out here, no anaphylactic little boys collapsing outside the church, though there were quite a few trains. At the diner Jack had seen two freighters rumble by, their horns reminding him of Peter, but his thoughts, as now, had lingered only briefly in the darkness before returning to the light of the present and future.

It's going to take time, but you will get through this, Jackie, I promise, his wife had said, and now he could genuinely believe it. Things were looking up and smiling at him. He wouldn't need any old friends here; instead he would meet new ones.

A new home.

A new town.

Far away from the darkness.

Chapter XI

"You forgot to pick up the brown sugar," Stephen Gibson groused, his new secretary hurrying in moments later to answer for another botched supply run.

"So sorry, Senator," she apologized, looking like a child in the principal's office. "Would you like anything else?"

"Never mind now. Pick it up tomorrow." Steve angrily waved her off, but made sure not to allow his frustration with her shortcomings to detract from his appreciation for her finer qualities. She was a cute, shapely little thing, tight in all the right places and curvy where it counted. If only his wife had such a physique – apparently childbirth had been the line in the sand, sexy yielding to uninspiring, and never again would Steve enjoy such a hot–

The damn cell phone was buzzing, Dad's number on the screen. Great, just what Steve needed. This was surely the call he'd been expecting. His father had lived out west for two weeks, and things were finally – inevitably – unraveling.

"I've got a meeting in ten minutes, Dad. Is everything all right?"

"Everything's great, Steve. Just wanted to check in and make sure you're not working too hard. You've done such a great job since taking office."

"Thanks, Dad. Same old stuff out here," Steve said impatiently, glancing at his watch. "How's Night? Still barking all the time?"

"Actually, she's gotten much better in the last week. She didn't bark at all last night, and I think she's starting to like this place. The mornings are so peaceful out here, son – me and Night always go for our morning walks."

Steve had set the phone to speaker and placed it on his desk. "Uh huh. That's great," he kept saying, his attention drawn to an email from his subcommittee chairman.

"I joined a chess club yesterday," Dad continued. "This guy I met at the diner, Oscar Montoya, I guess his father's a grandmaster who won thousands of dollars from tournaments. Oscar's the one who invited me to the club, nicest guy you could imagine."

"That's great. So happy for you, Dad, but I've gotta run. Can't be late for this meeting."

"Oh, no problem. Call me when you get some free time and I'll tell you more about the club. It's a great group of guys – never thought I'd actually join a chess club."

"Good for you, Dad. Have a good day now."

Steve ended the call, not caring whether he heard his father's response. A little current of irritation was running through him, one he didn't wish to acknowledge but couldn't deny, not unless he wanted to lie to himself. He wasn't at all pleased that his father was thriving out west after two weeks, for that meant he would stay out there longer and remain free of Steve's control. The perfect situation would be for Dad to fail and demand to move back home – then Steve could put him in a senior living community and be done with worrying about him and what he'd do next and what damage he might cause.

But for now Dad remained a liability, an unleashed dog that could make a mess at any moment. For all Steve knew, Dad would get sick and need to be hospitalized or try to cook something and burn down the house or kill another goddamn kid with his truck – and then the reporters would come with their questions and agendas.

"Damn it, Dad," Steve muttered, shaking his head at the idea of Dad eluding his control. Steve took great pains to ensure that every aspect of his life was exactly how he wanted it, right down to the cream and two teaspoons of brown sugar in his coffees, and Dad wasn't playing into the system, his glaring red crayon straying well outside the lines Steve

had set. It was almost like – no, Steve didn't want to think that – but it was almost like Dad had intentionally moved thousands of miles away to spite him. And even if things *weren't* going well at his new house, Dad was just stubborn enough to lie about it in an effort to prove his sons wrong, especially Steve. He clearly viewed this as a battle he could win, and that vexed Steve more than anything.

Life needed to be orderly, under control – under *his* control – not because Stephen Gibson was a control freak but instead because he knew he had better senses than most, senses that had propelled him through the governmental ranks, senses that would boost him all the way to the top if he aced the tiresome game.

And Dad – what could he possibly do for Steve at this point besides cause him more headaches?

Just then there was the most fleeting of thoughts surging through Steve's head, one that told him life would be much easier if his father were dead, the transitory notion quickly replaced by guilt and feelings of good will toward Dad. Sometimes Steve had similarly dark ephemeral thoughts about his wife, usually when they fought at length or he met particularly enticing, fresh-faced poli-sci interns at various functions, their youth making him yearn for days long past and filling him with sullenness at the realization that college women would find him perverse for fantasizing about them in the ways Steve did. To them, everyone over forty ranged in terms of oldness, and though youth would never return to Stephen Gibson, he often wondered if he could do better than his current hand. To succeed in the game, he would need to remain married and in strong control of the Great American Semblance, of course, but fidelity had begun to feel a little slippery of late, that helpless sense of the world passing you by sometimes constricting Steve to the point of claustrophobia, the remedy seemingly lying in the arms of another woman, a younger woman he could charm and flatter, a woman who enjoyed his power and money, a woman whose breasts were still immune to gravity.

Steve checked his watch again. Almost time for the meeting. "You're gonna stop this foolishness and sell that house, Dad," he muttered to the wall. "It's the only way."

Part III: In the Darkness

Chapter I

A loud bang against the hallway wall, then a series of heavy thuds in the blackness of the power outage.

Night is barking violently, as if something's coming at her in the darkness.

"Ahhhhhh, get off! Get off!" Stevie screams, and when the lights return I see Night standing on my cousin's back, pinning him to the floor, his arms flailing uselessly.

But Night isn't attacking Stevie. It seems like she's defending him, still barking but not as fiercely, her gaze cast down the hall.

The lights flicker. I will them to stay on.

It comes in the darkness.

"Come on, Night, get off him!" I shout, tugging the dog by her collar. She whimpers a little and then steps off Stevie, licking his bare legs apologetically.

Several pictures have fallen from the wall, coming down beside Stevie, one of them cracking, a jagged split in the glass between Grandma and Grandpa.

Stevie scrambles to his feet. "Night tackled me into the wall!" he exclaims, looking fearfully at the dog like she might do it again.

"I think she was trying to protect you. How could a forty-pound dog tackle you, anyway?"

"She took out my legs, man!" Almost as exasperated as he is embarrassed, Stevie stalks off to the living room.

"Wait up. We should light some candles, just in case the power goes out again." I follow him down the hall, Night lingering behind, seeming to realize she angered Stevie.

Together we round up as many candles as we can find and light them. "We should have gone to the motel," Stevie complains, thin lines of worry etched into his forehead.

"Yeah, the motel was definitely a better option," I mumble, thinking again of the book.

After depositing a spent match into Grandpa's ashtray on the coffee table, Stevie returns to the sofa and tugs the blankets to his chin, then, somewhat petulantly, pulls up his hood. He looks like a kid who's just been cut from the team or dumped by his girlfriend via text.

I wonder if I should leave him alone, fear besting me again. I can't help but worry about what would happen to Stevie if everything Grandpa wrote is somehow true, if...

...It comes in the darkness.

Chapter II

Jack was on the back deck, taking in the smell of grilled steak and watching Night rest in the cool autumn grass, when the coyotes began their distant howls. Night's chin lifted abruptly from her paws, her ears straightened sharply and eyes wide, but Jack wasn't afraid for her safety. Almost an acre of the back yard had been enclosed by wooden fences nearly two months ago, a project that had come at a steep price but had justified itself every day since.

Beginning at the back deck, the enclosure featured four gated entrances. From the rear of the house, the fences fanned out into the woods and extended well out of sight, forming a virtual rectangle that allowed Night more than enough wilderness to try her luck at chasing critters, every foxhound-lab mutt's dream. Jack relished watching her pursuits and knowing she was safe; sometimes she bounded so fast after something it seemed like she was flying.

Each time Jack witnessed the graceful freedom of Night reaching top speed was a reaffirmation that coming here had been the right decision. This was their new life, a good life, free of the troubles their old life had brought.

The coyotes. They were howling again, a sharp, hair-raising sound even from a considerable distance, spreading through the dark woods like a vapor. Jack, a little uneasy, slid a spatula beneath the final steak patty and transferred it from his grill to a plate, the aroma drawing Night up to the deck. Almost dinner time.

"You hungry, beggar?" Jack chuckled, but then he stopped rigidly just before the door. His smile disappeared.

The coyotes he'd heard before – those had only been the decoys, driving some poor animal toward the rest of the pack. Now there was an eruption of frenetic shrieks much closer to the house, so loud and grisly that Jack clenched his fists and gritted his teeth, the nearest attack he'd ever heard. The worst part, he could hear the victim's yelps as it was torn apart, an odious sound somehow distinguishable from the

disorienting, savage storm that seemed to come from everywhere – the forest alive and echoing with death – and then it all quickly died down, remaining briefly before the inevitable silence.

Tail lowered, Night was cowering by Jack's side, eyeing the woods with trepidation.

Oh no, no, no, no. This is terrible. That animal might have been someone's lost dog. All alone out there in the woods at night. It just couldn't find a safe place until morning.

And there they were – those seven words in his head again, coming to him for the first time in months.

Morning does not welcome those who die.

The words were accompanied by Peter's vivid memory, a little boy lying dead in the middle of the road, his blood spilled and shoe torn away. "Interstate Love Song" played briefly in Jack's head – *Breathing is the hardest thing to do* – and, the plate of steak still in his hand, he wavered, stumbled, shouldered against the back door, closed his eyes, tried to banish the final fear in Peter's eyes from his mind, the fear of certain death, the same fear that had just moments ago flashed into a defenseless animal's eyes when the coyotes sprang.

Dragging himself inside, Jack set the plate on the table, no longer hungry but dizzy. His stomach was suddenly sour, his breaths escaping in quick bursts, a coating of sweat developing on his forehead in spite of the cool night. He hadn't experienced many attacks of grief since coming here, but now the damn coyotes had dredged up thoughts of death; thoughts of Peter Elliott and his blonde, bloodstained hair and his spattered shirt and his little black shoe and his ruined father; thoughts of Mary and how she'd gone too soon, leaving him in a house crawling with memories; thoughts of someone's beloved dog being ripped up in the middle of the woods, all alone, never to see another morning because it would die, die, die, die, and now there was a call for Jack, a call from a very old friend, the most urgent call he'd received at his house in the middle of the woods.

Jack took a deep breath. *You can get through this. You can. Just calm yourself.*

Night was looking up at him, alternating glances between Jack and the plate of steak on the table, wagging her tail gently. Overwhelmed by gratefulness that Night was there for him – that he wasn't alone in this house with his renewed darkness – Jack kneeled and hugged his dog for a while, until finally Night grew tired of it and pulled away, nodding entreatingly at the steak and shaking her tail a little faster.

As if Jack didn't get the message, she even licked her lips.

"Okay, okay, you win," he said, and cut up a few chunks for her.

His appetite slowly returning, Jack microwaved a bowl of broccoli and selected a handful of strawberries from the fridge. He wished he could add corn on the cob to the meal, but summer was over and it was time to start getting ready for winter, gathering and chopping firewood daily for the next month to augment the supply he'd ordered two weeks ago. He could only imagine the silence of a winter here, snow weighing down the trees and making them feel like they were pressed even closer to the house, a season perhaps to be dominated less by peace than claustrophobia, he realized, especially if the snow piled up high around the house. But if Jack stayed inside and enjoyed his crackling fires, keeping the curtains drawn, then surely peace could be found before the hearth, a cup of hot chocolate to soothe him and Night to comfort him, his best friend curled up on the sofa or stretched out on the floor. It wouldn't be so bad with Night to keep him company, just different. And of course there would be his chess club meetings twice weekly, Oscar and the boys providing a little human companionship for an old man who lived in the woods. They were a good group, not the stiff, stodgy old coots Jack had always associated with chess clubs, with their endless grumbling about game etiquette and how this person took too long to move and how that person touched a piece inappropriately.

These guys didn't stare silently at the board for hours and then depart – they were like a little fraternity, daring to talk during games about what

was new and how you were doing (and even daring to eat snacks at the table, which Jack had once heard described as a chess sin).

The coyotes. They were at it again out there in the dimly moonlit woods, not attacking something else but howling sporadically, perhaps striving to repeat the same hunting tactic they'd employed before, with the first few members of the pack (the decoys) funneling the target toward the larger group lying in wait. It amazed Jack to consider the intelligence required for them to survive, relying nightly on cunning teamwork for every meal. Jack had once read somewhere that the coyote population was booming throughout the United States due to their adaptability and cleverness, capable even of surviving in cities and carrying people's pets away for dinner. During a discussion with one of his new chess club friends, Jack had learned the word coyote meant "trickster" in Native American, and the little devils were up to plenty of tricks in his woods tonight.

"Fog and coyotes and fishers," one chess club guy had said. "Pretty much sums up the nights in this town."

Jack closed the dining room window, then the kitchen window. Sacrificing the cool night air for a little relief from the sounds of nature's cruelty was a fair exchange, and Night certainly had no qualms about it, her focus remaining on Jack's food. After a while, though, Jack became annoyed by the thought of being forced to shut his windows. He'd moved out here to be at peace and experience the tranquil solitude the forest had to offer, not to hide from it. But these woods were undeniably forbidding, from the massive trees that blocked out the sky to the beasts that patrolled them by night.

The woods were deep.

BURN, DO NOT READ!

The woods were dark.

Robert Frost might have argued, but the woods weren't very lovely.

And nestled within them was Jack's little house, like a flea in a lion's mane, unseen and inconsequential to the rest of the wild.

Not for the first time Jack wondered if he'd moved too far out, a thought quickly dismissed by his pride, much like the fleeting worry of an ocean swimmer venturing out to the point where his feet lose contact with the sand. As in the swimmer's case, soon Jack's worries would be lost and the journey would continue along, carried on by pride and determination and perhaps even a little stubbornness. The swimmer would never retreat back to the shore and face inevitable regret, nor would Jack Gibson move out of his new home because a few things weren't perfect.

The positives far outweighed the negatives, he told himself as he finished up his steak, and then, after the last bits of broccoli were gone, he set the empty plate down for Night to lick clean.

But the dog was gone.

From the front of the house came low growling. When Jack hurried through the living room, he found Night staring at the basement door, her teeth bared and tail flicking.

"Easy, girl. There's nothing down there," he said, but that only sent Night into barking chaos, not the doorbell bark but the I'm-gonna-tear-someone's-throat-out roar.

Jack opened the door, and immediately Night shrank away from the opening. It was dark down there, too dark. Jack had been sure to leave a few of the basement lights on last time to discourage the growth of mold, but now he and Night were staring into blackness. Could the bulbs have burned out that quickly? No. One of them Jack had replaced maybe three weeks ago.

Confounded, he fetched a flashlight and descended into the basement, the stairs creaking with each step. At the bottom he noticed a faint but definite rotting smell, the kind that often indicates a dead animal

nearby. The smell built to a stench when he reached the workbench, and Jack beamed the light along the floor beneath it, then swept it

between boxes on the workbench shelves. No carcasses yet. Behind him, Night had warily clicked down the staircase and crept closer, though she refused to approach Jack at the workbench, no longer snarling and revealing her teeth but shaking.

"Come on, girl, check it out," Jack encouraged, pulling the string and turning on the nearest light (one of the bulbs he was almost certain he'd left on). The bulb brightened dutifully, leaving him with a little self-doubt and something else.

Something unmistakably worse, though not quite rising to the point of definition.

Jack pulled the other five strings and fully illuminated the basement – no dead bulbs down here. So why had they gone out?

Standing perplexed with his hands on his hips, watching his suddenly fearful dog, Jack tried to grasp that hitherto undefined emotion. It remained just out of reach, but Jack could vaguely see its shadowy color, could practically hear its dry, papery whisper – the color and sound of dread.

Lights don't go out by themselves unless they're dead. Or unless–

Night issued a weird, ululating whine. Still focused on the workbench, her head was tilted at an angle, and for a moment Jack thought he heard something skittering along the wall beneath the bench with little tick-tick-ticks. He shined the flashlight down there and again spotted nothing.

After searching each box on the workbench shelves (occupied only by dusty, cobwebbed items), Jack gave up in favor of a shower before bed. But he was sure to leave all six basement lights on, a knowledge that would be firm and absolute in his head tomorrow morning when he returned first thing to check them.

Chapter III

The abstract color of dread having dimly lit the insides of his eyelids last night, making for troubling sleep, Jack awoke early and hurried down into the basement, where he found each of the six light bulbs still burning brightly. The predawn hour, meanwhile, was dark and foggy, Night still sleeping on the bed, though she'd probably heard Jack close the bedroom door behind him and was now scratching at the door.

Pleased – perhaps even comforted – that the lights had stayed on, Jack shut four of them off and climbed the creaking stairs. Not all that tired in spite of enjoying limited rest, he took a walk through the house and eventually ambled out to the back deck. The fog was low and swirling, pleasurably cool against his stubbly cheeks. He hadn't shaved yesterday, and maybe he'd allow for the beginnings of a beard to form and see where they took him. Mary had always wanted him to be clean shaven – *Don't want to kiss a cactus, Jackie* – but now that he was out west, in his little house in the woods, what was stopping him?

The coyotes. Their howls were nearly remote enough to be inaudible, but riding did they come along the fog, funneling little chills through Jack's chest and thoughts of Peter into his head. He bit his lip. This wasn't good at all, the damn coyotes lifting themselves to the point of association. His new house was supposed to provide a fresh start, a sanctuary where the darkness of his past couldn't find him, but if every howl in the woods made him think of death and, therefore, of Peter Elliott, then this place would do him no good.

For a scared moment, Jack wondered if the guilt would find him anywhere, a darkness powerful enough to douse all lights – the price he paid for ending a little boy's life.

If it weren't for that Barfield and Brickley truck and the–

Ironically, a train horn drifted from miles off, cutting through the foggy forest and arriving at the deck just as Jack thought about the train back home, the one that had delayed him that sunny Sunday morning. He smiled dimly, unhappily, receiving thoughts that at first seemed like

madness but then, well...not so much. They were sleep-deprived thoughts as nebulous as the back yard, thoughts that told him maybe the ruler of life had orchestrated everything – the Barfield and Brickley truck, the train, the anaphylactic boy, Peter's death, Mary's death – to draw Jack to this very house in the middle of the woods. But why would any supreme being go through the trouble? Jack was one man, an old, unimportant man who loved his dog and preferred grilling over cooking. He didn't even believe in a higher power, so why would such a force waste his/her/its time on him?

Jack was about to head back to bed when he saw it. Something black. It was gliding quickly toward him from the depths of the yard, very much like a soaring shadow but darker, visible only because of the contrast supplied by the fog. It was coming straight at him, amorphous and eldritch, as wide and encompassing as the fog itself.

And then it was gone.

The coyotes howled distantly.

Another train horn trilled.

Jack thought of little Peter, lying dead in his Sunday suit, and where were his parents now?

Back in the master bedroom, Night began growling.

Chapter IV

Robert Gibson meant every word of his Thanksgiving dinner prayer when he thanked God for the company of family.

He was grateful to have his father and his wife's parents in the same room, along with his son, who'd returned from college, and his brother Paul, who'd flown in from Alaska. Unfortunately, Steve had family commitments down in D.C., not much of a surprise considering his wife's father practically compelled them to attend fancy holiday parties in Indiana each year. The guy was a millionaire – and a real ass, too, though that wasn't a very nice thought to have on Thanksgiving.

It was probably for the best that Steve hadn't come. Rob supposed his brother only would have darkened the mood by badgering Dad to move back east and reside in a senior community. Though Dad had provided mostly positive reports from his new home since moving there four months ago, Steve kept insisting that he was making a huge mistake and that something would eventually go wrong. For Rob, there was an expression about crossing a bridge that applied to Dad's new home. If he claimed to be happy and thriving, then what sense was there in encouraging him to move east? Rob and his wife and son were worried about Dad, of course, but there was nothing they could do outside of calling him regularly and asking how he was faring.

And apparently he was doing just fine.

"I'm looking forward to the first snow. They tell me the winters sometimes get pretty nasty out there," Dad said halfway through the meal, lifting a spoon of mashed potatoes to his mouth. "But Oscar's son Ernie said he'll plow my driveway for nothing. Real good kid, that Ernie, always doing what he can to help you out. And he's not half bad at chess, either."

"How's that club going?" Rob said. "You showing those guys all of your tricks?"

Dad chuckled, and Rob took a moment to appreciate seeing him laugh after everything he'd been through. A lot of people in his position would have turned back to alcohol, but Dad was strong and Rob was proud of him. If a new town out west and the people he met there kept him happy, then so be it. Screw the retirement community, as Dad would say.

Rob couldn't have known that Dad would return east only a few more times, and then he would never see his father alive again.

Chapter V

"Damn, Jack, looks like you've got me again," Henry Howard admitted, slapping a palm against his thigh. "I guess I'll start pushing pawns for the heck of it. Never like to tip that king – bad luck."

Jack looked up from the board. "It's not over yet, not with the way you put those pawn chains together."

Grinning, Henry brought a can of Pepsi to his lips and then proceeded to set a pawn into motion. White-haired, as pale as the fresh snow coating Main Street, Henry had been Night's veterinarian for over two years. It amazed Jack to think he'd lived here that long, but his little house in the woods had become a fine home, its history notwithstanding. New furniture had gone in, new paint had made its way to the walls, and new appliances had been added, including a television, Jack having found the silence to at times be a bit too dominant. Night had grown accustomed to the house as well, barking with less regularity and eventually abandoning her random rages targeting the basement, though she had torn through the house barking at nothing in particular one night last week.

The addition of the TV seemed to have done the dog a world of good, for she often left Jack's bedroom at night in favor of a place on the sofa before the TV, which Jack usually left running with low volume to keep his dog content.

"Supposed to be a real doozy of a storm," Henry said. "I heard well over a foot by noon tomorrow."

"It better not knock out the power," Oscar said from the next table over. "Whenever it snows, I just sit my ass down at the computer and play online chess for hours. My wife says it'll give me cataracts, but what's one more thing on the list for a fat, half-deaf, arthritic guy?"

"A fat, half-deaf, arthritic guy who stinks at chess," Henry added, and the others erupted in laughter.

Jack wasn't laughing. He'd gone into one of his occasional brooding sessions, but they hadn't been as bad in the last year, usually gripping him for a short while and then releasing him. It was impossible for him to avoid sometimes wondering what Peter Elliott would be doing if he hadn't died that sunny day. Right now, for instance – would he be finishing up his homework before dinner? Or would he have already eaten his mother's pasta and moved on to a bowl of ice cream? How many days had Jack robbed of him? How many vacations and birthdays and field trips and sporting victories and long laughs had been taken from him by a truck and its driver, an old man who hadn't been able to stop quickly enough? Jack liked to think little Peter was in a new place, a better place, but then his hopes always stopped just short of the next step – unable to set his heart free of its restraints and believe – and he scolded himself for wondering if some grand paradise was waiting beyond this world. What proof was there that such a place existed? If it was really out there, how come people had to suffer before getting to it?

Peter was nowhere, simple as that. Dead and nonexistent, his life stolen on a gorgeous Sunday morning. That was the cold, iron truth for Jack, far easier for him to settle for guarantees of nothing than it was to build faith in something unseen.

Jack came out of it quickly again, and his thoughts turned back to his friends, Henry and Oscar still ribbing each other and making jokes that were probably funny only to people over sixty, the kind of jokes at which young men would smile politely and teenagers would scoff or roll their eyes, the kind of jokes that stitched the fabric of their friendship, ten men who met twice weekly to play chess and enjoy each other's company, snow falling persistently outside tonight while their wives found an hour or two of peace and quiet at home. For Jack, there was no wife anymore, only his dog, but life moved on, never staying the same, and Jack had learned to embrace the small things, especially his friendships.

The chess club had not only been a source of social recreation for Jack but also a means of gaining knowledge, specifically insights into the history of his little house in the woods. Oscar, who'd served as a town councilor for thirty years and was regarded as the unofficial town historian, claimed to have met every resident who lived in town during the last three decades. But when Jack had gotten curious one night and asked Oscar about his house, the usually talkative former councilor had averted his gaze to the chess board, his eyes a little strange when he looked up again, flickering with reticence. Jack had pressed him, though, and then an odd thing had happened, the others seeming at once to shift their attention from their respective games to Oscar Montoya.

"The last person to own your house never had any problems there in ten years," Oscar had begun, and Jack had tensed with anticipation, the same way a high school boy might tense up when his girlfriend says, "You're a really sweet guy, but…"

"He was a pastor," Oscar continued. "Tommy Talbot and his family never had one incident, so don't get yourselves all carried away," he said, addressing the room before returning his attention to Jack. "There've been a lot of stories about your house, Jack. All because of the things that happened there before Tommy."

"What things?"

Oscar bit his lip, looking increasingly uncomfortable. "Well, the woman who lived there before Tommy was a little left of center…actually, way left of center."

"She was nuts," one of the guys said. "It's no wonder she killed herself. Has nothing to do with the house."

Jack gasped. "She killed herself? In *my* house?"

There was a brief, uneasy silence, Oscar lifting a captured bishop from the side of the board and fidgeting with it. "She hung herself in the basement," he said flatly, then quickly added, "But this was twenty years ago. The place was empty for years before Tommy moved in."

Jack felt cold and hollow, unsure of what to think about this revelation, but before he could begin to process the news someone said, "Didn't another guy who lived there die of a heart attack?"

Oscar nodded solemnly, probably dreading his wellspring of knowledge. "His name was Randall Poulin, and he died of a stroke. This was way back in the early eighties, though."

Oscar coughed, took a sip of water. "There was another man who died on the property, too – got lost in the woods in sixty-eight and froze, just a few months after he moved in. Everyone blamed it on the fog, said he lost his way and just kept walking further and further out." He shook his head disapprovingly. "First thing they tell you if you're lost is to stay put. Who knows what got into his head, but they found him dead five days after he was reported missing. Somewhat of a recluse, that guy – only reason they knew he was gone was because his brother happened to come over one day. Anyway, I remember searching the woods with my wife and parents for hours. They had cops and dogs out there, and we all must've gone through the place where they found his body a hundred times. It was so close to the house he could have hit it with a rock."

"So three people have died on my property?" Jack said, unwilling to believe what he was being told.

"Three of them *on* the property," Oscar corrected. "A married couple lived there for a few years in the mid-eighties, but they died in a car accident just outside town. Their kid was sent away to live with the grandparents, and the house was sold to Mrs. Scrivens, the lady who hung herself in the basement."

Oscar was speaking freely now, letting history flow unimpeded from mind to mouth, like a tour guide showing off a city's most prominent features and informing passengers precisely when and where certain significant happenings took place. Overwhelmed and disillusioned, Jack could only listen and nod, left dazed by the past and its miseries. His little house in the woods hadn't been such a peaceful place for others.

The snow was strengthening when Jack left the senior center. He climbed into his Ford Taurus and switched on the windshield wipers (a few months ago he'd finally gotten around to trading in his F-150, the truck that had killed Peter Elliott, a great relief spreading over him at the first realization that the truck was gone forever). Now, with a different house and a different vehicle, Jack could be the new and improved Jack Gibson, a feat he'd managed well in recent months, staying on top of his thoughts for the most part and allowing time to continue its healing process. The dark thoughts could only get to him if he let them in, he kept telling himself, and whenever he found his thoughts clinging too long to Peter or the people who'd died in his new house, he would force himself to think of Mary and the good times.

There were so many memories to choose from – holding their kids and grandkids for the first time; weddings; graduations; eating cotton candy and bashing into each other's bumper cars and kissing on the ferris wheel every year at the carnival; autumn weekend rides on the motorcycle; Christmases and birthdays with the boys – and all of these memories, Jack had realized, were the lights that kept the darkness away. It helped immensely to be in a new place, empowered to harness the cherished recollections that would stay with him always. Even if Mary was gone forever, she would never leave him.

The snow was driving down hard when Jack let Night out for her bedtime walk hours later, almost half a foot already piled up on the back deck. Watching Night bound through the snow, taking in the smoke billowing from the chimney, listening to the silence of another winter night – only the softest sweep of biting wind to be heard – Jack nearly fell asleep right there on the deck, standing in the little cleared out path he'd shoveled for Night.

Unsurprisingly, the dog didn't remain outside for very long, doing her business and returning swiftly to the deck.

"Ready for bed, girl?" Jack said, patting Night's snow-dusted back with a gloved hand.

Aggravated by the moisture on her coat, Night rubbed her sides against the sofas as she always did, walking back and forth and using the furniture as towels, a habit for which Mary had always scolded her. Jack didn't care. He never had any visitors to impress with an immaculate house, and even if he was expecting company he wouldn't concern himself with cleaning the place to sparkling levels like Mary had.

Finished drying herself, Night slipped off to the bedroom, leaving Jack to turn off the lights. When the kitchen was fully dark he peered out the window at the back yard, which was nothing more than a world of white. Peaceful. Certainly not insufferably claustrophobic as he'd once feared. Tomorrow Ernie Montoya would plow the driveway and Jack would take care of the walkways with his little snowblower, gladdened to feel like he was still useful and capable. Tomorrow Jack's adventurous dog would hop through the snow in search of the deer who'd left their prints. Tomorrow there would be another fire and more glasses of hot chocolate and maybe an old movie or two.

But for now the storm and sleep would rule.

Jack smiled when he came to the dining room, content with the way things were out here and the life he and Night shared, even if their past and that of the house was limned in black. It wasn't much, this life, but it worked for them. Simple, fulfilling, serene – embodied perfectly by the still, quiet night. And maybe in the spring Jack would finally get around to restoring that classic car he'd often thought about, a Chevy Nova or a Ford Falcon, an old gal he could detail and paint and return to her former glory.

What a great time that'd be.

147

Still smiling, Jack switched off the light mounted above the back deck, his reflection coming to life in the glass door. But there was another reflection behind him, black and briefly there. He whirled around and faced an empty, darkened room, his chest tight with the shock and fear that had accompanied what he'd seen.

Outside, the snow fell.

In the living room, the grandfather clock was ticking rather noisily. Unusually so?

Too dark.

Although Jack was almost positive the living room lamp had been on just seconds ago, the room was now completely dark, only the little glowing embers in the double-sided fireplace breaking the blackness. Beyond that large room the hallway light had winked out as well, and now Jack was scared because he was certain he hadn't clicked off that light yet.

Am I losing my mind? he wondered, fumbling and shuffling through the dark, banging hard into a dining room chair. *No, that damn light was on! I'm sure of it.*

In the bedroom, Night began growling.

Chapter VI

Excluding half an hour of thin, unproductive sleep, Jack found himself listening and worrying and questioning himself into the earliest hours of the morning. This hadn't been the first time the lights had befuddled him. There'd been that night in the basement in his first year here, and a few months later the bedroom light had puzzled him in the same way. There'd been other times when he'd gone for a morning walk with Night and returned an hour later to find the house lit only by the sunlight (despite his near certainty that he'd left at least a few lights on).

Only once had he been able to ascribe the strangeness to a bad bulb.

People died in this house, he thought, turning onto his side. *A woman hung herself and a man died of a stroke. And another guy died outside in the woods.*

There was nothing immediately searching in these thoughts in terms of a pattern connecting the past and present, no inchoate traces of a supposition. Jack simply thought it strange that the lights kept fooling him and thought it sad that people had died here and thought it confusing that he sometimes saw things that couldn't be explained, flashes of black that flourished and then evaporated, perhaps manifestations of his inner darkness, a darkness that could never be fully vanquished? A momentary whisper of ghosts and spirits fluttered through the clouded outskirts of his mind, but it was quickly driven off by gusting worries about dementia. His grandfather had suffered from Alzheimer's disease, eventually forgetting his name and the names of his children, the world around him fading to a frightening, unrecognizable void – and how terrifying it must have been to feel trapped and helpless, essentially dead, his family reduced to a bunch of strangers surrounding him and asking him questions to which the answers would never come.

The fear of following his grandfather down that bleak road to death kept Jack changing positions throughout the night. Through the curtains a dim wintry glow seeped inside, eroding the darkness. Within the house silence prevailed, only Night's soft sighs and her occasional adjustments to remind Jack that he wasn't alone. He couldn't imagine being without a friend in this place, where the silence sometimes felt like a presence and dark thoughts crept at him from their hiding places and occasionally freed themselves entirely, to the point that they became ephemerally visible entities?

No, no, it's not that bad here. Things are good...for the most part. I'm just forgetful, that's all. Mind isn't as sharp as it once was, I guess. It's like this for everyone my age. Need to start reading more.

Far too edgy to sleep, Jack kicked into his slippers and creaked through the room. Woken by her master's movements, Night sighed at length, stretched, and repositioned herself, curling up by the warm pillows.

"Good girl. You go back to sleep now. I'll just be a minute."

Willing Night not to bark, Jack stepped into the hallway. Listened. Continued to cogitate at a highly unsafe hour to do so. From the living room came the *TICK-TOCK, TICK-TOCK, TICK-TOCK* of the grandfather clock, Jack remembering the day Mary had picked it out. Jack hadn't himself been a grandfather when they'd purchased that clock. He'd barely even been a father, but now those times were gone, never to be had again by some miraculous fortune or repeated in an afterlife where everyone wore white robes and sang. The best times were gone and the clock was tick-tocking again and again, another second and then another marked by the incessant little noises. Time only moved one way, and morning could never welcome those who died.

It only welcomed those who lived, not Peter Elliott and not Mary, only those who lived.

Soon enough Jack would be welcomed no longer, his soul to depart in the silent hours preceding one of those foggy mornings, a new pack of coyotes to mark the predawn wilderness with howling, Night left all alone. And then she would be gone, too, but the clock would always

tick-tock, tick-tock, tick-tock, and little Peter's bones would be reduced to dust in the earth back east, his little suit long ago claimed by nothingness, and Barfield and Brickley would eventually go out of business, damn them, and people would still be listening to "Interstate Love Song" because music lives forever, but hopefully the song would always bring them happiness, never agony.

Jack rubbed his eyes. He was pacing the hallway, clutching his stomach as if nauseous. But he was only nauseous of thought, languid, his head feeling heavy, his feet sweating in his slippers. Surely it was still snowing outside, snow gathering in the boughs of the trees and accumulating on the driveway, snow packing itself into every crevice, leaving not an inch unoccupied, oppressing soundlessly in the night. The morning would be bright and peaceful, no doubt. It was always bright after storms, and Jack wanted to enjoy the morning, wanted to stand on the back deck with his dog and savor the winter morning because time only moved one way, but he needed to stop the bleeding tonight, needed to come through this and find some sleep. This was a bad one, worsened by the stupid lights last night, but he just had to work through it!

He thought of Mary, tried to cling to what came into his head – Mary leaning into him on the ferris wheel; Mary holding him on rainy nights when there was nothing but their love and its indescribable warmth; Mary cooking a meal, humming as she peeled the potatoes; Mary cheering on the boys at a baseball game, indifferent to the stifling heat that lifted others to complaint…

Morning does not welcome those who die.

Jack felt a familiar urge. Frighteningly strong. An old friend was out there on the porch, standing in the wind-driven snow with a fedora

151

shadowing his face and a briefcase in hand and a cheerful smile, patiently waiting to be let in.

Let's get through this stormy night together, Jackie, and there'll be nothing but blue skies tomorrow morning.

In the bedroom, Night began growling.

Chapter VII

Stevie and I have been talking for a long time.

We talked about Grandpa and his house, about Night, about the funeral, our families, my job insecurity at the newspaper, and the stress of his college application process (his father, Uncle Steve the Senator, would surely tolerate nothing short of Ivy League for Stevie Jr.). We talked about his soccer team and the most recent women in our lives, each of us currently between girlfriends. We talked about why women do the things they do to us. We talked about the weather. How else can we pass the time on a stormy night, with sleep maintaining its distance? The wind is wailing and the rain is beating down against the roof and Night, having slipped in from the guest bedroom and curled up beside me on the sofa, finally closes her eyes for a few minutes, seemingly not the result of desire but resignation. The windows drip with streaks of moisture. The chill of the house has abated but not the loneliness and certainly not the heaviness.

Time moves slowly. I check my watch. 11:23.

"It's working again," Stevie says, surprised.

"What's working?"

He points to the grandfather clock, which is indeed ticking again, its sounds drowned by the wind and rain.

"Maybe it's haunted." Stevie shoots me a half-grin, but I don't find the comment amusing, not after BURN, DO NOT READ!

It comes in the darkness.

I glance at the other clocks, which remain stuck at 11:57. "The battery must be weak," I assume, though I've never seen a clock stop for a prolonged stretch and then restart.

"No, man. I heard those things are haunted."

I toss a pillow at Stevie. "I need another beer."

"Seriously. Me too," and he turns onto his side, propping himself up on an elbow.

I saw it and it saw me.

I wish I could find a way to force the contents of that book from my mind. They keep eating at me from the inside. Corrosive.

MORNING DOES NOT WELCOME THOSE WHO DIE!

But I know I have to finish the book. Alone. Stevie would only add distractions about ghosts and demons and the crap he's seen on those paranormal reality TV shows. There's no time for all that, not tonight. I desperately want to know what was in Grandpa's head when he wrote and painted those foreboding things. Knowledge won't bring him back. It won't lighten the aura of this house, but still I must seek the truth, if only to form my own sense of closure. What is It? And why did he choose the most personal of first-person perspectives, going as far as including Grandma's name?

And why did he cover the windows with newspaper?

I take a deep breath, trying not to get too overwhelmed. I wonder if I should just call my father and let him deal with the book. I know I'm not in the best frame of mind, strained after a long, hard day.

But strained or not, Grandpa wrote BURN, DO NOT READ!, and now I need to read. I wasn't there for Grandpa in his final years, wasn't there when he sealed up his house and missed all his appointments and told his neighbors to go away.

It won't let me leave.

Even though Grandpa titled his book, Burn, Do Not Read!, I feel I owe it to him to finish, all the way to the end, to join him in his final journey as I failed to do in life.

Chapter VIII

Each year, Jack honored the anniversary of Peter's tragedy by making a contribution to the foundation that had been established in the boy's name. Mary had helped set up the Peter Elliott Foundation, and it uplifted Jack to donate yearly to the cause, his money supporting a scholarship given each spring to a graduating high school senior. The Peter Elliott Scholarship. It was always strange for Jack to visit the foundation's website and scroll through the countless photos of Peter, knowing with every click that *he* was the reason this child before him was dead. In some of the photos Peter posed with his parents; others captured the boy with his soccer and hockey teams; in one of Jack's favorite photos, Peter stood with a bursting grin at the entrance to a roller coaster. Looking at that photo always reduced Jack to tears, the joy and spirit in the boy's eyes making it seem like he'd live forever.

So many years taken away.

Jack settled in before one of the library computers. The morning was still encumbered with thick fog, the brick building enshrouded by a wall of watchful gray. The little one-story structure was virtually empty, the librarian tapping away at her computer behind the main desk. Five years ago Jack had been driving down Main Street on a bright Sunday morning, shortly after finding himself delayed by a train and two old ladies in a crosswalk and the careless maneuvers of a furniture delivery truck driver, "Interstate Love Song" playing on his radio. Peter had darted out into the street, turned toward Jack with eyes of absolute terror – and now those blue eyes stared at him from the computer screen.

Time only moved one way.

Jack sipped from the styrofoam cup of coffee he'd purchased at the doughnut shop, then looked past the computer at the far wall, where an angry yellow sign read:

ABSOLUTELY NO FOOD OR DRINKS AT THE COMPUTERS!

Shrugging, Jack snuck a glance at the librarian, who was still engrossed by her computer, a pair of glasses resting on her nose. He'd probably get yelled at, Jack supposed, but worse things had happened on this date.

Jack was about to click on the website's DONATE tab when he saw the short message about halfway down the page. The words nearly made him choke on his own breaths, and quickly he was searching the internet for confirmation, his eyes expanding and mouth falling open when he read about Peter's father. He'd been found dead in his home two months ago; the police hadn't released the cause of death, but the article indicated a previous OUI incident that had landed David Elliott in jail around Christmas.

He couldn't take it anymore and killed himself, Jack assumed, bringing both hands to his cheeks. *Or maybe he mixed alcohol with antidepressants. Shit, that was probably it. Didn't one of Mary's old college friends die that way?*

From there Jack's conscious decisions gave way to mindless instinctual reactions. He stood, hurried to the exit, forgetting his task and his cup of coffee, and then he was outside in the cool, miserable fog, jogging toward his Taurus, guilt jabbing repeatedly at him.

It's all my fault. He's dead because of me. Both of them are dead because of me!

For a while Jack just sat there in his car, gripping the steering wheel and shaking his head. This was never a good day, not back east and not in his new town. It had been such a good year, but on this loathsome day the darkness always came for him. Had he been a spiritual man, this tragic news might have brought him a sliver of solace, based chiefly on his faith that father and son had been reunited in Heaven. But Jack Gibson had never been steered toward spiritual inclination, not even when Mary spoke to him of "God's grace", sometimes even warning him that they could only be together again in Heaven if he

believed. She'd said he would be very sad and lonely without faith, that he'd have no direction. There'd been other things she'd said, too, things about salvation and the importance of a baptism, Jack half-listening as she rambled on.

Sitting in his car, the fog swirling around him, the distant red traffic signals dimmed to spectral eyes peering out from the grayness, Jack briefly wished he was a religious man. *It would be nice to have faith*, he thought, *but it's just a farce. What God would have let Peter die in the road?*

Jack had heard statements of a great variety uttered by Mary and other spiritual people when describing tragic events – God needed him/her in Heaven; it was his/her time; God works in mysterious ways – but how could anyone know that? Did they speak to God on the phone about these mysterious ways? Did they sit down with God at a coffee shop somewhere and chat? Their rationalizations and justifications inevitably surrounded the Bible, a book written ages ago by people with five fingers and five toes, not some prophetic, divine text but a massive collection of fictional works. It seemed odd that such an ancient book could be considered infallible when people didn't even agree on who discovered America – but you couldn't argue with the believers, couldn't get them to even consider that the end might actually be just that.

Jack's eyes lingered on the traffic lights – watching the continual shifts from green to yellow to red – his mind fixed on another place, another street, held firmly by the darkness. He remembered Peter's face, both before and after the fatal collision, and then he remembered his discussion with David Elliott, who'd looked straight into Jack's eyes and said he didn't blame him for his son's death.

Jack inhaled deeply. Let out a tearful, shivery breath. Watched the inevitable shift: green, yellow, red.

Saw something moving in the fog, just in front of his car.

Something dark and sidling.

It sunk down low, impossible to see below the bumper.

Jack scrambled out of the car, remembering the last inscrutable sighting of black. It had been wintertime, Jack having fallen asleep on the sofa, Night curled up on the seat beside him, an empty glass of hot chocolate on the table. The fire had nearly gone out and a chill had crept into the house. There'd been a noise, rousing Jack from a strange dream – one about a group of precocious boys who challenged Death one moonlit night, repeatedly outrunning it and slamming the door in its face and taunting it from the safety of their locked house, then venturing again into the midnight black to taunt Death some more because Death was slow and old. But Death, in its invariable hood and cloak, tricked the daring boys later that night, hanging its uniform upon a distant moonlit post, and when the boys opened the door and hollered at the decoy – Come get us, you slow, old, smelly creep! – Death snatched them all at once and dragged them screaming and flailing back to its den, where it locked them away for a while and eventually, one by one, dealt with them as it eventually deals with every living creature.

Upon waking that frigid winter night, within the first few seconds of consciousness, Jack had been aware of two things: Night growling quietly beside him and a fleeting darkness crossing before the dying firelight, momentarily blocking it before vanishing, a popped ember drifting upward when the hearth was fully visible again. Night had immediately quieted when the thing was gone, and Jack had been left cold and numb, wondering if what'd he'd just seen had really been there, his neck tingling and chest tight with pressure. Gripped by remnant thoughts of Death and those stupid boys, he'd flicked on multiple lights and huddled on the sofa with Night, both of them blanketed and uneasy. Many hours later, with sunlight saturating the house and winter white overspreading the lawn, the darkness so briefly seen had transformed from a frightening thing to a harmless extension of a nightmare.

Now, quickly remembering that night and others, Jack dropped achingly to his knees and searched beneath his car. Nothing there, only fog on the other side. Had he imagined it? Of course he'd imagined it.

Feeling foolish, he got back to his feet, dusted off his corduroys, and made a slow, searching circle of the fog. To his left, an old woman was exiting the library. To his right, sparse morning traffic progressed carefully along Main Street – if a little kid ran out into the road in these conditions…

Jack climbed back into his car. For some reason he felt compelled to slide the moonroof cover shut. He half-expected to hear a little thud when he eased the car into motion, but there were no strange sounds or sights, not now, and Jack again wondered why he occasionally experienced these frightful little glimpses of black. There'd been that night in the dining room, of course, when he'd shut off the light and briefly seen something in the reflection, something standing behind him. And, as now, there'd been a handful of times when he thought he detected something in the fog.

Alzheimer's disease? Were these the initial stages of an insidious storm?

By the time it got done with Grandpa, his brain didn't even tell him when he was full. He just kept eating and eating and eating till someone took the damn food away.

An old friend nudged Jack's arm on the way home. He was passing the package store, a freight train rumbling parallel to the road, the bright headlights cutting through the fog, reminding Jack of the date and Peter and Peter's father, everything connected in chronological horror.

It would always be connected in this way.

Jack fought an urge to stop at the package store, concentrating on memories of Mary until he rounded a bend and the store was gone.

There's always tomorrow, came a dark thought, and with it, *Morning does not welcome those who die.*

Chapter IX

Jack's eldest grandson called him that evening, the sound of his voice offering a needed reprieve from tireless thoughts. Talking with Jon made him feel connected to the world beyond his little house in the woods, made him feel like he and Night weren't out here all alone, surrounded by the stubborn fog.

Jack was proud of his grandchildren, especially Jon, who wrote for a community newspaper, one of those old-school papers that paid the price for wanting to stick with tradition and provide news the tangible way, not through misspelled internet headlines, overreliance on user comments to generate traffic, and terse, poorly written stories. But a new era of endless videos and social networking sites had dawned – and so Jon's company had undergone an expected series of layoffs recently, only the best writers surviving the cuts. Jon, with his unfaltering humility, said he'd simply gotten lucky, but Jack kept telling him he was a great writer.

"You keep at it, and you'll be at the New York Times one day, kid."

Jack knew he was being corny, but corniness and light talk made the fog outside seem a little less imposing. It kept the bad thoughts from his head…mostly.

Jack drew the living room curtains, took a seat on the sofa beside Night, the TV flashing with local news. He spoke a while longer with Jon and then let him go, knowing Jon was busy with work and his girlfriend. Not everyone lived in a house way out in the woods, after all, and time only moved one way; those who didn't believe it needn't require any further proof than the tick-tick-ticks echoing from one corner or another, one wall or another. For Jack, it was the grandfather clock that tracked the hours most prominently – otherwise he might have occasionally been fooled into thinking life stood still out here in the wilderness.

Later, Jack called a few more family members (the ones he assumed would call him back). He seldom spoke to Paul's four kids – all

between the ages of fourteen and nineteen – but it wasn't their fault. Their grandparents on their mother's side lived twenty minutes away from them in Alaska, Paul having firmly entrenched his life in the Last Frontier, and they simply weren't very close to Jack anymore.

When it came to Steve's children, Jack usually only spoke with his twelve-year-old granddaughter Jenny when Steve or her mother called out, "Hey, Jenny, Grandpa's on the phone. Do you want to talk?" During such instances Jack could always envision a frowning Jenny reluctantly extricating her gaze from the TV.

Steve's other sons, Stevie Jr. and Matt, sometimes called him, Stevie far more often than Matt. Whenever Jack talked to Stevie, the kid seemed engaged in their conversation and even asked Jack about life out west, but Matt – two years younger than Stevie – usually just muttered, *Uh-huh, Uh-huh*, and tried to get off the line as quickly as possible, taking after his father.

Jack didn't have Matt's cell phone number, but Stevie had offered his number at Thanksgiving and welcomed Jack to call whenever he wanted. Still longing for the connection of family, Jack found himself dialing the number.

Stevie answered after the first ring. "Hey, Grandpa." He sounded excited, and that brought a smile to Jack. It was nice to think his grandkids were still interested in him, even though he'd moved across the country and rarely saw them.

"Hey there, Stevie, how are you? Staying out of detention lately?" Stevie didn't take school very seriously, much to the displeasure of his father, who'd enrolled him in some fancy-schmancy prep school. Jack hadn't liked school much at Stevie's age, and the idea of dressing up in a uniform for school abhorred him.

164

Stevie laughed dutifully. "I've almost gone two weeks – I think it might be a record for me at this stupid school. How's Night doing?" Jack glanced at his sleeping dog. "She never runs out of squirrels to chase, that's for sure," and Stevie gave another obligatory laugh. "How's your dad doing, anyway? I left a couple messages for him these last few days, but he must be real busy, I assume."

"He's always busy," Stevie blurted, sounding unhappy. "I wish he'd never gotten elected. Then I could still see my old friends."

"Haven't you made some new friends at your school by now?" Jack remembered Stevie complaining about his school at Thanksgiving, his father making it seem like it was Stevie's fault, and Jack had felt bad for him. Now he found himself asking the same question he'd asked back in November.

"A few," the kid said, "but they're not like my old friends. They're all rich and fake, like younger versions of my dad."

Jack couldn't suppress a laugh. "Give them some time. Even rich, fake, snobby kids can be all right sometimes if you give them a shot. What about your baseball team? Last time I spoke with your dad, he told me you guys are doing well."

"We're still undefeated, but it's not that big a deal, I guess."

"Not a big deal? Your dad said you're one of the best hitters."

"Yeah, the best hitter on a bad team in a horrible league," and they both enjoyed a genuine laugh at that one.

Stevie went on to ask how Jack's chess club was going, and then proceeded to bring up the topic of metal detecting. It surprised Jack that the kid had remembered him mentioning wanting to buy a metal detector at Thanksgiving, a purchase he'd been putting off since moving (he'd never quite made it out to the Wal-Mart that allegedly existed two towns over, a half-hour drive, according to Oscar).

165

"Still haven't gotten around to buying the damn thing," he admitted. "One day."

When their conversation was on its deathbed, Stevie told Jack, "Love you, Grandpa," reminding Jack of the child he'd once been, and it occurred sadly to him that Stevie was his only grandchild who still said that to him – in fact, he was his only family member who said that.

"I love you, too, kid," Jack said, and set down the phone, feeling heavy, staring contemplatively at the coffee table, loneliness settling in like the dampening fog. For a few moments he wondered if moving closer to his family would be for the best, but then he remembered Steve's insistences that he move to a retirement home. He'd been at it again on Thanksgiving, still refusing to accept that Jack could live successfully on his own, still asking him things like, "What happens when the shoe eventually drops, Dad?", and the thought forced Jack into an indignant mindset.

To leave now would surely be to forfeit his freedoms.

But what if living on his own became too much, he worried. What if strange things like this morning's experience kept happening and he drove himself mad out in the middle of the woods?

People have died in this house, he thought with a sudden brisk discomfort, his eyes landing on the oak grandfather clock, its resonant hourly chimes sounding particularly doomful.

Another hour had passed.

A new hour had come.

Time only moved one way.

At the chiming calls, Night sprang from sleep and studied the room, tilting her head to the ceiling and sniffing, sniffing, sniffing with rising energy. Then, apparently satisfied, she collapsed back to the sofa and closed her eyes.

Chapter X

Steve was indulging in a fine selection of internet pornography when Rob called.

"What's up, Rob?" he said with irritation, wishing he could be undisturbed for just a few minutes of peace and pleasure. He was playing by the goddamn rules, resisting urges to go to clubs and meet women because that was how you lost the game; resisting urges to approach his secretary with a new set of directives because that was how you lost the game; resisting the occasionally strong impulse to touch interns in interpretable ways because that was not only how you lost the game but also how you got disqualified from future games and became the subject of lawsuits.

So why couldn't he be left to enjoy his brief, completely harmless pleasures without someone interrupting him? First it had been his wife calling, then Stevie calling to bitch about his school again, and now it was Rob.

"Hey, Steve. Have you talked to Dad today?"

Steve threw his hands behind his head, exasperated by that increasingly embittering three-letter d-word. "No, why?"

"Well, he was pretty upset when I spoke to him yesterday. I left you a message this morning, but long story short, he found out about Peter Elliott's father."

"Perfect," Steve muttered, shaking his head. "See, this is exactly what I knew would happen. He'll go off the grid for a while, and now we're stuck worrying. Tell me how that's fair. When we get old, I pray we're not a burden to our children."

"He'll get through this," Rob assured. "He just needs some time. I wish he would return my calls, though. I've tried the landline and his cell all day, but no response. Last thing I want is to contact one of his friends, only to find out he took a drive or something."

"He didn't even want to give us their numbers," Steve remembered. "Everything's always gotta be so damn hard with him – it's like pulling teeth."

"It's still early out west," Rob said. "I'll give it a few more hours, but eleven o'clock's the deadline. Meanwhile, I'm gonna give Paul a quick call, but I doubt he's been in touch with Dad."

"Doubt it," Steve said, staring angrily at his laptop screen. The video wouldn't be nearly as pleasurable now, he realized, not when Dad could be crumpled up somewhere after falling down or in the police station after killing another kid.

Damn it, Dad. Only you can screw things up from across the country.

KEVIN FLANDERS

Part IV: The House in the Woods

Chapter I

It was almost dark when Jack finally retired to his little house for the
night. He'd been drifting about the back yard for the better part of the
afternoon, Night watching him interestedly as he followed the beeps
and boops of the metal detector he'd purchased that morning, his arm
sweeping heavily – and with increasing discomfort – back and forth
until it was time to dig for treasures. Though Jack had only unearthed a
shredded, rusty can, a rusty nail, and a rusty rod that looked very much
like a railroad spike, the thrill of the hunt had been addictive, keeping
him at it even though his back had gotten sore and his arms had tired
out. He dreaded predicting how his body would respond tomorrow
morning, but the activity had served its purpose, getting him out of the
house and away from his thoughts. There'd been peace out there in the
yard today, with the sun glinting through the trees and Night
occasionally racing after a squirrel or a rabbit, coming up empty just
like her master but never quitting on a hunt. The morning fog had worn
off quickly, and a warm, sunny day of metal detecting had settled him
like an antacid of the mind (thankfully Stevie had reminded him
yesterday about his idea).

But now Jack found himself growing wary.

Darkness stalked through the woods, and he was back in his house
again, listening to the grandfather clock. The stillness bothered him,
made him feel like he was in a tomb. If it weren't for the clock and the
hum of the refrigerator, the place would have surely been as silent as a
coffin.

Jack switched on the television, then paced circumspectly into the
kitchen, half-expecting with every glance into a mirror to see
something behind him. Night, sharing his unease, perhaps drawing

from it, followed Jack closely and sat near the refrigerator, searching the kitchen and dining room with troubling alertness.

Jack's cell phone rang then, and he realized he'd left his phone charging on the countertop all day. The boys were probably worried sick, especially Rob, who he always called during the early evening. But in the back yard, with the metal detector beeping and sending him in circles, the day had gotten away from him.

He scooped up the phone and disconnected it from the charger cable. "Hey, Rob. I'm so sorry I didn't call – was out in the yard all day with my new metal detector."

Jack could hear his son decompressing on the other end. "No, problem, Dad. You'll find a bunch of messages from me on your home phone, too, but it's all good now. I hope you didn't wear yourself out with that thing."

"Oh, definitely not. It was good exercise, keeps the body moving." Jack was selecting delis from the fridge for a turkey sandwich, Night still staring into the dining room. "I bought the detector this morning and just couldn't seem to stop, like a little kid with a new birthday present. It's one of those fancy ones that tells you how far down something is – I dug eight inches to find a crappy old can."

"You find any coins?"

"No, not today, but you can bet I'll be back out there tomorrow. Weather's supposed to be great all week."

"Good for you, Dad. I'm glad you had fun today. We were a little worried about how you were taking the David Elliott news."

"Can't worry about that. Not in my control," Jack said abruptly, not wanting to think or talk about David Elliott.

171

"That's the spirit," Rob said, and, perhaps sensing his father's discomfort with the subject, shifted their conversation to Jack's chess club.

They spoke a while longer and then Rob was gone, Jack left to his sandwich and his loneliness. He wished Mary were here, wished he had someone to talk to. Night was a great companion and the chess club guys were terrific friends, but he missed talking to his wife over dinner and holding her in bed and watching her water flowers in her garden and knowing that, no matter how bad things got, she would always be there for him. He missed his Sunday morning breakfasts with her at Chestnut Ridge Diner. He missed watching Wheel of Fortune and Jeopardy with her. He missed seeing her delicate unwrapping of birthday and Christmas gifts, never wanting to tear open the paper. There were little things and big things he missed, important things and trivial things, but they all added up to an amazing person he would never see again because time only moved one way and morning did not welcome those who died.

Mary. My sweet Mary, how I wish we could have another day.

Mary had always wanted what was best for Jack. She'd kept him straight, guided him when he was without direction, loved him when he'd hated himself – but now she was gone and he was alone in a little house in the woods, feeling as small and insignificant as the house itself, darkness sliding in all around him. The clock was tick-tocking in the living room. Night's paw was perched atop his foot beneath the table, subtle canine pressure to throw down a scrap of turkey. Jack obliged, smiling at his dog, whose loving brown eyes followed his every move. The white spot on her chest and the slight tilt of her head made him feel a little gooey, as did the simplicity of the realization that Night was here with him, ready to usher in the darkness with him, as loyal a friend as he'd ever known.

"I love you, girl," Jack said, scratching Night behind the ears and beneath the collar.

Night smiled as she sometimes did when Jack found the spot, but her happiness didn't last long. Moments later she was tearing through the house, barking at every window and eventually stopping before the closed basement door and growling.

It was happening again.

With a stiff gust of wind the house stirred – curtains fluttering, a door creaking shut down the hall, something thudding lightly in the basement. Night stopped barking and backed away from the door, whimpering and then falling silent. Jack's chest went cold as he crossed through the living room.

Opening the basement door, clicking on the stairwell light, Jack listened for a long time but heard only the residual whispers of wind and the distant ticking of the clock. Night remained quiet behind him, waiting for her master's decision.

"You want to check it out with me, girl?" he said, realizing he'd carried his dinner plate with him when Night had raced angrily through the house. Though the turkey sandwich and potato chips were calling, Jack knew he wouldn't be able to enjoy his dinner without confirming…confirming what? That there were no intruders? The idea seemed ridiculous, but Night wasn't completely mad, only half-crazed at times.

Yet she hadn't been barking at the air, had she?

Jack took the stairs quickly, hurrying down into the basement and turning on the lights, wanting to get the investigation over with. Night followed him and stared at the workbench, then growled lowly and gave Jack a quick dose of déjà vu. As before, there was nothing beneath the bench, no little gremlins weaving between the boxes of tools and appliances, no rabid rats glowering at him with red eyes, no apparitions or shadows. The longer he remained in the basement, searching for things that simply weren't there, the greater Jack's irritation became with himself.

I have to handle this place better. This is my house. I own it, not the other way around! It's been years. Time to be done with this foolishness.

At that thought, Peter Elliott's face came flashing into his head, almost as if the house had…no, no, no, it was a damn house, comprised of wood and glass and plaster and shingles just like any other house. *He* was the problem, specifically his head. His guilt and loneliness were doing all of this, messing with him now that he knew about David Elliott, and Night was making it worse. She'd probably just heard mice in the walls or something, he figured, desperate for any explanation. That one seemed to make sense, and so he settled upon it, forcing himself back upstairs to finish his meal.

And muttering the entire way.

Chapter II

The next day Jack finally decided to bring a little zest into the house, and when he thought about what Mary would do, it instantly came to him. She'd always loved the sound of wind chimes, so much so that she'd ordered several of them online over the years and asked Jack to hang them from the porch. There'd been brass chimes and aluminum chimes and even wooden chimes that made hollow little thunks like baseball bats coming gently together. Mary's chimes had featured decorations of all kinds – stars, moons, suns, cats, frogs, dogs, leprechauns, daisies, fairies, on and on it went – and Jack would always remember standing on the porch and listening to the chimes clanging and rattling as a storm came in, something intrinsically peaceful about them, instruments capable of slowing time. Mary had often left the living room windows cracked, even on colder nights, just so the voices of the chimes could slide in and soothe her.

But Jack had sold or given away his wife's wind chimes – time to start afresh.

At the only Wal-Mart for fifty miles, Jack carefully selected five chimes he could hang from the porch. He picked out the basic, undecorated ones to avoid working himself into a sentimental state in public. This was no time to start getting moist-eyed with memories of cribbage games in the living room, the chimes spritzing the night with simple melodies.

Satisfied with his new collection of chimes, Jack meandered through the aisles until he came to the nursery, where he purchased a few flower pots and boxes, followed by colorful annuals that could intersperse a little red and orange and violet into those endlessly gray-green mornings. As he did so, he thought of Mary and what she'd think of him buying flowers and chimes.

Jackie Gibson, she might say, *you're finally developing an appreciation for life's small treasures.*

175

Jack spent an hour hanging his chimes and nurturing his flowers, the porch transformed from bland and uninviting to energetic. A paint job would be next, he decided.

Time for this place to get a makeover. That's just what it needs. A good old makeover to get rid of the bad memories.

Still can't believe people died in this house.

Night watched Jack work from the front lawn, the grass matted down beneath her. She'd whiled away the last few minutes rolling on her back, her tail wagging whenever Jack called out to her. Now she was resting with her head on her forepaws, blinking contentedly at Jack, drifting closer to naptime, a bowl of water and a rawhide bone at her side. Jack wished she could enjoy such peace all the time – and then it struck him that her violent barking fits rarely happened during the day or outside, almost all of them occurring in the house after dark.

Could she hear the coyotes many miles off, maybe? Did they frighten her into rushing around the house like a lunatic? But distant coyotes didn't explain her often sustained, adamant barking at the basement door.

Jack shrugged, wondering. *If only she could talk. Too bad she can't tell me what gets her so upset.*

A gravelly crunching sound grew steadily louder. Moments later a gray Buick Century eased around the driveway curve into view, just past the pond, dust kicked up around the wheels. It took a moment, but Jack recognized the Buick as Oscar Montoya's car.

"The hell's he doing here?" Displeased, Jack stuffed his hands into his pockets.

Night, meanwhile, went hollering after the car, coming up alongside it and forcing Oscar to stop. Jack's repeated calls were initially ignored,

Night returning to him only after she decided she'd supplied sufficient warning of a stranger's arrival.

The driver's window came down. An excited smile flashed into existence. "Ready, Jack?"

"Ready for what?" he shouted from the lawn.

Oscar removed his glasses and squinted out at him. "The show, remember? You and I are supposed to take the afternoon shift."

Jack, embarrassed, whisking Night toward the porch, tried to remember. *Oh, right, the show, the damn show.*

He'd agreed at a chess club meeting some time ago, mostly out of politeness, to help man the tent for a few afternoon hours; he'd even confirmed his availability at the last meeting. Apparently the guys and their wives participated every year in a crafts festival at the center of town, many of them selling homemade knick-knacks, the kind of stuff Mary had always loved to buy, dragging Jack to the festivals when he'd wanted to sleep in. (*Jack, look at these beautiful photographs. And these lovely Christmas ornaments. And this book, my goodness, that looks scary, and from a local author, too!*)

The guys had asked Jack if he'd like to sell anything – you get to keep the proceeds of each sale, Oscar had informed – but Jack had declined, said good company and good weather was all he needed for a fun time.

But now he was dreading the festival. He just wanted to stay home and rest, maybe do some more metal detecting if his back and knees didn't bother him too much.

"How long we supposed to be there?" Jack asked, strolling up to the Buick once he'd gotten Night inside.

Oscar rubbed his chin. "Till about six or so – then Charlie, Curt, and their ladies will come for the night shift. Always a great time." Oscar

seemed to detect the reluctance on Jack's face. "You don't have to come if you're not up for it. I can handle it myself, I guess."
"No, no, I'll come. Absolutely." Jack was rounding the car, coming to the passenger side, roped into an event he wanted no part of, Oscar smiling joyfully when he hauled himself into the seat – and it was like being a kid all over again, going with the gang on an adventure, except there was nothing dangerous or illegal about this excursion, only a trip to the annual crafts festival.

How bad can it be?

Whitley Park, occupying a sprawling expanse near the town center, its tennis courts and baseball diamond usually sparsely populated, was packed with rows of tents. Vehicles flanked the length of the entry road, a few of them parked at careless diagonals, others backed fussily into openings scarcely wider than their bumpers, a handful left in illegal spots (the ones with orange tickets tucked beneath the windshield wipers).

Oscar parked about as far away as possible, in a little clearing at the edge of Main Street. The bright red banner proclaiming, **WELCOME TO LIBERTY DAYS FESTIVAL**, was barely visible in the distance.

"Are you a bad parker, or just looking for exercise?" Jack said, eyebrows raised, annoyed by the prospect of a long walk.

Oscar laughed, deep and hearty. "These decrepit legs of mine certainly don't need any more exercise, but parking's never been my strong suit. I need three empty spaces on either side to feel comfortable," and they were both laughing now, following the sinuous entry road toward the hub of noise and color, gnats harassing them the whole way.

The slightly uphill walk, with the help of good conversation, didn't seem all that daunting after a while, and soon they were passing beneath the banner and joining the fray. Ahead, the baseball field and tennis courts were lined with tents of varying sizes and colors. Some looked like they'd been erected by a team of professionals, with side walls and sturdy canopies; others, slanted and woebegone, seemed like they could be blown over by a gentle breeze.

"We're always set up in the same spot each year, a little ways ahead on the left," Oscar said, leading Jack through a maze of shoppers – little children capering about and old couples studiously analyzing products and vendors drawing attention to their wares.

It was a lively atmosphere, a large crowd gathered around the gazebo, where a group of men in tuxedos was playing crisp big band music. The air was redolent with popcorn, couples holding hands or locking arms as they walked, thoughts of Mary springing at Jack. She would have delighted in a day like this, though she and Jack surely would have come in the morning when it was cool, then gone for a motorcycle ride or had themselves a picnic in the afternoon.

"Jack? Hey, Jack, you tired?"

Jack didn't realize he'd stopped. He was taking it all in with a strengthening mawkishness, Oscar coming quickly back to him, oblivious to Jack's sudden discomfort. He felt weak for allowing himself to be dictated by emotion, but it was still so hard sometimes to accept that *this* was his life, that Mary was gone forever, that events like these could never again be had with her dainty hand in his.

The kids. They were all around, brightly dressed, young families everywhere, and how Jack yearned to be given an opportunity to repeat and relive, but time, of course, only moved one way.

"Just a little sore, that's all," Jack feigned, taking a stab at a smile. "Knees aren't what they once were."

"Amen to that. Used to be the best damn roofer around – then my legs gave out. They kicked me off the last job, told me to go home after the first day, you're all done, old guy, take your money and scoot." Oscar waited patiently for him, recounting the indignities with a scowl, and at last Jack carried on, not wanting to delay his friend further.

179

They passed a big blue tent with apparel of all kinds, the dresses hung from lines and T-shirts stacked on tables. Next, on the right, was the **SUPPORT OUR HIGH SCHOOL SPORTS!!!** food and ice cream tent, the parents and coaches up front waving to potential customers while the athletes, relaxed in lawn chairs, matching windbreakers partially zipped, were staring down at their cell phones, tapping messages of grave adolescent importance.

Jack had never understood the lure of texting, those buttons so damn small, anyway.

On they went, past a gloomy author whose dourness contradicted the factitious smile plastered upon his posters; past the cheerful balloon man whose gut was far more inflated than his creations; past the little waif of a woman selling yarn inventions; and now Jack was locking gazes with a smiling, ebullient vendor, a black vest over his red dress shirt, a strange magnetism existing between the two men, Jack caught and held by his dazzling stare.

Then, like all moments, it was over, the man searching with high spirits for his next target. "Step right up, don't be shy!" he shouted gaily. "The Great Frankie Esperanza has magic of all kinds for you today! Coins, strings, cards – the choice is yours, ladies and gentlemen."

The chess club's tent was two down from The Great Esperanza's setup, and directly across from a tent filled with oddly shaped mirrors. A good distance from the gazebo, the customer traffic out this way was much lighter.

Oscar greeted the guys they would be relieving for the afternoon shift, but Jack's focus quickly returned to Esperanza, a sixtyish man with a thin build and tapering white hair. His snowy mustache was neatly trimmed, his glasses silver and somehow regal in their glint of sunlight angling through the side of his tent. There were three boys and a little girl behind him in the deeper shade of the tent, snow cones in hand – grandchildren? – each watching Esperanza with what Jack perceived as proud interest.

"Step right up, don't be shy!" the magician encouraged, beckoning with his hands, and Jack willed the guests to oblige, hoping to see a trick

from this vantage point, perfectly sidelong. Maybe he'd even figure out how it was done.

"So what do you think of our wares, Jack?" came Oscar's voice to his left.

Jack settled into the cushioned metal chair that was his only option, one of those cheap pieces of crap they lined up at graduations, surely designed by the makers of Advil or Tylenol.

Jack's eyes roamed the chess club's tables of inventory – little glass squares of varying colors, wooden pegs glued to their bases; larger ceramic tiles that looked like they'd been pried out of someone's floor; bizarre items fashioned out of twisted paper clips; lower, in front of the tables, there were logs crudely carved to resemble animals, the paint seemingly splashed on; higher, dangling from fishing line, were model airplanes absent detail. How much did these guys earn selling this stuff, a few dozen bucks?

But Oscar was excited enough. Hefting up one of the ceramic tiles with a grimace, he said, "They tell me two of my babies sold today, and that's a record!"

Mindful of his proximity to the invisible line that, if crossed, would result in hurt feelings, Jack carefully selected his comment. "Wow, that's great, Oscar. Do people buy them for their gardens, you think?"

"Nah, these are cutting boards." Oscar tilted the cream-colored tile, as if analyzing it from a slightly different angle would somehow make its purpose self-evident. Then he selected another, a black tile with little swirls of pink. "These are usually our least popular item, unfortunately for me – Henry's coasters sell like hotcakes.

Jack, confused, scooped up one of the colored glass squares that were apparently coasters and examined its underside, where four wooden pegs had been glued somewhat askew at the corners.

2 for $5, a sign placed before the squares read. **Get them while they last.**

"So who makes the log animals?" Jack said. Two tents to their right, The Great Esperanza was still merrily soliciting guests, his smile remaining even when they passed on by, and what an inspiring thing that was, something to be learned from it, Jack decided, impressed to the point of nodding.

Oscar crossed his arms, beaming. "Those are my bread and butter." He shook his head as if caught in a wondrous reverie, his eyes falling to his log creations. "Countless hours go into each one, such a precise hobby, you know? Gotta get every cut just right to bring out the details."

Jack didn't dare ask more about the animals – one of them resembled a bear, but it might well have been a very angry badger. Another seemed to be a cat, but who knew?

"Step right up, don't be shy!" The magician was trying his luck at a new throng of guests, and two of them turned – *yes, yes, come on, go for it, kids* – and sure enough, they drifted to the magician's tent. About nine or ten, the little girls were pigtailed and metal-mouthed, their youthful smiles like lights you never wanted to see turned off.

"How are we today, ladies? Ready to see some *magic*?" Esperanza's eyes gleamed, his hands waving in a flourish, the girls nodding excitedly, Jack equally as excited from his seat, ignoring two old ladies who observed the highly acclaimed coasters.

"Sí, sí, very well, and what shall it be?" Esperanza was saying. "Coins? Strings? Cards?" The magician was sliding quarters across the table, back and forth, back and forth, hands flashing, and then, deftly, those two quarters were gone.

"Whoa!" one of the little girls marveled, the other's lips falling open, blue eyes lifting to Esperanza.

"And what about these strings, ladies? What shall we do with them?" The yellow strings were extracted swiftly from the magician's vest pocket, then laid with precision across the table to demonstrate three different lengths, the shorty on the left and, twice its length, the big boy farthest to the right. "As you can see, we have three sizes of string, yes?" Simultaneous nods from the little ones, Jack's eyes narrowed, searching, intent on descrying. "But these strings, you see, are *magic* strings, for they can change at a moment's notice."

The parents had joined their daughters, wearing curious smiles as Esperanza collected the strings and let them dangle from his fingers, still revealing the disparity in length. Then he bunched them into a ball and, with nonchalant grace, tossed them to the table for the girls to inspect.

"Go ahead, check out how these magic strings have changed," Esperanza urged, and the girls quickly sorted them out, lined them up, and giggled at their discovery, each string the same length, identical from end to end.

Esperanza bowed at the reception of applause, the girls imploring him to do it again, their braces sparkling in the sun. Behind Esperanza, his grandchildren, the oldest perhaps ten, were grinning at the successful display. Their snow cones had dwindled but not their interest, for two of them were dutifully up from their seats to fetch red-covered books from a box beneath the table, which were presented to the little girls for their review.

"I'll make you a deal, yes?" The magician, with his dapper vest and thin, square-rimmed glasses and gold-chained pocket watch, nodded jovially at each girl. "One more trick if you buy my special magic book here, only ten dollars." He pulled open one of the books and directed the girls' attention to a caricatured magician on the first page, black-suited and caped, with a top hat, of course, and a wand giving rise to streams of color. "You see, ladies, a magician worth his salt will never reveal a trick, but this little book here – it will tell you exactly how to impress your friends. Just ten dollars."

In unison, the girls turned to their parents. "Pulleez. We want to see another trick. Pulleez," and who in their sane mind could resist such fervent beseeching?
Jack glanced absently toward the old women at the chess club table, the coasters still under the puritanical scrutiny of eyes wrinkled from age and perhaps excessive glaring. Back to the magician's tent, where cash had been coaxed from a wallet and handed over to the Great Frankie Esperanza, and a little frisson went spiriting into Jack's gut at the thought of what the next trick might be.

Out came the deck of cards, Jack feeling like a schoolboy. *Yes! I knew it'd be the cards!*

In Esperanza's hands, the cards seemed to shuffle themselves, fleet and airy in their sorting, snapped firmly yet gracefully together and then spread across the table into a slightly arcing line. The girls watched him closely, as did Jack and the parents and a few other people, everyone waiting. Unseen, the old women departed without a purchase, shrinking wordlessly away like smoke, their deaths drawing another minute closer – time only moves one way – yet they weren't the slightest bit friendlier for it.

"Choose a card, ladies, any card, one for each of you – but don't show them to me," Esperanza instructed, and the girls made their hasty selections, a blue-backed card in each of their hands.

"Can we show it to each other," one girl asked.

"Of course, of course," and the magician turned his back to them, flitting his hands up above his head and fluttering his fingers. "Now, if you'll give me just a moment, and, what's this I feel in my pocket?" To the vest pocket he went, two cards withdrawn and flattened across the table, one a red suit and the other black, further details impossible to gather without a closer look.

Between the chess club tent and Esperanza's tent was a jewelry tent occupied by two middle-aged women, who, until now, had shown little interest in the magician. But even they were held rapt as the little girls

giggled and clapped, the parents equally impressed behind them. "That's amazing," the father said. "How did he do that, girls?"

"Again! Again! Pulleez!" came the encore requests, and, stunningly, Esperanza obliged.

"Very well. For two special ladies like yourselves, one more trick it shall be."

Puzzled, Jack brought his arms to his hips, determined to pick up the trick. Mirrors? Furtive communication with someone standing behind the girls, tucked away somewhere with binoculars? No, none of that – the guy simply spun around once more and fluttered his fingers, then pulled the correct cards from his vest pocket, the little girls wowed again, the parents spellbound.

Magic. Indeed, magic, or about as close as one could venture to its seemingly unreachable plateau.

But too soon it was over, everyone dispersing, chattering as they went away fulfilled, another moment in time complete, the grandfather clock ticking away back home, the little red magic instruction book in the father's hand, not a single look from the family toward the chess club table. And rightfully so. Content and humble, Esperanza was organizing his accoutrements, the strings put away and cards shuffled, the tricks of the trade readied for their next act, Jack left to ponder why a man of such immense talent was performing at a smalltown festival and not in Vegas. Here was an unassuming diamond ensconced comfortably in the rough, in search not of fame nor fortune – yet another lesson to be learned.

185

If you look close enough, there's always a lesson.

"That guy's pretty good, isn't he?" Oscar said. Jack had forgotten about Oscar to his left.

"Yeah, I'll say. Couldn't for the life of me figure out how he was doing it."

Later, when the clouds came in and a light drizzle overspread the festival and darkness got loosened up in the bullpen, Jack ambled over to the magician's tent. He'd been watching Esperanza's tricks for the better part of the afternoon, and here he was, hours later, just as befuddled as he'd been following the very first one. The man was as charming as he was dexterous, his accented words smooth and flowing, like a twilight tide weltering in and whispering its receding course.

"You're good, real good," Jack said, their eyes meeting again. Maybe twenty minutes earlier, a sprightly old woman with gray-black hair and a face that had seen much laughter, had delivered a vanilla ice cream cone to Esperanza, a chocolate cone in her other hand – and together they'd savored their ice creams and talked, seeming peaceful, happy, reminding Jack very much of him and Mary and the way they'd once been, with the grandchildren all around them. It was like looking at a younger version of himself, a sight not without its sharp twinges of longing, a sight that had inspired Jack to stand when he otherwise would have remained seated, a sight that had impelled him, back aching a little, toward the magician's tent.

"Thank you, sir. I appreciate it very much." Esperanza's smile was deep and genuine, Jack impressed yet again.

"How long have you been at it?" After finishing their ice cream cones, Esperanza's wife had taken the grandchildren to explore the festival a few minutes ago. Now it was just Jack and the magician.

A reminiscing twinkle slipped into Esperanza's eyes. "I started with magic real young, maybe six or seven when my father taught me that very first trick." He brought a quarter to its edge and spun it on the table, absently letting it balance and whirl like a figure skater, Jack expecting it to disappear or transform. But it flattened out heads up, nothing more, the magician spinning it again, speaking fondly of his parents and their early life in Ecuador, where his father had overseen a hat manufacturing factory. "Panama hats, you see, are not made in Panama but Ecuador. Beautiful country, always wanted to return."

"Do you host a lot of magic shows each year?" Jack, having scooped up one of Esperanza's books, was flipping through the pages and taking in the detailed illustrations.

Esperanza waved an olive hand. "Oh, Heaven's no, just a few a year. Gets me out of the house – and the kids love it. I used to be on tour, started out with the circus giving palm readings and telling fortunes. Whenever someone demanded their money back thinking I was a fraud," he said with a laugh, "I would make something disappear. Say, how about I give you a trick, yes?"

Jack smiled shruggingly, feeling like a boy invited to throw out the ball game's first pitch. "Well, in that case, I better buy the book." He pointed to his right, his voice lowering. "We're two tents down, the one with all the oddball stuff. I'm part of the chess club, thought I'd come down and help 'em out for the afternoon."

"Oscar Montoya's a fine man, real fine man. Heck of a chessman, too, yes?" Esperanza, having accepted Jack's money and nodded his appreciation, was twirling two quarters now, Jack reminded of the many weekends he'd taken his grandkids to the science museum, the youngsters always excited upon standing before the coin funnel, their eyes following those rolling quarters around and around, sometimes the smallest things in life providing the most enduring memories.

And now many of those kids were adults or close to adulthood, time not merely moving one way but sprinting.

Esperanza extended his hand over the table. "Francisco Esperanza, by the way."

"Jack Gibson," and the men shook hands – but Esperanza grimaced as if burned, his mouth agape, his hand pulled rapidly away, his eyes searching Jack with darting flashes of shock and…fear?

"Could you see my future?" Jack said, chuckling, a little uneasy, wondering if this was all part of the trick.

The magician's expression had darkened considerably, his legs taking him a few involuntary, almost stumbling steps backward. "I'd need a…a closer inspection for that, but I" – an awkward hesitation – "how about that trick, yes?" The deck of cards was hurriedly shuffled and finessed across the table. "Choose any one you'd like, sir," and he turned from Jack, this time forgetting the fluttering finger ritual, instead pivoting and pulling a card from his vest pocket, nine of diamonds, the very card Jack had selected.

Yet Jack was less interested in the magic than what had happened moments earlier. Something disquieting never to be revealed, the previously fun and easygoing magician having broken out in sweat. His eyes were wide and distressed. Suddenly nighttime felt very close.

"Well, thanks for the book," Jack said, offering his hand, just to see Esperanza's response. "My youngest granddaughter will love it. You're a phenomenal magician, mister."

"Much appreciated, sir. I hope she enjoys it." Ignoring Jack's handshake attempt, the magician retreated to the back of his tent, eyes failing to maintain contact, sliding past Jack to passing guests. "You have a great day, Jack, and God bless. God bless you now."

Heading back to the chess club tent, Jack glanced over his shoulder at Esperanza, who was staring at him with a face of wan terror, the way a recently released hostage might watch the fleeing gunman.

And all Jack could think was, *morning does not welcome those who die!*

Chapter III

That night was the turning point, the line separating past from present, the night Jack would remember often and with great agitation, until the pen of death scratched a red X across his name.

Awakening to a painful pressure on his back, it took him a few somnolent seconds to realize what was happening. Night was standing on him as he lied facedown, growling at the bedroom door with increasing rage, louder and louder and louder, until she was barking wildly. But this time she didn't leap off the bed – no, she remained planted on her master's back, her barks lashing purposefully out into the darkness, directed at something close, something threatening.

Jack, momentarily paralyzed with fear, still not free of sleep's web, at last glanced at the digital clock, its numbers glowing an angry red – 11:57.

"Come, on, girl, get off," he groaned drowsily, thinking he heard something then – perhaps even sensing someone in the room, *no, no, don't be foolish* – but Night held her ground, still barking but no longer as severely. Soon her barks downgraded to little growls and worried *bwoofs*, yet she remained on his back.

"Down! Now! Get off me, girl!"

Even with his voice elevated, Jack still thought he heard the sound of creaking footsteps, just beyond the closed bedroom door. Night having hopped down, Jack rolled onto his back and was blasted from within by an explosive fear.

The hallway light was out.

But Jack was positive he'd left it on. Just hours ago he'd lain in bed staring regretfully at the little sliver of light beneath the door, too lazy to leave the comfort of the covers to turn it out. His body was sore after a long day, and he'd reluctantly decided to take the minor hit on his next electric bill.

Now the hallway light was out, though, and Night was scratching the door and sniffing and growling intermittently, unseen in the darkness. Jack, briefly motionless in the throes of a senseless, repeating fear – *There's someone in the house. There's someone in the house* – eventually stumbled to the door and through it, his chest tightening when Night sprinted about the grave-dark house with a flood of barks.

Jack groped for the hallway light switch and found it, flipped it, hoping a dead bulb would end his fears. But the light came on without delay, and Jack felt as if the house had lost forty degrees, his arms and chest heavy, his legs rubbery. For a threatened, confounded moment he stood there in the hallway, listening to Night's continued barking, half-certain he'd just missed seeing an intruder, wishing he'd applied for a firearm license like he'd intended.

Soon Night returned to the hallway, concentrating her barks yet again on the basement door. Still standing outside the bedroom door, Jack called out, "Who's there?"
Moments later: "I've got a gun, so you better get out!"

Quiet now, tail lowered, Night looked up at him with despair, an expression that conveyed a grim combination of frustration with her master's inability to understand her and hopelessness at their situation. There was fear in her eyes, too, but something greater than fear, a glinting turmoil that cut deep beneath Jack's skin, right down to his bones.

They looked at each other for a while, two alarmed souls in the dead of night, listening carefully, interpretatively, to the clock in the living room. Otherwise the house was silent and still as always, though there was something watchful about it tonight, Jack troubled by a strengthening feeling that they weren't alone, troubled also by memories, most recently of Frankie Esperanza, a man with a wife and grandchildren who loved him deeply, a man who had everything, it seemed, an adoring family and respect and talent and kindness – and then Jack had come into his world.

What had the magician felt during their handshake?

What had the magician *seen*?

It came at Jack with velocity, the same train of thought as before but this time carrying many passengers, ones that hadn't previously been there.

People died in this house. What if they're still here?

Coyotes, somewhere out there in the fog, preying again. Their maniacal attacking storm whisked through the cracked living room windows, along with the shrieks of the suffering, dying victim, Jack filled with thoughts of Peter and his father, then a familiar urge.

An old friend was at the door again.

"Get out of my head!" Jack shouted, forcing himself into motion. From the bedroom closet he gathered his Louisville slugger, then soldiered through the house ready to pound anything that moved, Night loyally following him from room to room as he switched on lights. "Every damn night with the coyotes, always have to kill, kill, kill, don't you? Bastards! Can't you just go somewhere else, anywhere else?"

The house was empty. No intruders. No further noises. No sightings of shadows or strangers. Nothing in the mirrors but the reflections of a tired old man and his devoted dog.

Leaving Night inside, Jack stepped onto the back deck and found himself enveloped in thick, cool fog, his face dampened and chilled – and he remembered the story of the man who'd gotten lost here and died in the woods.

We all must've gone through the place where they found his body a hundred times, Oscar had said. *It was so close to the house he could have hit it with a rock.*

Jack shivered at the creations of imagination and how menacingly they slouched through the fog, his stomach roiling and sour. The trees, rising up through swirls of vapor, seemed to be leaning in at him, reaching for him, but they were still, of course, still and watchful, fog-skirted sentinels guarding the little house in the woods. At a time like this, oppressed by the night wilderness, it was hard to imagine a world beyond the woods, where nightclubs and casinos and diners were bustling at this hour. It was hard to imagine anything existing beyond the trees…and harder still to imagine morning arriving to welcome–

From the other side of the door Night scratched the glass, her ears raised to pick up sounds beyond Jack's auditory limits, keen on joining her master. Hesitant, Jack ultimately gave in and let her out into the fog.

"Be careful, girl," he said as she slipped into the obscurity of the back yard, his thoughts returning to the hallway light.

How did it go out? It wasn't dead, so how? Someone must've turned it off, and the chill on his arms seemed to worsen by the second, until it felt like he was standing outside on a winter night. Another coyote attack flared up moments later; much further, a locomotive's horn echoed, its bells dinging; and within the back yard fence, Night was tearing through the woods, pursuing whatever scent or sight had come to her at this strange hour, Jack again immensely thankful for the fence.

Something's wrong with my house. Very wrong! All those things I saw, all those times Night went crazy – this has been happening for a long time. Whatever's going on, it–

Jack felt a panging, twitching urge, the most powerful one he'd experienced since killing Peter Elliott. His old friend was at it again.

There's no problem I can't solve, Jackie, nothing your old pal can't handle. Let's just get through this one night. Let's do it together.

"Just one night," Jack murmured, the coyote attack replaying in his head, another poor animal dead and torn apart out there in the foggy, ruthless forest, another animal that hadn't survived the night and would

never know another sunrise because morning does not welcome those who die.

"Mary's not here," Jack said with an eager smile, his thirst steadily building, and it was almost as if he could feel his old friend's hand upon his shoulder, guiding him to the door.

"Come on, Night!" he called. "Come on, girl! We need to get out of here tonight. Let's go for a ride."

Chapter IV

Away from the house, safe with Night inside the Taurus, slowly rolling through the fog, Jack was capable of resisting his old friend's requests. Yet even if willpower had eluded him, flying away into the fog like a nighthawk, there weren't many establishments to which his friend could guide him at this hour. The only tavern in town was long closed; so, too, were the grocery store and the package store down by the railroad tracks.

Though Jack was tired and overwrought, getting away from the house helped provide him with a much needed change of perspective. Distance was good, very good. He could take a breath now and allow himself a laugh at his own foolish thoughts.

I can't believe I let myself get that carried away, he thought, remembering the instances over the years in which lights had mysteriously gone out. *Must be a few kinks in the place's wiring, that's all, nothing an electrician can't handle. No intruders. Certainly no ghosts.*

But what about the footsteps...and all the other weird stuff?

"You think it's kids breaking into the house and messing with me?" Jack asked his dog many minutes later. They were parked in the lot outside Grimley's Diner, hidden amidst the fog, Night poking her head through the passenger window. "Is that what's been going on, girl? Have a bunch of kids been going through the house making mischief?" He patted Night's hind legs. "You know, I heard the footsteps tonight, too, or at least I thought I did. I was half asleep, after all."

Night briefly receded into the car and wagged her tail at Jack, then stuck her head back through the window, gathering whatever scents might be creeping in. It was quiet out here, a distant sodium vapor lamp tingeing the fog with hazy, ominous orange, the railroad tracks dark and spectral, the lonely street flashing with an occasional set of headlights. Oscar and Henry and the others were all probably snoring in bed beside their wives, comfortable and happy, but Jack no longer had

a wife. He tried to think how Mary would handle this situation. She'd be uneasy, no doubt, but in the end she would come up with a practicable solution to quash the problem.

Locks – it was a simple enough solution. Jack would lock all of his doors before bed, though he was reluctant to lock the windows and deprive himself of the cool night air. He could always buy some of those threatening signs, he supposed, the ones that read, **NO TRESSPASSING! VIOLATORS WILL BE SHOT! SURVIVORS WILL BE SHOT AGAIN!** But if there really were kids breaking into his house – and they were bold enough to do so in spite of hearing the owner's barking dog – then they probably wouldn't get scared off by signs.

But if they're not stealing anything, what are they doing?

Jack scratched his chin, new ideas springing up. Cameras just might do the trick as an added layer of security, and he would call the electrician first thing tomorrow to examine the wiring and perhaps rule out that possibility.

"I'll get to the bottom of it. Yes, sir, you can count on that," Jack said, feeling comforted when a freight train clattered by. Usually the sight and sound of trains distressed him with memories of a sunny, awful morning, but tonight was different. Enshrouded by fog in an otherwise empty parking lot and harried by his thoughts, the sight of the train's bright headlight made him feel like there was a world out there and he was connected to it.

When the engineer sounded his horn, it warmed Jack like soup on a sick throat.

"We're not alone, Night. Not alone, girl. We'll be just fine." Jack scratched his dog's belly. "I'm as sharp as I ever was, girl, you know that. Just tired, that's all. Need to get some rest."

Jack returned to the Wal-Mart the next morning, enlivened and emboldened by the bright, cheerful sunlight. The fog had burned off like a bad memory, and Jack, who'd slept in his car in the parking lot and awoken to the sound of vehicle doors opening and shutting at seven a.m., rubbed his eyes and yawned as he further familiarized himself with Wal-Mart's many aisles.

Accidentally, while searching for surveillance equipment, he found another product that could be highly useful – nightlights. They were discreet, decorative plug-in lights that turned on automatically in the absence of light, just what he needed.

Can't let that place get too dark anymore.

Jack chose four nightlights, then moved on to the costly stuff. The inventory in stock didn't exactly appeal to him, but a friendly young employee came by and told him the store sold additional surveillance products online.

"I don't have a computer at home," Jack admitted, realizing as he said so that the young lady probably assumed he was one of those technologically incompetent dinosaur grandfathers who couldn't send an email. "I guess I could drop by the library, though."

"That's a great idea," she said with a smile. Lola, her nametag read, a pretty, high-school age girl. *Hard worker*, Jack noted. *And very nice. Kind of reminds me of a young Mary,* and he went a little sad and cold at that thought.

"We offer free shipping and free store pickup, if you prefer to do it that way," Lola continued, then described an array of products, taking her time as if Jack were the only customer in the store.

He stopped listening after a while, enjoying Lola's smile and remembering the early days with Mary, when time had seemed of limitless supply.

Chapter V

Unusually tired, Jack decided to put off his trip to the library to order surveillance equipment online. He would do it later, he figured, or maybe he wouldn't buy the cameras at all. It was beginning to seem like a waste of time and money to rig all of the equipment, especially when locking his doors was probably all it would take to keep the kids out. They'd simply taken advantage of an easy entry…if they'd been there at all.

He completely forgot about calling the electrician.

Following the final curve of the driveway, Jack's jaw clenched when the little house came into view. The trees towered above it like skyscrapers, peering down on the house as they'd done for centuries. The smell of resin and the songs of birds greeted him when he opened the driver's door, Night hopping out of the car and promptly doing her business on the front lawn.

Jack stood there for a few moments, squinting out at the pond and then observing his house, reluctant to go inside. He kept thinking about the possibility of intruders, but if they'd been bent on making a little mischief, then why not link all of the coat hangers together in the closet or wrap toilet paper in the trees? Why just flick off one light?

Jack felt something strange – a change in pressure? – upon entering the house. It wriggled its way into his ears, causing them to ache a little, then climbed higher and brought a spurt of lightheadedness. Even sleepier now, he yawned and stretched, which only worsened the vertiginous feeling and forced him to sit for a while on the sofa, listening to the ticking clock and carefully studying the house. All of the lights were off, the house bright with sunlight, though Jack could have sworn he'd left at least a few of the lights on during his hurried, panicked departure. Bringing the house to darkness certainly hadn't been a priority at the time, but again he was left doubting himself.

The kids.

Had they come back after he'd left, wanting to mess with him some more?

Before heading to bed, Jack went through the house to make sure the intruder(s) hadn't taken anything. Three twenty-dollar bills remained on a decorative dish in the kitchen, and none of his valuables had been stolen, not even his metal detector, which leaned conspicuously against a living room wall.

Was anyone here at all, or am I just imagining things?

Jack finished his inventory tour by checking the cedar chest in the master bedroom, sighing in relief at the sight of Mary's dearest pieces of jewelry still tucked away in their burnished oak box, diamonds catching the sunlight and gleaming happily, briefly free of the confining darkness.

Heavy with nostalgia, Jack took some time to examine each piece. He stood in a little rectangle of sunlight and remembered his wife – she'd loved to wear her jewelry, and how striking she'd looked with that sapphire and diamond pendant around her neck, those ruby earrings bringing an extra sparkle to her eyes. There'd been times when Jack stood in awe of his wife, thinking to himself, *I can't believe she wants to be with me. Of all the guys out there, she loves me.*

Brought to the verge of moistened eyes, Jack snapped the jewelry box shut and returned it with mildly shaking hands to the cedar chest, where it was surrounded by stacks of old documents and a few significant trinkets. The chest's lock had long ago broken, but Jack had never thought he would need to replace it. His other house had been nestled in a safe neighborhood, and this place – the realtor had said no one locked their doors in this town, but…

"There could be more crime than you think, buddy," Jack growled, shaking his head at the thought that his house might have been targeted.

Brooding about the matter at length, Jack supposed he should have prepared for the possibility of break-ins after Oscar told him about the house's past. After all, people had died in this place, and kids were always drawn to cemeteries and "haunted houses" and abandoned mental hospitals, places where they could smoke pot and show their little girlfriends how brave they were, the sorts of things Jack had done as a teenager, before he'd enlisted in the Navy and spent the better part of four years aboard an aircraft carrier. He'd had a far different plan for his life then, but time, with its uncompromising direction, had a funny way of changing the ground rules without notice.

Uncomfortably aware of the house's overwhelming silence, Jack crossed the bedroom to the window and cursed Randy Thomas, the realtor who'd neglected to reveal the darkness of this house. Had Jack known a woman had hanged herself in the basement and a man had suffered a stroke and yet another man had died in the woods, he never would have bought the place. He would have settled for another little house in the woods – surely this town had plenty to choose from.

The basement.

It had often been the target of Night's barking rages.

The poor lady hung herself in the basement.

This time, Jack quickly dismissed the thought of ghosts. He took a deep breath, gazing out the bedroom window at the back yard, pleased by the brightness of the morning, yet he wasn't without an icy truth sliding unpleasantly through his veins. When it was sunny and the hour was early, the house stood starkly different. The ticking of the clock wasn't as foreboding. The stillness wasn't as profound. The surrounding trees weren't nearly as daunting. And the lights didn't announce themselves the way they did at night, when Jack relied on them to keep from the darkness.

Yes, it was a different house by day, and Jack knew the night would come as it always did. It would come and things would be even worse

200

tonight, Jack feared, wondering if he might glimpse faces peering hungrily at him from the windows at dusk, when the sky beyond the trees was tinted orange and pink, darkness falling steadily over the little house in the woods. Or perhaps he'd envision shadowy figures hovering above the pond in tomorrow morning's fog, a thought that sometimes came to him at the edges of sleep.

Jack exhaled deeply. Listened. He wasn't sure what he was listening for, but he stayed very still for a few minutes and received the full quietude of the house. With the bedroom door closed, he couldn't even hear the clock in the living room, and again came the wild thought that no one existed but him and Night. Outside, there would be no sounds of distant traffic or lawnmowers or airplanes, no rumbling garbage trucks or blaring fire engines, no motorized hums or children's voices, only the birds and crickets and faint jingles of wind chimes in a gentle morning breeze, the house itself as silent as a mausoleum.

Jack straightened, almost jumped, when his cell phone rang, Stevie's number flashing on the screen.

"Hey, Stevie, how are you, buddy?" There was a wave of relief at the sound of Stevie's voice.

"Hey, Grandpa. I thought I'd call and let you know my streak's over. I got detention for being late again." He laughed almost triumphantly. "This school's such a joke."

"Good for you, kid," Jack heard himself say, surprised by the words that had escaped his lips. He was so overjoyed to be talking with a family member that, if asked, he might have agreed to pack everything up and fly back east.

There was a brief silence. Then Stevie said, "Don't tell my dad I got detention, okay?"

"It'll be our secret," Jack said, returning to the bedroom window and peering into the woods, dreading how they would look when it was dark – how they always looked – watchful and impenetrable, concealing the coyotes that ended countless lives between sunrise and

sunset. This place certainly wasn't what he'd thought it would be, not even close.

"So how's your day been?" Stevie said. "Better than mine, I bet."

His voice has really changed in the last year, Jack noted. *He's growing up, becoming a man* – and these thoughts inevitably took Jack to Peter and all that had been robbed of the boy.

"Good, real good," Jack lied, memories flying back to him of a little boy's terrified blue eyes and his bloody face; memories of his blonde hair and ruined clothes; memories of his fair skin and how the blood had menaced it; memories of Peter's little shoe torn away and "Interstate Love Song" on the radio.

"I think" – Jack was surprised to be fighting tears – "I'll go for a walk with Night around the yard here soon. Then maybe do some metal detecting."

"You bought the metal detector?" Stevie said excitedly. "That's awesome! Maybe you'll find, like, an old treasure chest or something."

"I sure hope so. I'd settle for a few old coins," Jack said, trying to stay in the moment with his grandson. He was resisting not only the memories and tears but the unfairness that swept over him – it wasn't fair that his grandchildren and millions of other kids got to live their lives while Peter's bones were crumbling in the ground. It wasn't fair that Peter's little life had only lasted six years. None of it was fair, none of it!

"It must be hard digging in your yard with rocks and stuff, huh?"

"Yeah, it is." Jack closed his eyes, rubbed his chin, tried to think of something to say, something that would keep Stevie engaged, but nothing came to him. He was tired and frayed.

Damn kids keep breaking into my house. I'll show them.
"Well, I guess I'll go eat some of that crappy caf food," Stevie said. "It's so horrible. I bet prisoners get better food."
"You hang in there, Stevie. Everything will eventually work out."

"Thanks, Grandpa. Love you."

"I love you, too, Stevie."

Jack felt a cold draft on his neck just then, but it was more than a draft, pointed and intense, like fingers on his neck. For a moment, just a moment in time, the phone clutched in his hand, he was afraid to turn around. But Night wasn't barking, no, not yet, too early for that, and Jack did turn around, turned around to find a sunlit bedroom, the house quiet and still, his greatest enemy perhaps lurking between his ears.

Chapter VI

When the call came in, Stephen Gibson was in his office, fantasizing about his secretary and wondering how he could sate his strengthening thirst without jeopardizing his enviable position in the game.

Though his wife said all the right things and attended the important functions, it had become clear to Steve that his marriage couldn't sustain the satisfaction of his needs. Somewhere along the way his attraction had been lost, and now their union seemed more like a mutual agreement to go through the expected motions in public and exist separately when the game wasn't in session. The fire simply wasn't there anymore, not even a little flickering glow, Steve's heart burning for younger women with smooth skin and flat stomachs and impressionable minds. He didn't feel guilty for craving women half his age, for in his heart he was, at times, still a twenty-year-old college kid brimming with promise.

Then there were other occasions, the ones when Steve felt like he was up against it. Where had the time gone? The game. He'd played so long and hard that he'd lost sense of things, his youth draining away like a once full bubble bath – and now the sudsy water was getting even lower, time running out. He felt constrained and miserable and cold on such occasions. What good was power if he couldn't get what he wanted, when he wanted it?

He knew he had to make a major change to feel alive again.

The call. Oh no, it was Melvin Bishop, the headmaster of Stevie's school.

"Melvin, good morning. How have you been?" Steve turned unhappily to face the window. It had only been a month since their last conversation, and Steve had a feeling Bishop hadn't called to talk about Stevie's success on the baseball diamond.

"I'm doing well, Senator. And yourself?"

"Very good, thanks. And, please, call me Steve." He frowned at the window. He'd been hoping the generous donation he made to the school in January would buy Stevie a little slack, but the kid was a screw-up, plain and simple, and schools of prestige only tolerated screw-ups if their parents kept paying up. Steve wondered what this most recent trouble would cost him.

The men made obligatory small talk for a bit, and then it was down to business. "The reason I called, Senator, is due to your son's continued disciplinary problems." There was an uncomfortable pause, as if Bishop were waiting for an admission of parental failure. "Continued tardiness, unexcused absences, sleeping in class, disrespecting staff members – all of which I believe we discussed previously."

"Yes, I spoke to Stevie about those things. This is very disappointing news, Melvin."

"Indeed, it is," the headmaster said in a tone blending between haughtiness and boredom. "And yesterday Stevie was involved in a skirmish with another student, a boy with no previous history of delinquency. Anyway, I've discussed your son's problems at length with his teachers and the dean, and we all feel it might be in his best interest to attend another school next year, perhaps a public facility whose administrators are better experienced in dealing with…such matters. Looking on the bright side, perhaps all the boy needs is a simple change of scenery."

Steve's face went hot. Springing up from the chair, his voice rose nearly to a shout. "I won't have my kid in some public school! You listen here and listen good – I've been very generous to your school, but that money can just as easily go to another school that doesn't call me every time my kid misses class!"

"Of course, yes, Senator, I completely understand your frustrations." Even before Bishop had responded, Steve knew he held the advantage over the headmaster. He hadn't advanced to his current position in the game without stepping over a thousand mealy-mouthed squirrels in

suits like Melvin Bishop. Even during Steve's early political days of crushing a former high school classmate and friend in the primary election for state representative, he'd always been ruthless in his quest for success.

"Perhaps," Bishop continued, "we could figure out–"

"I'll tell you how we're gonna handle this," Steve interrupted. "First, you're gonna stop calling me over trivial nonsense like this. Unless the kid gets arrested or injured, I don't want to hear about it, understand? The best way to handle Stevie is to be hard on him. He acts tough, but trust me, it's all an act. He'll cave in – I don't care if you have to lock him in detention all day. Whatever you need to do to break him, you have my permission."

"I understand, Senator, but it's not our policy to–"

"I'm not interested in your policies. I'm giving you my permission to make his life a living hell, got it? Break him down, make him afraid to act up. When he calls me whining about how much school sucks, I'll threaten him with boot camp. Trust me, it'll work."

"I suppose it could, with reinforcement from your end, of course."

"Absolutely, but I don't have time to waste talking about this stuff. I've got a busy schedule, Melvin, and I need to know he's on the Ivy League track. It doesn't matter how he behaves – he'll shape up eventually and become a man. What matters is that he stays on track, and I'm entrusting you and your staff with that job. Can you get it done, or is my money going elsewhere next year?"

"We'll figure out a way to make it work," Bishop said hastily. "Thanks so much for your time, Senator."

Chapter VII

Jack awoke from a long nap doubting himself, though his doubts didn't distress him but instead brought hope. What if all this time he'd been somehow misremembering which lights he'd left on and off, giving rise to needless fears?

I can't be one hundred percent sure, I guess. There's a chance I could have been wrong.

And that was a good thing, because the thought of kids – or anyone – breaking into a house simply to turn off a few lights here and there made no sense. The effort of venturing out into the middle of the woods, not to mention the inherent risks of injury and/or arrest, wouldn't have been worth it unless they'd taken something valuable. And none of Jack's valuables were missing.

It's possible I've been wrong, he kept telling himself. *What a relief that would be.*

The damn electrician! I still need to call the electrician out to have a look at the wires.

Jack forgot about the electrician.

He spent much of the afternoon metal detecting, working on the lawnmower, and tending to his flower boxes, the sound of the showering hose taking him back to Mary, with her flower-patterned gloves and summer hats and tanned legs and clinking glasses of lemonade. In each of his memories she was smiling, happy to be completing whatever task occupied her, even the dirty jobs, and it came to him that she appeared this way in his recollections not because she'd been brimming with joy at the sight of her gardens but that of her husband. She'd always been smiling at *him* and, if nothing else, that was a gift he hoped would always stay with him, even if he submerged into the black waters of dementia like his grandfather, who'd been able to write one day and not the next. But if Jack could somehow manage to keep his head above the water, remembering always to think of

Mary's smile in dire times, then he could get through anything, he thought.

Just think of her smile, and it'll all be okay.

Jack looked up from the flowers. It would be getting dark soon, another night to descend. He stood slack-jawed for a moment on the porch and gazed up to the treetops, where birds flitted among the highest branches, well beyond the circular clearing that held the little house in the woods. It was a different world up there, a world free of worries about coyotes and other four-legged beasts. Jack wished he could see what the birds saw, wished he could share their perspective for a moment and look down on the house like they did. But what had the birds seen here over the decades? What had they heard? Had other residents stared up at them like Jack, feeling small and subjugated by the surrounding woods?

It was a strange thing to wonder about, but Jack found himself going there as a way to avoid sliding into a familiar pit and thinking about…other things. He'd been imagining lately the woman who'd hanged herself, Mrs. Scrivens, and now, inevitably, he was doing it again, brooding about what might have sent her to such despair. Even after the struggles Jack had endured, the idea of taking his own life seemed insane. What about those left behind? What would his death do to them?

But what if that lady didn't have anyone to love? What if she was all alone and just didn't want to live anymore? What if (and this thought was exceedingly strange) *the house was just too much for her?*

Jack shook his head to wrest his thoughts free of that dark place, a tactic he sometimes employed when dominated by memories of Peter. Still gripping the hose nozzle, there was an impulse to shower his face with cold water – that would sure shake him up good – but he sensed his mind drifting into safer waters, away from the rocks.

Just don't think about it anymore. Everything will be fine. Just fine. Jack headed inside, clicked on the TV, tried to keep himself locked firmly in the moment, twice remembering Mary's smile to push away dark thoughts.

Scrolling across the bottom of the TV screen was a severe thunderstorm watch for several counties. Jack smiled, feeling a familiar excitement in his gut. He'd always loved watching storms.

This will be a great night. I'll see the storm, order a pizza, and watch TV, maybe a baseball game or the hockey playoffs. Nothing to it.

Outside, the wind chimes jingled with greater intensity, the late afternoon going gray.

The scent of rain crept through the windows.

A distant train horn bellowed.

Jack did not remember to call the electrician.

Night, sitting on the sofa with lifted ears, let out a single bark.

Chapter VIII

Jack kept the lights on that night, within reason, of course. He hadn't hustled through the rooms illuminating every lamp and flashlight he could find, but all of the primary lights were on as darkness made its approach. And the doors were locked.

The storm had missed the house, Jack standing for almost an hour on the porch, watching and thinking as the wind strengthened and the clouds became sharp and gray. There'd been brief spatters of rain and far-off thunder but no visible lightning, not with the surrounding wall of trees that largely succeeded in screening out the sky.

Sometimes Jack wondered how many prodigious lightning bolts he'd missed living out here in the woods, the kind that danced across the sky if you had a decent view. It was a regretful thing, he'd decided, to not enjoy storms to the fullest, especially for a man of his age. But whenever he became overly pensive about such matters, his thoughts shifted to a little boy who'd died in his Sunday best, a boy who could no longer feel the joy and excitement and laughter of experiences grand or small because Jack had killed him. He'd hit him with an F-150 pickup truck, split his head open, and killed him. He'd stripped him of everything he would have become. He'd sent him to his funeral, all while the warm May sun beat down and "Interstate Love Song" played on the radio and a bee-stung boy was jabbed with an EpiPen and brought away from the edge of darkness over which Peter had helplessly fallen.

The pizza delivery guy was very friendly, a chubby college-age kid with pimples and an oily face. He wore glasses and spoke quickly.

"I didn't even know they had houses out here. I don't think I've ever been so lost in my life," His smile was nervously overdone. "Can you believe those storms? Lightning was unbelievable!"

Jack sighed, retrieving cash from his wallet. "It didn't come out this way. Must've just gone off to the north, I guess."

The kid nodded repeatedly. "Yeah, definitely. I was making a delivery up in Lakemore – lightning was insane the whole ride home. Rain was so heavy I almost drove off the road."

Night began barking off to Jack's left, causing the kid to flinch. But she wasn't barking at the delivery guy – no, Jack glanced over and spotted her at the basement door, barking and scratching.

"You didn't see any kids hanging around my property when you pulled in?" Jack blurted, a little alarmed by the aggression in his voice.

The kid shook his head. "No, I haven't seen a person for miles. Why?"

Jack shrugged, looking past the delivery guy to the driveway and beyond, down to the glassy pond. "I've been having some trouble lately with kids trespassing."

"Kids in this town don't have anything better to do but find trouble," he replied, shaking his head with disapprobation. "There's a growing heroin problem in town – have you heard? It's an epidemic. Three kids from my high school class alone are in the clinker."

"Yeah, the guys at chess club have mentioned that a time or two. Real shame."

Night quieted for a few moments, then came trotting over to Jack. Surprisingly, she wagged her tail at the delivery guy.

"Cute dog," the kid said, kneeling and holding out his hand. "Hey, doggie, how are you?"

Night stepped cautiously forward and licked the guy's hand. She usually warmed up to people pretty quickly, but this time she hadn't even bothered to bark at the stranger.

Jack, peering out into the almost full dark, was convinced he saw something move just inside the woods near the pond. He hadn't gotten a good enough look to determine size or shape, but he was certain something had drifted from right to left.

"Well, I better get back to base," the kid said, and he jogged unathletically to his car, red delivery bag in hand.

When the pizza guy was gone, the sound of crickets dominated once more, Jack taking a few moments to scan the spot in the woods where he'd been sure something had moved. But there was nothing there now, not even any crunches of receding footsteps, and Jack was hungry.

"Come on, girl, let's eat," he said, and locked the front door behind him.

Chapter IX

Jack was watching a playoff hockey game, five pizza crusts remaining on his plate atop the TV table, when a crack of thunder shook the house, scaring him so much that he leaped up from the sofa. A new storm had snuck up on him. Switching briefly to the local news channel, he saw the expected warnings scrolling across the bottom of the screen.

The storm hadn't snuck up on Night, who'd sensed its approach and left the living room a while back, probably cowering beneath Jack's bed like she always did when storms came.

"Night, where are you, girl?" Moments later the dog, tail between her legs, crept out of the master bedroom, coming to Jack with wide, fearful eyes. "It's all right, girl, just a storm," but that never worked; it only made Night shake as he patted her.

Jack turned up the volume on the TV, and Night bravely remained in the living room, tucking herself into a den behind the TV cabinet. Only her tail was visible, which wiggled distressfully back and forth when thunder crashed again. The rain and wind quickly strengthened, chimes clanging wildly from the porch, lightning pulsing through the windows, where the curtains were fluttering and flickering blue.

Jack hurriedly went through the house and closed the windows; he wanted to watch the lightning from his porch, but leaving Night alone inside seemed cruel. He'd left her here at home during a thunderstorm once, when he was at chess club last July, only to come home and find a puddle on the dining room floor.

"It's just fine, lady. I'll stay with you. We'll get through it together."

The power was knocked out with the next lightning bolt, plunging Jack and his dog into darkness. Even the nightlights had clicked off, for they were plug-in lights, not battery-powered devices, and now the house was completely black, the loudest clout of thunder yet reverberating in the walls.

The wind-driven rain was slanting in at the windows, ticking oddly as though there might be a few hail pellets mixed in, and Jack, using subsequent bursts of lightning to guide him, made it to the kitchen and retrieved a flashlight from the drawer.

Suddenly and inexplicably alarmed, feeling not quite threatened but close, he shined the light in every room, giving rise to strange shadows and catching something in the dining room, beneath the table, something moving, shrinking away from him.

Eyes glowing green when turned into the light, they left Jack momentarily breathless before he realized Night was blinking back at him, nothing but those fearful eyes to give her away.

"You scared me half to death, girl," Jack laughed, holding his briefly aching chest. It had felt like something dropped in there when he'd first glimpsed the movement, and now his apprehension was mounting again, building with each pass of the flashlight into a new room.

In the living room the TV had gone out, but the grandfather clock could not be relieved of its guard so easily. Jack directed his light upon it, half-expecting the thing to lurch scrapingly forward. Its sounds, interspersed with those of the storm, were exceedingly portentous, and Jack yearned for Mary's conversation, her laughter, her hands in his.

"I miss you, sweetheart. I miss you very much."

Jack perimetered the living room with his flashlight. It was empty, nothing on the sofa, nothing in the corners. Of course it was empty. Why wouldn't it be empty?

Just calm down, he told himself, angling the flashlight down the hallway. *You're a grown man, for crying out loud.*

The hall seemed much longer in the blackout, like a tunnel, baleful somehow, the flashlight's beam passing over a little wooden credenza Jack had built last year and a bench – Mary's old foyer bench – which he'd felt compelled to place between the master bedroom and study doors, where it would serve prominent reminders of better days.

Lightning flooded the house, then a return to darkness, Jack's little flashlight cutting through the black. Taking deep breaths, he began to calm himself, his ridiculous fears diminishing. With Night trailing him through the house, he lit a few candles and placed them in different rooms. Then, satisfied, he returned to the sofa and watched the lightning play across the walls and ceiling, the thunder eventually becoming a rolling rumble, not as incisive as before.

The storm was moving away.

Night returned to her makeshift den behind the TV cabinet, and Jack gathered his cell phone to notify the electric company about the outage. Finished, he set down the phone and listened, not quite sure what he was hearing down the hall. It sounded like a series of creaking noises near the bedroom, the faintest of thumps mixed in. Then came a slow, brief dragging shuffle reminiscent of his slippers against the rug, a sound that whisked shavings of ice between his shoulder blades.

Someone was stirring stealthily in the night, limited to the darkness but limitless in possibility. The ideas of what might be coming toward Jack from the hall were somehow worse than the appearance of an intruder, for the blackness of the hallway was an unknowable enigma of concealment, undisturbed by the candlelight, and thus exponentially more horrifying.

Jack grabbed his flashlight from the coffee table and lit up the hall, thinking for just a moment he saw something that shouldn't have been there, a hunkering shadow between the credenza and Mary's bench.

Night barked once from behind the TV cabinet, a cautious, frightened sound, just enough to let him know something was amiss. She'd repositioned herself and was now staring down the hall.

Too afraid to leave her hiding place, Night didn't join Jack this time as he returned to the hall and examined each of the connecting rooms.

No one in the master bedroom, no kids hiding beneath the bed or in the closet, the window shut and locked.

No one in the box-filled study, which Jack used almost exclusively for storage.

No one in the guest bedroom.

No one in the other little storage room.

That left the basement. Swallowing hard, Jack opened the door and pointed the light down the stairwell. He listened carefully, wondering if he'd heard that strange shuffling sound spring up elsewhere in the house.

Jack crouched a little lower, cocked his head, strained his ears. Heard only abating rain and thunder.

Then there was a shattering sound, Jack sent stumbling backward, away from the basement. His cell phone – he must have accidentally set the ringer on high, and now it was screeching in his pocket.

Frustrated by his jumpiness, Jack fished out the phone and checked the screen, surprised to see an unfamiliar number. He'd been expecting Rob, whose call he'd missed earlier.

"Hello?" he said somewhat warily, his body tensing with anticipation as he snapped the basement door shut, lightning invading the house and revealing nothing untoward.

But whose voice would fill the line? Who the hell was calling?

"Jack, how are you? It's Oscar."

Relaxing, smiling at the sound of his friend's voice, though he couldn't remember giving Oscar his cell phone number, Jack said, "Oh, hey, Oscar. I'm doing well. Power just went out at my place from the storm, but they should get it back on soon, I imagine. What can I do for you?"

"Oh, wow, the power's out over there?" Something about Oscar's tone unnerved Jack, something about those last two words that troubled him deeply. "Well, the lights are on at my house if you want to come over. Maybe we could play a little chess, if you'd like. Anyhow, reason I called is to let you know about a chess tournament taking place next month in Lakemore." The connection went sour, making Oscar's voice sound crackly and distant, but Jack thought he heard him add, "We could go together. What do you say, Jackie?"

But Oscar never called him Jackie. No one in this town called him Jackie.

"What did you say?" Jack demanded, but the connection was lost. Jack returned to the living room, where reception was usually optimal in the house, and called Oscar back. The call went straight to voicemail.

"Dammit!" he shouted, glancing down the hallway. There was an extended spell of dim lightning as he did so, illuminating the house just long enough for Jack to see the tilted face, the one that had haunted countless nightmares, dripping with blood, Peter Elliott peering out at him from the basement stairwell, his blonde hair soaked…and he was grinning at Jack with gapped teeth.

Darkness again. Footsteps, impossibly soft, descending the stairwell, and by the time Jack snatched the flashlight from his pocket and clicked it on, Peter was gone, the basement door closed as Jack had left it.

Something brushed against his leg. Shaking, rendered immobile, Jack was powerless to act as Night looked up at him. She wasn't barking, though, no, not this time, not tonight because there was nothing to bark at – and now Jack was far more afraid than he'd ever been. The

problem didn't lie with the house or the woods. It wasn't rooted in the history of the place. It couldn't be blamed on faulty wires or intruding kids.

He was the problem, John Robert Gibson, a realization that drifted silently and slowly down on Jack like snowflakes.

The lights came back on then, and Jack, staring at the basement door, knew with sudden and profound terror that there was no need to go clomping down the basement stairs in pursuit of what he'd just seen.

What's wrong with me? What's going on? Is this...it? Is this the start of it? He shrunk down achingly to his knees, clung to his dog, feeling lost and hopeless and scared and alone. *This must be it. It came for Grandpa, and now it's coming for me.*

I never should have come here.

Jack watched the basement door for what might have been ten minutes or an hour, shocked by the extent of what he could only describe as guilt-driven insanity. It was like looking into a mirror and finally seeing a scar that could have been there ever since Peter's death, growing and growing until recognition of its existence was inevitable. He knew he couldn't blame the hallucination of Peter on a trick of the lightning or a brief imaginary creation; no, Peter's face had been vivid and real, his grin searing into Jack's soul.

This is what I deserve. He's dead because of me.

Jack smiled resignedly. He didn't need a shrink to tell him what was happening. The hallucination had been partly inspired by his gnawing guilt, day after day of swelling pressure – and now he was breaking down physically as well. He'd thought he was getting better, but the guilt had only been festering as his mind slowly crumbled. Maybe it was PTSD combined with dementia; whatever it was, Jack knew it would soon get worse. Unless…

He took hold of a hand extended by a very old friend.
A friend who could cast out the guilt.

Wobbly, Jack got to his feet. "Come on, girl," and it was like his legs were in control and the rest of his body was along for the ride. It wasn't until he was through the front door that he realized where he was going.

Yes, that's it, Jackie, old pal. This is no way to live.

"No way to live!" Jack shouted, stepping off the porch into the rain.

Distant lightning revealed the watchful trees all around, which seemed to be looming even closer, right on top of him, wanting to get a better look. Jack kept his eyes level on the Taurus.

Just get to the car, Jackie. That's it. Don't look back. I'm here for you, guy. Just a little bit longer and we'll sort all this out. Time to get rid of that guilt. It's an infection, Jackie, and I'm here to help you clear it up.

There were dim, scattered thoughts of Mary as he slid into the car, forgetting to open the passenger door for Night as he always did when it was time for a ride.

"Mary isn't here, so what does it matter? I just need to stop the guilt, need to stop the bleeding – I can't do this anymore."

He was pulling away now, Night barking desperately in the muddy driveway, ready to run after the car, but the lightning came again, scaring her back to the porch, where she trembled and whimpered and watched Jack drive off.

219

The package store's still open, Jackie, but not for long. You've gotta drive faster. Faster! Do you want to see Peter all night? Do you want to see him in every corner of every room and in your dreams because he was just a little boy and you killed him? You killed him, Jackie, cracked him open in his little church suit. Do you want to see his Sunday bloody best all night, Jackie?

Jack accelerated. Pounding over potholes, the car jolted and slewed and barely remained on the road. Faster. He was gripping the steering wheel, biting his lip, lost so deep in his head that it might take a rescue team to get him out.

"Why was he wearing a damn suit, anyway?" Jack murmured, his voice calm and level. He tore out onto the dark main road without stopping, skidding on the slick blacktop and then quickly charging up to sixty. "Kids don't wear suits and ties to church anymore, do they?" He squinted and shook his head wonderingly as he crested a hill, nearly losing control around the next bend. "Oh, right, his neighbor's Confirmation, I remember. Whatever that is. Mary would know."

That's it, Jackie, you're almost there, buddy.

"Damn right I'm almost there." He thought it odd that he could hear his old friend's voice so clearly in his head, a coarse, entreating voice.

So close now, Jackie.

There were no hesitations or deliberations this time when Jack reached the package store. Sneakers squeaking, he didn't take long to find his old buddy, grabbing two bottles of Jack Daniels and then a 36-pack of Budweiser.

"Gotta get rid of the guilt," he mumbled. "It's making everything worse."

The clerk eyed him suspiciously when he set his friends on the counter. There was a nervous, dreading moment, Jack fearing the guy might turn him away for some reason, but then he was ringing him up and Jack was walking out of the store, back to his Taurus.

"Night!" he gasped, realizing he'd forgotten her. Lightning glazed over the horizon, leaving Jack sick with worry.

The drive home found him rushing even faster than before. The back road potholes were like manholes at such speeds, brutal and unforgiving, but he didn't care about his car. He only wanted to get back home and find Night, then settle down with an old friend and drink until the sky lightened with morning's mercy.

Chapter X

"That's it, I've waited long enough," Rob said. He was sitting on the side of the bed in his pajama pants and T-shirt, his wife leaning against the backboard and grading science tests, a pile of papers and folders in her lap. The room was lamplit and cold, even though Rob had switched off the air conditioner half an hour ago.

Maybe he was simply cold with worry after failing to reach Dad all day, several cell phone and landline messages unreturned. It was almost midnight, and Rob would have a long day in court tomorrow. He couldn't afford to be up all night worrying about Dad.

"Are you sure you want to disturb the poor man?" Rob's wife asked, referring to his decision to contact Oscar Montoya, one of Dad's closest friends in his new town.

Rob grabbed his cell phone from the nightstand. "Absolutely. He told me not to think twice about calling him if I thought Dad might be in trouble. Plus, it's not even nine o'clock there yet."

Sighing, his wife set down her red pen. "He probably just forgot to call back. Maybe he got tired and fell asleep early."

"That's unacceptable," Rob said angrily. "Dad and I agreed that if he was gonna live thousands of miles away, in some house in the middle of the godforsaken forest, then one of us had to speak to him every day. He can't just check out on us and say he fell asleep – that's setting a very dangerous precedent. What's next, is he gonna go days without getting in touch, weeks?"

A worried smile spread across her lips. "All right, you win, counselor. Go ahead and call him. Lord knows Steve and Paul aren't going to."

After leaving a long and rambling message, Rob didn't receive a call back from Oscar Montoya until over an hour later.

Chapter XI

There was a car in Jack's driveway when he returned home – and an intruder on the porch. Jack couldn't remember leaving the porch lights on, but what good were his recollections anymore? No good. He knew he couldn't even trust what his eyes were showing him – a distressing realization – but the man on the porch didn't vanish or transmogrify as Jack pulled up. He turned toward the driveway, his face coming into view.

"Oscar, what are you doing here?" Jack said when he stepped out of the car, fraught with displeasure at the sight of his friend. He was trembling with the need to find Night and then reunite with Jackie D., to finally deal with his infection, but here Oscar was pestering him.

"Hey, Jack, I see they got the lights back on for you," Oscar said amiably. The trees were dripping themselves dry, remnants of lightning peeking in the distance. "By the way, I found Night on the porch when I got here. She was shaking in her boots, so I let her inside. Hope you don't mind."

"No problem. I really appreciate it." Jack felt himself rising with relief, but quickly his annoyance redoubled, his focus drifting to his purchases in the Taurus.

Reemploying a tactic from his drunken days, Jack took a deep breath and prepared to pretend. He'd always been able to fool Mary and buy himself another opportunity to drink if he'd exuded a calm, controlled exterior, lying if necessary, omitting truths if necessary, making promises if necessary, basically doing whatever it took to free himself up for the bottle. Work had often been his go-to excuse, but the lies had been difficult to maintain after he'd gotten himself fired – and so he'd usually found another job quickly, if for no other reason than to provide a cover. Those had been the days when he'd put his friend before his family, the days when Jackie D. had ruled Jackie G., strange times when Jack had gone through life in a fog thicker than the ones that constantly hung over his little house in the woods.

"So what brings you out here so late, Oscar?" Jack said, putting a leg down on the first porch step and forcing a smile for his friend.

Oscar, remaining on the porch, crossed his arms sternly. He looked Jack over for a few moments, resembling an angry father whose daughter has returned home hours late from the prom.

Eyes narrowing beyond his glasses, Oscar said, "Your son Rob called a while back, said you hadn't returned any of his calls all day. He's real worried about you, Jack."

Jack felt the sting of regret through his irritation. "Kids, all they do is worry, right?"

Oscar seemed unconvinced. Usually Jack could get him laughing, but tonight he was a wall of stone. At least he uncrossed his arms. "Is everything okay?" he said at last. "You seem a little, I don't know...off."

Relying on experience, Jack stayed committed to the prize, not allowing himself to get ruffled but instead rolling with the punches, using the questioner's words as ammunition for his next excuse. He rubbed his head, feigning discomfort. "I actually haven't been feeling so hot today. Head's been aching pretty bad. I better go in and hit the hay."

Oscar nodded. "Maybe you should see the doc tomorrow, get yourself checked out," and Jack could see the worry in his eyes. Oscar was genuinely concerned about his health, and for a wishful moment – an aching brevity – Jack wanted to reveal everything to his friend, his former irritation evaporating. But no one in this town knew about little Peter, and how could Jack unload such a heavy burden now, at such a late hour, when Oscar surely just wanted to get back home to his wife?

He'd been kind enough to drive all the way out here at Rob's request, and Jack couldn't keep him any longer.

No, his new friends couldn't help him with this one, only a very old pal.

Jack fudged through a bunch of garbage about seeing the doctor and taking vitamins, talking, talking, and talking, until finally Oscar appeared satisfied (or perhaps just talked out). "Give your son a call, Jack," he said, coming down the porch steps and patting Jack on the shoulder. "Poor guy's worried out of his mind."

"I will. Absolutely. Thanks a million for everything, Oscar. You're a great friend."

Oscar waved a hand. "You're in the club, kid. Once you join the fraternity, you're stuck with us." Just when it looked like he'd climb inside his Buick, he turned to Jack. "Say, if you ever need a friend out here, maybe just someone to talk to or play a few games with, you know my number."

"Yes, sir," Jack said, and he had to turn away so the porch lights wouldn't catch the glistening tears. He suddenly felt like he was drowning, his skin heavy and cold, not his own. He wondered if he could survive the darkness that had been there since Peter's death, at first dribbling little frightening drops on a mental canvas but eventually painting a full, vicious portrait whose subject had finally been unveiled as a boy poking out from a basement stairwell, his grinning, bloody face limned with lightning.

Please stay. I really could use a real friend out here.

Jack watched miserably as the lights of Oscar's car were consumed by the woods, feeling like a boy abandoned in a strange, frightening place. Worst of all, he knew there was no one he could turn to, no one who could free him of his torments. They could try to say the right things and offer assurances, but Jack had realized he was on the other side

225

now, separated from society by Peter's death and his grandfather's curse. He was diseased, beyond repair, capable only of dulling the pain. He didn't want to be a burden. He didn't want to drag people into his

problems, and it scared him to feel so isolated, surrounded by the darkness, unable to escape it, his friends and family on the other side of things. Even if they were here, each of them giving him a long hug, they would always be on the other side because they'd never killed a little boy. They'd never stared into Peter's lifeless eyes and seen the awful blood on his face and wished he would move a finger. They'd never seen how far a little black shoe can be tossed from its owner. They'd never smelled the blood of death mixed with fresh asphalt. They'd never seen innocence shattered in such a way, a young, fragile life extinguished, fear swelling in Peter's eyes before the impact – and so they would remain on the other side, the side of light and weightlessness, the side of peaceful nights and happiness, the side where guilt didn't rise with every sight of a child on a sidewalk.

"Once you cross over, you can never go back," he murmured.

The world, it's so much different on this side, isn't it, Jackie? Come on now, pal, that's enough thinking for one night. Let's take that edge off.

But eventually I won't be able to remember any of it. I won't need you then.

There was maddened laughter, then tears.

BURN, DO NOT READ!

Part V: Old Friend

Chapter I

Returning to the guest room at 11:45, Night dutifully following me like a bodyguard, I turn on all of the lights I can find (overhead lamp, bedside lamp, flashlight) and pull open the book.

Grandpa left many pages blank in the middle of the book. As I riffle through these yellowed pages until I find the writing again, I'm not without a thought that I, too, am slipping into the same anathematic mire that plagued Grandpa in this house. But my eyes act on their own, falling upon the words as if tugged by magnetic attraction, pulled along with each sentence...

If you're reading this far, you may have failed to get it to go back. That's okay, there's still time. Just keep the lights on, all of them. Don't let it get dark, and whatever you do, don't fall asleep. If it knows you're onto it, it won't let you leave. If you sleep, it might try to kill you. I've tried to leave but I can't. You likely won't be able to leave now either, at least not until you get it back into that room. Don't look around! Don't go searching for it! I know you want to, but it's watching. Don't make it angry, especially not at night. It will turn out the lights, one at a time, and it's your job to keep them on. If it gets too close, Night will let you know. Just stay out of its way.

The door creaks open opposite the guest bedroom - the door to Grandpa's bedroom - leaving a column of darkness a few inches wide. Night growls, staring at the door as well.

As if governed by Grandpa's words, the hallway light clicks out.

Night barks once, twice, three times, and then comes a familiar bark-snarl flurry, the dog hurtling off the bed and challenging something unseen in the hallway.

Every muscle going rigid, I call Stevie's name. "Is that you?"

No reply.

Night's rage builds steadily, her eyes tracing something in the hallway as she bellows, her fur bristled all the way down her back. These aren't the absent barks of a dog suspicious of a muffled sound. She's barking at something specific.

I shine the flashlight into the hallway. Are those footsteps in the distance, thumping softly?

With Night at my heels, I hurry down the hallway toward the dark living room. But Stevie is on his stomach on the sofa,

beneath the blankets, mumbling about the dog. There's no way he could have made those sounds.

My ears ring slightly, vibrating with a sudden change of pressure like they do when I'm in an airplane. The grandfather clock is exceedingly loud now, somehow overwhelming nature's wrath outside.

Smoke. I notice the candle nearest Stevie on the coffee table, one of the candles we lit earlier in anticipation of another power outage. The flame has just died, a trail of smoke telling of its recent extinguishment, not a matter of minutes ago but seconds.

My throat goes tight. The heaviness of the house seems to crush me. For a moment I can't breathe.

Now I'm jogging through the house, bringing to life every light, perhaps acting with the same desperation these walls saw from Grandpa. In a dark epiphany, I understand why he covered the mirrors, possibly facing the very fear that ravages me, the fear of seeing something - It - behind me. But what is It? What

229

does It look like? What was Grandpa envisioning when he described It?

MORNING DOES NOT WELCOME THOSE WHO DIE!

The basement! I still haven't searched the basement for the room where Grandpa found It.

Chapter II

Jack delighted in his reunion. Nearing the bottom of the J.D. bottle, he realized the darkness had sailed off, the little house perfused with gray morning light. It was foggy out there, and Jack was feeling better. He'd gone slowly, paced himself, for he knew well the finer points of this ritual and the art of dulling the senses without overdoing it. His mind had been operating with excessive speed, and he'd finally – mercifully – been able to slow it down to a manageable pace.

His old friend had been right. He'd simply needed to take the edge off. All would soon be well again.

Jack leisurely lifted the bottle to his lips and took another pop. He'd been giggling intermittently about life's cruelty these past few hours, but now he was quiet and calm, sitting on the floor with his back to the living room wall. Night was curled up on the sofa, and whenever she stirred or changed positions, Jack would call to her with slurred words, telling her, "Almost supper time, doggie. Few more hours till supper."

Jack finally slept, the ultimate goal of the process. When he woke, the grandfather clock told him it was almost noon, except he didn't realize the clock wasn't tick-tocking anymore. It had stopped the previous night just before midnight, and Jack – his head hurting and back sore – went through much of the day assuming it was three hours earlier than the actual time. Resultantly, Night received strange-houred meals and Jack found primetime TV shows when he wanted the local news, not that it mattered. Much of the good oblivious day he spent with a can of beer in hand, sipping every time an unfavorable thought came to mind.

Four cans found their way to the sink before dinner, another crunched underfoot, before Jack decided to cut it out for a while. He felt a little loopy but largely unburdened, last night's debacle now seeming more like a distant nightmare. In the depths of his heart there was dim regret over giving in, but this was the only way to keep from going crazy, he'd decided. With no one to turn to who'd understand, everyone

231

separated by that indomitable wall, the only man in his corner was a very old friend.

Jack fell asleep again before he made much progress with his second round of J.D., even before he could let Night out for a long overdue walk. Whimpering after several failed attempts to wake her master, the dog found a place in the corner of Jack's bedroom closet and remained there for the better part of the night, holding her bladder until she could do so no longer.

Chapter III

Jack felt great the next day, as tip-top as he'd been in a long time. He woke energized and sharp, ready to take on whatever project he came up against. His previous fears and despondence had drifted off like late-night clouds, replaced by a fine blue-skied morning, warm with a gentle breeze and the songs of birds. And there was something different about the house – it felt lighter and just…different.

Excited, Jack went out to the porch and stood there, hands flat on the railing, his gaze drawn to the trees. "It's beautiful out here, absolutely gorgeous."

Acting on a sudden impulse, he walked across the driveway to the garage and hefted an old pool lounge chair back to the front lawn, Night watching him curiously from the thick grass. After situating the chair to face the morning sun, Jack stripped off his clothes and lied naked on the worn, faded cushion. Squinting, he shook his head at the sight of his pale skin and vowed to get a little tanning in.

What good is living out in the woods if you can't do things like this? he thought, closing his eyes and letting the sun wash over him.

The rest of the morning was spent making up for lost time with Night. Jack fed her a big breakfast – with a few deli bits mixed in as heartfelt apologies – then took her for a long ride in the car, followed by a walk around the park. His old friend began to beckon halfway home, but he could wait a little longer – that 36-pack would keep his afternoons tension-free, the perfect appetizers preceding his nightly sessions with J.D.

Speaking of J.D., Jack stopped by the package store on his way home and reloaded, adding a few new names to the roster. This wouldn't be an exclusive, invitation-only party – friends of friends were welcome.

When Jack got home, he stood on the porch and took a few reluctant minutes to return all of the calls he'd missed from his family, beers at the ready on the railing. He wished everyone didn't get so damn bent out of shape if he didn't call them back right away. They were always assuming the worst, those people; ever since Peter's death they'd assumed nothing but the worst. They could never just give him a break.

Jack's mood soured as he called Rob back. The thought of his son asking Oscar Montoya to check in on him was mortifying. Now Oscar knew incontrovertibly that Jack's family didn't feel he was cut out for life on his own.

They all might as well put a tracking device on my car.

The worst part was that Jack knew they were right in thinking he shouldn't live alone, which only made him more bitter.

What good is a man who can't do things for himself? Better get the damn coffin ready now.

"Hey, Dad, how are you?" Rob said, his tone settling Jack. *How can I be angry at him for caring?*

Jack took a long sip of beer. "Just fine, son. Thought I'd check in early so you don't go worrying about me."

Rob laughed uneasily. "That's my job, Dad. And I'm afraid you can't fire me from it. Seriously, though, we all just want to make sure you're doing well. You and Mom always put everyone before yourselves, every single day, and you deserve to be taken care of. I wish you'd reconsider about moving closer – we all miss you."

Jack looked exasperatedly to the sky. *Do they ever stop trying to control me?* "Maybe one day," he said. "Meanwhile, I better get back to building a new workbench for the garage – it's coming out great." Jack smiled at the ease with which he was able to lie; he hadn't yet lost his former skills.

234

"Wow, that sounds like a big project. I hope you're not working too hard."

He thinks I'm weak and old. They all do. "No, it's nothing. I could build these things in my sleep."

"What about metal detecting? Have you found that diamond ring yet?"

Of course not. I metal detect in the yard, damn it, not the beach! "Not yet, but you never know. Could be just one beep away."

Jack's first beer was nearly empty by the conclusion of their talk. Next on the list of calls to return was Jon, and by the time that conversation wrapped up, Jack had almost downed the second beer.

Gotta take it slower, he thought, *but these people are driving me to drink. Why are they always so worried? I had one terrible accident in fifty years, and now I'm a walking, talking disaster waiting to happen.*

You know damn well why they're worried.

But it isn't fair, not fair! Why is this happening to me?

Returning inside, Jack suddenly realized what had been different about the house all day. The grandfather clock. It was stopped just before noon, or midnight.

How long has it been like that? he wondered, well aware of how infrequently he needed to change the clock's batteries. He could only recall doing so on two occasions, the trusty old clock keeping better time than Father T. himself.

But now, examining the clock's gilded face and pendulum, his eyes beginning to roam somewhat warily up and down, taking in its roman numerals and ornate pediments and polished veneers and the ever-watchful carved eagle at the top, Jack felt a little intimidated by the grand keeper of time. He thought briefly of Peter Elliott and how time only moves one way and how morning never welcomes those who die, then mulled whether he still wanted to hear the clock's ticking every second and chiming every daytime hour.

Maybe it'd be best to just get rid of the damn thing. It only reminds me that I'm another second closer to death.

But Mary had loved this clock, cherishing its elegant songs.

Reluctantly, acting solely in his wife's memory, Jack fished the needed batteries from a kitchen drawer and brought the clock back to life. He gazed through the beveled glass into another decade, a happier time, and began to hum "Ave Maria" in preparation of the next hour.

Later, it was pizza night at the chess club, a monthly get-together for the guys and their families that always injected sadness into Jack's heart. When the pizza boxes were empty and it was finally time to get down to some chess, the wives unfailingly took a table and gossiped, while the grandkids watched the chess games with varying degrees of interest, the little boys usually yapping about how they could see some great imminent move as the little girls amused themselves with movies and computer games and artwork in the next room.

Jack usually found himself painfully aware that he was the only man in the room without a single guest. Sometimes the pain was like a dull, pressing ache, while other occasions brought sharp agony, especially when one of the guys kissed his wife and said those three words, or when they challenged their grandkids to a few matches. These were the kinds of moments that had prompted Jack to fill a coffee thermos with J.D. that evening and bring it to chess club, sipping whenever he felt the twinge of jealousy, sipping at every sight of a kiss, sipping each time a blond-haired boy – Henry's grandson – caught his attention, for the boy somewhat resembled an older, chubbier version of Peter.

Enjoying his whiskey, Jack wondered how he'd ever endured pizza night without an old friend at the table. How had he made small talk with these women and allowed these kids to watch his games? How had he walked out of the place by himself without breaking down, a lonely man's shadow interspersed among those of handholding couples and youngsters?

"Check," said Charlie Andersen, his gaze seeming briefly to linger on Jack's thermos from across the table.

A little flicker of paranoia went through him. *I wonder if Charlie can smell the whiskey. I sure hope not.*

But Charlie kept eyeing the thermos, or at least it seemed so. *Why can't you just look at the board? Keep your eyes on the pieces, you old turkey. Stop looking around.*

"Goshdarnit," Charlie said when Jack captured a knight and gained a decided advantage in material. Once an avid profanity machine, Charlie's New Year's resolution last year had been to cut down on the swear words, though Jack would have preferred a few four-letter zingers over Charlie's annoying substitutes – goshdarnit, goddangit, phooey, shoot. It was like listening to those ridiculous TV movie replacements for swears.

"You always pounce on my mistakes," Charlie continued, his grandson adding, "He's a machine," and then the kid made a series of strange onomatopoeic sounds that got Jack thinking of intergalactic warfare.

"Nah, I just get lucky half the time." Jack took another pop, beginning to relax. *The pizza was good*, he thought, *and these people are all very nice. Who am I to feel sorry for myself?* He glanced out the window at the street as Charlie put an elbow on the table and rested his bearded chin in his hands, staring intently at the cluttered board.

It's a great night. But there are people in hospitals right now who can't enjoy it because they're hooked up to machines and fighting for their lives. So who am I to feel sorry for myself? It's such a nice summer night. Look at that, those two kids holding hands and eating ice cream cones – what a great thing to do on a summer night.

Jack smiled down at the board, infused with gratitude for his friends and his dedicated little dog, who was waiting for him back home, probably sitting up on her sofa perch and watching the driveway for headlights. She always put on such a jubilant show when he came home, jumping and barking and racing around the house, as though he'd been gone a week (Mary had called it "the pony run").

Charlie studied the board a while longer, evaluating his options and looking increasingly frustrated with each one, his lips stretching into a grimace when he finally decided to dispatch his queen on a very dangerous solo mission. She was captured four moves later, and Charlie tipped his king.

"Wow, Grandpa, he destroyed you," Charlie's grandson remarked, the sting of defeat surely worsened by the candor of a child's postgame analysis. Maybe the kid would grow up to be a sports radio talk show host.

"I wouldn't say *killed*, more like wriggled by," Jack said, wanting to make Charlie feel a little better about his game. The truth was that Charlie stunk at chess, always putting his forces in overaggressively untenable positions and using pieces to protect endangered material rather than mobilizing them for a coordinated, balanced attack. Whenever Jack played Charlie, he envisioned the guy's reckless pieces as miniature ambulance drivers rushing around to the next accident. On one side of the board a knight would be in dire need of rescue, and then, a few moves later, it would be a bishop in distress on the other side. But Charlie was a good guy. He didn't grumble about losing or make strange excuses, taking his frequent defeats with grace.

"I'll get him one of these days," Charlie told his grandson, his smile slight and rueful. He was about to expand on the matter, but his older brother Patrick came bumping up beside him, cane in hand.

"You get your *bee*-hind spanked again, Charlie?" the half-blind Patrick Andersen jested, poking his brother in the arm. Patrick's good eye – the one not covered by a worn black pirate's patch – leveled on Jack. "I'm betting you didn't need more than thirty moves to take this patzer down, eh? Charlie makes more blunders than a rookie quarterback, ain't that right, brother?" He jabbed Charlie again, his wheezing laughter quickly worsening to a hacking cough.

When Patrick regained respiratory control, he extended a gnarled hand to Jack. "Name's Pat Andersen – I don't believe we've met."

Now it was Charlie's turn to rib his brother, which began with an amused chortle. "Pat, you God…goshdarn amnesiac, you've met Jack before. You two talked just a few months ago."

"We did," Jack remembered. "You were a schoolteacher in town, right?"

Patrick nodded proudly. "Taught for thirty years and can remember almost every student, first *and* last names. Even remember the bastard school committee members, sons-a-bitches, corrupt as the day is long." His blue eye seemed to roam searchingly over Jack's face. "Strange, though, I just can't recall meeting you, mister. You live in town?"

"Yeah, sure do," Jack said, then told Patrick his street.

It was as if Jack's words had been a pair of arms gently shoving Patrick Andersen backward. His eye dilated with dread or something worse, his face losing a little color.

Charlie shifted uncomfortably, looked down to the table.

"*You* live at the house of tricks?" Patrick said, his eye locked on Jack. He took a single, cautious step forward, acting like Jack was plagued by a deadly pathogen.

"The house of tricks?" Jack said, an unpleasant little shiver creeping up from his stomach.

"Don't start that stupid stuff, Pat," Charlie warned, looking worried. His grandson ran off at his mother's request, joining her at the ladies' table, and now it was just the three of them, Patrick still eyeing Jack

with what might have been fear or pity. It was impossible to tell, but whatever lurked behind that stare was decidedly awful.

"You better not get him all worked up," Charlie said. "Last thing he needs is more hearsay."

Jack took a needed sip from his thermos, his eagerness to hear more tempered with unease. It had risen swiftly and coldly into his chest, like a tiny, gravity-defying ice cube. The longer Pat stared at him, the colder it seemed to get.

"Why do you call it the house of tricks?" Jack said, his question seeming to take an hour to form.

Do I even want to know?

Pat's eye shifted sidelong to his brother before returning to Jack. "It's not me who first called it that – I just like the name." He shook his head thoughtfully, consulting his memory. "You heard about Tommy Talbot, the pastor who owned the place before you?"

Jack nodded. Took a quick pop.

"Well, Tommy's kid came up with the name, and I thought it fit just fine considering everything that's gone down there." Regarding Charlie, he said, "He does know about everything that's–"

"He knows, he knows," Charlie said irritably, fidgeting with his defeated king. "What he doesn't need is all the rumors."

"It's fine," Jack assured, wanting to get through this morass as quickly as possible. The conversation was like sitting in a dentist's chair and watching him prepare the needle.

Just get it over with already.

"Tommy's son, Richie, wrote about the house of tricks for one of my creative writing assignments," Patrick expanded, ignoring his huffing, head-shaking brother. "He wrote all kinds of spooky stuff in that piece, *seriously* spooky stuff about hearing whispers in the night and seeing things in the woods. He kept writing about the woods coming alive and the fog and nightmares and parents who didn't believe – a house that writes its own story, I think he mentioned a time or two." Patrick stuffed his hands into his jeans pockets. "There was so much detail in that damn story, I thought I was reading a horror novel – and Charlie'll be the first one to tell you I don't like that kind of stuff. Not for a second. I asked the kid about his inspiration, told him it was solid fiction work for his age, but he gave me a look I'll never forget and said it was all true, every bit of it." He pointed adamantly at Jack. "You know the stories about that place, mister. I don't need to tell you more, but suffice it to say Richie and his house of tricks never left me, never will, either. I've heard tons of rumors, ungodly rumors–" Patrick's lips trembled with the need to say more, but Charlie was standing, grabbing him by the shoulder.

"Enough, Pat. Enough of all this nonsense. Tommy Talbot and his family lived there for years without a problem – same with Jack."

Patrick's gaze, hard and frigid, remained on Jack. "Really? You mean, you haven't had any…*strange* experiences there?"

Their talk was interrupted by a dinging bell. At the head of the room, Oscar was ready to address the group, probably to make an announcement about an upcoming Relay for Life program (he and his wife were the proud organizers of the local chapter).

241

"We'll talk later," Patrick whispered with a conspiratorial wink, patting Jack on the arm.

Jack said nothing, the thermos rising to his lips.

Chapter IV

Jack found comfort that night in the fine company of an old friend, the pattering rain and the insistent clock ignored, the blanketing darkness forgotten. He was aware of Night's movements through the house in a vague, dimly sentient way, and he also detected little creaks and thuds occasionally rising from various shadowy corners and announcing themselves above the TV.

But Jack didn't think much of these noises, not when the sofa was comfortable and the company was good. It didn't matter when his friend was present; none of it mattered.

Jack had long ago ceased brooding over what Patrick Andersen told him about the house and the rumors surrounding it. A house of tricks, he'd said, but Jack had later forced him to confirm that no harm had come to Tommy Talbot and his family while living within these walls. They'd called this place home for ten years, and apparently the most frightening thing to emerge from their ownership had been a creative writing assignment. Patrick, a worried look glinting in his eye, had revealed some of the other rumors to Jack – stuff about poltergeists and demons and even aliens – but the icy unease in Jack's chest had melted to a lukewarm pool with each one.

Clearly, Jack had decided on the way home, the townspeople were obsessed with the negativity that had previously visited the house. *They* were haunted, not the house, constructing their little canards about a house in the middle of the woods, each person adding a different twist or fabrication, until finally the house morphed into a menace capable of swallowing all who entered it.

And Jack, with his acidic guilt, easily could have blamed the house for his troubles. He could have ascribed his hallucination of Peter on the basement stairwell to a haunted house of tricks, but he knew better, far better.

People are haunted, he'd kept telling himself. *Not places.*

Returning home from chess club, Jack had finished off the contents of his thermos in the driveway, the sky swathed in layers of dusky orange and pink, darkness overspreading the woods like hot tar. There'd been a momentary reluctance on Jack's part to enter his home, rumors scuttling through his head – and the sky had been so baleful, reminding him with every fading color that full dark wasn't far off, that he would be alone again in the woods, that he would never hold Mary again, that morning does not welcome those who die. Glancing up to the meager patch of sky afforded him by the ageless trees, Jack had forced his thoughts back to the lights of the carnival. What a view it had been looking down from the ferris wheel, their hands interlocked. Talking with Mary, holding her, kissing her – the wheel flashing yellow and red – Jack had often wished they could sit up there together forever with the cool autumn wind in their hair. Those times would hopefully always stay with Jack, the lights and the kisses and the laughter and the closeness he'd felt to her, the realization that such a kind, beautiful woman wanted to spend the rest of her life with him, *HIM*, Jack Gibson. Of all the millionaires and geniuses, of all the trilingual courtiers and doctors and musclemen who could heft boulders around, of all the celebrities and famous athletes, Mary had wanted to be with him, John Robert Gibson, a smalltown guy who'd seen the world during his Navy years, only to return home and fix cars. Sometimes it had all seemed like a dream, like he would wake and there would be no Mary, but now, though Jack felt immensely fortunate to have enjoyed the years he did with his wife, he knew it hadn't been nearly enough, not when there was nothing but death and darkness ahead.

Inside the house, wanting to enjoy what he could while he was still around to enjoy it – but also wanting to push back his slithering guilt – Jack had found his old friend and proceeded to get the night underway. He'd fed his dog and grilled chicken for himself, and then it had been time to reconvene with Jackie D., with whom he'd chatted about the old days and those carnival lights. There'd been cotton candy and squirt gun games and stuffed animals; there'd been rides and hamburgers and

French fries and sodas; the funhouse and, much later with the kids, a haunted house; but the best part had always been strolling through the

fairgrounds with Mary and talking – talking about everything, hand in hand until closing.

Jack was no longer reminiscing. It was getting late now. Seated on the sofa, a nearly empty bottle of J.D. in hand, he stared mindlessly at the TV, slipping deeper into a familiar haze. A peaceful place. Somewhere in the house Night had started barking unenthusiastically, her little discontented chirps barely penetrating Jack's virtually trancelike calm. When the barking grew more insistent, he glanced toward the hallway but realized tiredly that he didn't have the energy to check it out.

She's barking at the wind, pal. Always trying to get you riled up.

I wonder if that woman died right away after hanging herself. Did she suffer, you think?

It's too late for that, Jackie. Just relax.

"Quiet down, girl," Jack murmured, finishing off his J.D., a few parting words offered by his friend on the way out the door.

Atta boy, Jackie. Ready for bed now, kid?

***

It was just after ten o'clock. The rain was falling faster now, the wind ratcheting up and buffeting the house. Lightning pulsed at the windows, and Oscar Montoya, having just concluded an hour of online chess, was preparing for bed.

"I'm worried about him," Oscar told his wife. "Did you see him tonight? He doesn't have any family for thousands of miles. It's just him and his dog out there, and something isn't right."

Annie Montoya stretched the new sheets into place, tucking them neatly beneath the mattress. "I still can't believe you went over there at night, Oscar."

"Me, neither, but his son called me. What else could I do? The guy was fearing the worst." He shook his head. "I'm telling you, there's something weird happening with Jack. It's like he isn't all there anymore – I don't think living alone is good for him, especially in that place."

Frowning, Annie worked the pillows into their covers. "All the awful things that have happened there – I'd hate to go to a place like that at night."

Oscar felt a brief tenseness at the memories. "I got a bad vibe, a real bad vibe. The storm was pulling away, but there was still a little lightning, and the woods…they're just so deep. I tried not to stare at them for too long while I was waiting. With the lightning and the wind, you don't want your imagination getting too active over there."

"Has he heard all of the stories?"

A rumble of distant thunder. Oscar lowered the windows almost fully shut. "I sure hope not, but he was talking to Pat Andersen tonight. I can't even begin to guess what ideas he put into Jack's head."

"At least Pat doesn't know about what happened to Tommy."

Shuddering, Oscar felt like he could use a sweatshirt. "Not yet. In time he'll probably find out, though, and then everyone will know."

Chapter V

Stephen Gibson sighed with satisfaction, feeling twenty years younger and as happy as he'd been in a very long time. Myndi, or maybe her name was Mandi, slid out of bed and began to dress, Steve admiring her ample breasts, among other attributes.

All good things must come to an end.

Steve knew his time was up, but he felt confident and important and young again, to the extent that he'd forgotten the nature of their arrangement halfway through the exchange. The fantasy of enticing a younger woman with his power had, for a short time, become real, and Maddy had been his lover, her passion conveyed with each moan and gasp, visible in her eyes, electrified by every rhythmic burst.

Steve had rather easily let thoughts of the escort agency fall away, but that hadn't been enough. To fulfill the fantasy, he'd needed to dismiss thoughts of his wife and children altogether, his guilt quickly shriveling at the notion that a man whose wife has done nothing to keep herself up for him should harbor no regrets.

A man has needs, the line had often repeated in his head, his desire rising in recent months from an aching simmer to a blood-boiling necessity – and finally he'd done it, pulled the trigger, felt young again, the way he used to feel before the first gray hairs had sprung up. There hadn't been room for guilt or disappointment during the convulsive pleasure tonight. After a short while, there hadn't been thoughts of his family. There certainly hadn't been any reminders of his age.

Now, though, it was all coming back to him, and the heavy, suffocating reality of it made him miserable. Alone in the hotel bed, his sense of superiority fading, though still half-believing he'd made Macy want him, he said, "Why don't you stay a while and have a few drinks?"

"You know the rules," she said flatly, buttoning her blouse with a flaunting self-importance that made Steve hot with rage. He wanted to leap from the bed and throttle her, wanted to teach the bitch a lesson, to show her where she stood. Who did she think she was dealing with, some portfolio manager schmuck who ran a hedge fund or a dime-a-dozen idiot in charge of an insurance company?

You don't talk to Senator Stephen Gibson like that, you filthy whore, he wanted to shout, but instead he watched Marnie gather her things and leave, the quiet click of the door closing behind her somehow infinitely worse than a slammed, angry door, her perfume lingering cloyingly in the room. Steve couldn't believe she was gone so soon. The deal was the deal, of course, and he'd known that shining black hair wouldn't last forever, but there hadn't been any steamy parting words or call-you-laters, no financial discussions because the fee had been paid in advance, no drinks to prolong their rendezvous, nothing but an ache in Steve's gut and the sobering knowledge that his fantasy would always be just that. Younger women only wanted his money, not him.

Now that Melanie was gone, there was an awful, self-loathing silence, broken eventually by Steve's cell phone. His father was calling – again – and the thought of Dad made Steve want to puke. He had a long drive back to D.C. awaiting him now that his "conference" was finished, and talking to his father wasn't on the night's agenda.

Deeply downcast, Steve finished his drink and, with the last long swallow, repined over all that was wrong with his life. Macy didn't want him and he would have to look in the mirror yet again and admit that he was getting older each day, older and older and older, and Dad just kept on calling, and his stupid kid couldn't finish the school year without getting into more trouble, and his wife, goddammit, she just kept getting bigger.

Why can't she renew her gym membership or, I wouldn't want to tax her, maybe skip a fucking dessert here or there?

"Fuck off!" he shouted, and he might as well have been shouting at all of them as he fired the pillows against the far wall. "All of you, just fuck off!"

Chapter VI

Jack awoke startled and disoriented on the sofa. Dim gray light spread through the house, and Jack knew without touching the curtains what he'd see outside, another morning cloaked in fog, the first curve of the driveway barely visible from the porch.

Night was lying in front of the softly-volumed TV, watching Jack alertly. Ears raised, she flicked her tail a few times upon making eye contact with Jack.

"How're you doing, girl?" he mumbled, lifting his cell phone from his stomach and checking the time.

It was seven on the nose, the grandfather clock chiming dutifully. If Mary were still alive it would begin another rendition of "Ave Maria", but Mary was dead and Jack preferred to keep the clock on its normal setting. He couldn't bring himself to silence the hourly calls, though, even if they often whisked bad thoughts into his headspace.

At least now the clock couldn't perturb him with its previous totality, not with J.D. keeping watch over the house.

Rising groggily from the sofa, rubbing his eyes, Jack remembered his nightmare. Night had escaped her fenced enclosure somehow, and she'd been lost in the foggy predawn woods, running and running in search of Jack, the coyotes at her heels, but every turn had led her farther away, deeper into the woods. It had been so dark and horrible out there, and the coyotes, with gleaming yellow eyes, had marauded through the trees, roving in packs until they converged on Night. But Jack's little mutt had sprinted away from them, weaving and charging through the fog, the house coming into view, so close, and that was all Jack could remember.

Squatting, he gave Night a long scratch behind the ears and beneath the collar, her funny little smile forming when he hit the right spots. "I love you, girl," he whispered. "I know I've been a little off lately, but I've

Gotta do whatever it takes to get my head straight. You know that, right? Right, girl?"

Night, looking at him quizzically, seemed to understand. In a moment she trotted off to the dining room and scratched the glass door, ready to patrol the fog. Jack went out there with her this time, making sure each of the gates was latched before returning to the deck, where he watched the fog curling through the woods, thick in spots and shallow in others. He listened for coyotes but heard only morning quiet, their hunting hour apparently concluded.

Leaning comfortably over the deck rail, Jack watched Night cavorting through the fog, a little black dart zipping around with the carefree exuberance of a puppy. He wished humans could be more like their canine friends, capable of living each day to the fullest and then moving on to the next one, never brooding about the past because yesterday was over, never fretting about the future because tomorrow hadn't happened yet, never worrying in general because worrying was a waste of time.

I could go for a beer. Get these thoughts out of my head.

Yeah, that sounds good, kid.

Just one for now. Don't want to get carried away.

Just one? Really?

Jack spent a few minutes making the obligatory calls after a breakfast of beer and toast, calling Rob and then Paul. He had great conversations with both of them (he even found himself laughing so hard at one of Rob's stories that his belly hurt). Steve was another matter. His youngest son hadn't returned his calls yesterday, and he wasn't picking up this morning, either.

But Jack wouldn't allow fear to get the better of him. He wasn't a worry wart like the rest of his family; Steve was just busy, plain and simple. He would call when he found the time.

"I hope he's happy," Jack said to Night, setting the phone down on the kitchen countertop.

Night didn't care about Steve. Scratching the cabinet door behind which the biscuits and rawhides were stored, she only had one concern in that little head of hers, and it had nothing to do with Stephen Gibson.

"You're right, girl, screw worrying." Jack gave Night a choice between biscuit and rawhide, holding one in each hand for a careful sniffing evaluation, and away she went with the biscuit, a change of the usual pace.

"Time to get on with the day," he said after Night retreated to the sofa, but the dog wasn't the only one possessing a treat.

Jack permitted himself a second morning beer, the crack of the pull tab bringing with it a little guilty pang in his chest. He knew he wouldn't have needed another one so early if that stupid nightmare hadn't struck him.

But it wasn't just the nightmare that made him crave a second beer – even after a mostly oblivious night with his old friend, three persistent words refused to be expunged from his head.

House of tricks.

Chapter VII

Over the next two months Steve found himself arranging several nighttime appointments, his wife often inquiring about the nature of these impromptu events that caused him to break family commitments. She'd quietly accepted the first few weird-houred engagements, but Steve's latest announcements had been met with probing, mistrustful stares and rounds of questioning that had angered Steve. What right did a fattening woman with a virtually nonexistent libido have to question him? Did she spend an hour at the gym each morning? No. Did she ever ask him to make love anymore? No. Did she even come close to matching his diligence in image preservation? Absolutely not.

Yet she expected him to happily watch as she ordered an extra appetizer at every dinner and then follow up the meal with a slice of godforsaken cheesecake, Steve feeling defrauded each time. When he'd spoken his vows, they hadn't been given to a fat woman!

But his wife never used to order dessert, never, and it was utterly loathsome to envision what she'd look like in a few years, not to mention a decade or two, a pattern that was becoming very disturbing to Steve. He assumed she had gained ten or fifteen pounds in the last year alone – eating and eating and eating at every goddamn function – and if that alarming trend kept up, she might damage the presidential bid he had planned ten years down the road. For a man of such prodigious aspirations, every single detail had to be taken into careful consideration, and Steve knew he couldn't be seen with a woman whose breasts and stomach could barely be differentiated. Whenever he began his campaign for the Oval Office, his wife would need to spearhead programs educating schoolchildren on the importance of a healthy diet. She would need to promote regular exercise and athletic involvement. She would need to be a role model whose image complemented his. That was the plan, and, quite literally, she wasn't fitting into it, though the potential liability of her weight was clearly a conversation for another day, a day that found Steve with far greater patience.

Right now he simply wanted to convene with another young tart, preferably one who wouldn't look him over too closely (just another rich guy in a suit was the desired perception, and thus far Steve was confident he'd eluded recognition).

"What did I tell you about repeats?" Steve shouted into the phone one Saturday afternoon when no one was home. "I made it very clear that I don't want the same girl twice. No goddamn girlfriend effect!"

He was talking to his contact at the escort agency, a contact he'd established through incredibly methodical and painstaking means, going as far as creating an alias and purchasing a new cell phone, in addition to making advance payments each time he arranged a new meeting. The process, he'd found, very much reminded him of his high school days, when one or two or five girls had never sustained him. No, he'd been the quarterback, the most popular kid at school, and the more girls he'd slept with, the deeper his urges had become to sleep with new girls, redheads and brunettes and skinny girls and chesty girls, young girls and shy girls and loud girls and religious girls and rebellious girls, until he'd run out of potential partners at his school senior year and had needed to expand his scope to the community colleges, where he'd found more than a few older girls who'd very much enjoyed their alcohol.

But he wasn't in high school anymore, the goddamn mirror confirming as much. He was a U.S. senator who upheld the virtues of this great nation and blah, blah, blah, a man with immense power who had to be discerning with his private affairs. He couldn't let things get out of control – otherwise he might end up swimming in the same pile of shit that had claimed Dad the year before he got sober, when he'd come home early all the time because he was out of another job. "They cut me loose, kid, but that's all right, I'll find another gig tomorrow. Tell you what, I'm gonna head downstairs for a few hours and get caught up on some projects," Dad had told Steve one day before disappearing into the basement to drink. "Call me up when Mom gets home, will you?"

Last girl this month, Steve promised himself, remembering Dad's reeking breath and how easily a man could be toppled by his vices.

Then he proceeded to complete his order, securing another partner who could make him feel young again.

Chapter VIII

With the boundless support of old friends, Jack's next two months went about as well as could be expected. Some days were better than others, the ones when he didn't go too desperately to the well, the ones when a few beers by day and a touch of J.D.'s company at night were more than sufficient to breed solid, undisturbed sleep. Those were the days when he could go to chess club without a thermos, the days when Night got her meals at the right times, the days when he felt ambitious enough to wander around the yard with the metal detector or find himself a little woodworking project to embark on.

But there were other days, too, darker days when the beers rolled by morning and J.D. and the others were busy friends at night. Such days were usually precipitated by a coyote attack and the wrong thoughts, but J.D. and his friends were very caring guys who knew just how to chase the darkness off.

Even on Jack's worst days there were no hallucinations and very few nightmares, only a doused light here or there that he thought he'd left on, or an inexplicable noise that angered Night to barking, two months marked by relative peace. Jack didn't see Peter or anyone else grinning at him from the basement stairway, not even on the stormy nights of heightened imagination, and so he continued his guilt-numbing, mild-stabilizing regimen, dosing as needed. Perhaps alcohol could prevent dementia, cure PTSD, and ward off the whole evil lot of other maladies that might be afflicting him in some form or another – who knew? Regardless, this was the best deal, Jack supposed, that life had to offer a man in his position, and whenever thoughts came into his head telling him he deserved better, he inevitably remembered who he was and what he'd done, considerations that shut down each and every want for change.

Tonight was different, though. Autumn was like an expanding sail on the horizon. Soon the days would be shorter and cooler, the darkness heavier. The snow would eventually fall, and the pristine quiet of winter would ease over Jack's little house in the woods. There would be no metal detecting and far fewer daytime walks about the yard, Jack

and his dog confined on the coldest days to the house, where his stately clock would provide its constant reminders of time's velocity.

Can I handle another winter here?

Jack, seated beneath an umbrella at one of the picnic tables outside Lucky's Drive-In, a quickly melting vanilla soft-serve cone in hand, watched a passing train and wondered if he should sell his house. With each intermodal car that rattled on by, the idea seemed to gain a stronger hold. He could move closer to both Rob and Steve, maybe buy a house somewhere between Boston and D.C. That way, he could see his grandchildren more often, but without the hassle of people coming by every day to check on him. He could probably even manage to keep his old friend around, too; on days when he planned to see his family, he would simply limit J.D. to the nighttime.

That could work. Then I wouldn't have to live all the way out here anymore.

The last car of the train rolled through, its blinking red light fading into the twilight.

But what if they stop by unannounced one day? And what if they try to force me into a home? I know Steve'll try it again, I just know it.

Jack licked his way around the cone, trying to keep pace with the influence of a hot, muggy night. It was quickly getting dark, a line of customers swatting at mosquitoes as they waited to place their orders at the lighted window. To Jack's right, a youth baseball team and their parents/coaches occupied four tables, the kids eating ice cream cones and chasing each other around in their uniforms and high blue socks. To Jack's left, closer to the railroad tracks, the other tables were taken by high school kids on dates and old couples and a motorcycle gang clad in black, a few of them bare-skinned beneath their vests.

Getting down to the cone, Jack realized with stinging speed how lonely he was, an old man with no one but his faithful dog to come home to. Later, these kids and couples and friends would be playing games and watching movies and, for the motorcycle guys, raising hell in some bar. That's what Friday nights were meant for, but when Jack Gibson finished his cone, there'd be nothing to do but return to a dark house in the middle of the big woods.

Man, Mary would love this place. She'd get the clam chowder every time, I bet, and a twist afterward. She used to love her soft-serve twists so much.

Jack smiled, but then his roaming eyes stopped on a little boy standing in line with his parents. He was laughing, and he looked somewhat like Peter Elliott, blonde-haired and happy. Jack's dwindling cone fell to the grass, to be finished off by the ants. His jaw fell open. The boy laughed again at something his father said, and Jack felt like someone had punched him in the stomach, his hands shaking.

"Peter will never eat another ice cream cone," he said absently, unaware that words had escaped him. Like a strong thirst, he was overcome by the need to see his old friend.

Jack stood. He hurried back to his Taurus, the one he'd purchased because he could no longer tolerate driving a truck that had killed a little boy.

Jack didn't look back.

If he'd been home that very moment, he would have heard it happening again – another coyote attack in the woods.

Jack was seeing blurry a few hours later. He'd overdone his discussion with his dearest friend, a productive discussion, but now he was in an unusually bad place. He was dizzy, his stomach hurt, and his legs nearly failed upon standing. When he pissed it stung, and his ears were ringing.

For a while he stood very still beneath the harsh bathroom light, staring grimly into the mirror and feeling the angry churn of chicken tenders and french fries and beers and ice cream and J.D. digesting in his gut. His face seemed pasty, his eyes a little different somehow, sunken. He wondered what he'd look like if he was sober. He wondered what those motorcycle guys were doing right about now.

Night barked once, twice, a sound having preceded her barks – Jack's bedroom door creaking shut.

He straightened. Listened. Stumbled into the bedroom. Listened.

Poking his head out into the hallway, there was nothing to hear but muddled chimes and distant ticking. With his vision blurry, though, every shadow could be quickly transformed into a threat, and so he forced himself to breathe deeply.

"Nothing's there. Don't get yourself all worked up again."

Then his blood went cold, his body seizing up, his heart feeling like a heavy stone, when the grandfather clock chimed to mark eleven, a distorted, hollow sound that swirled windily in Jack's head.

But the clock was set on nighttime silent mode as it had been since he'd purchased it – this much he knew even after a long night with an old friend.

He also knew the clock had never done this before, its rigid sequence inexplicably broken.

Suddenly Jack remembered, memories spanning his ownership of the house coming back to him at once – the lights that had gone off, the black, shadowy sightings, Peter grinning at him from the basement. That grin would stay with him forever, as appropriate an expression as he'd ever seen, even if it hadn't been real. Jack was slowly breaking down, and Peter would surely be happy to see him suffer, wouldn't he?

259

The man who'd ended his life one sunny morning was paying, paying at last, his mind fritzing again.

Maybe I imagined the clock chiming and the door shutting. I feel like I've got a damn seashell stuck to my ear – who knows what I'm hearing?

Jack staggered dizzily into the hallway. Night had been shuttling menacingly about the house these last few minutes and was now taking aim at the basement door. Again. She kept looking over at Jack, as if expecting him to do something; she even tilted her head and made little circles and whined, trying everything in her power to spur Jack to action.

"What do you want me to do, girl?" His voice sounded completely foreign, strained and fragile. "There's nothing down there."

Night whined again, scratched the basement door. When Jack opened it and clicked on the stairwell light, she went charging quietly into the basement, taking a hard, skidding right at the base of the stairs and pursuing something with the single-minded focus that usually marked her outdoor hunts. Out of sight, at the other end of the basement, there was a clattering sound like trashcan lids coming together and then a roaring-snarling frenzy that sounded like a dogfight.

Jack stumbled downstairs – clinging to the railing for support, nearly falling – and found Night jumping wildly against the workbench, intent on getting up there, barking so profusely that one might assume Jack owned five dogs.

Jack grabbed her by the collar, patted her hackled fur. "Night, it's okay, girl, calm down!" He tried to look her over, panic exploding through his veins, but he couldn't see clearly enough to make out any injuries, Night's fur a blurry mop of black.

Jack rubbed desperately at his eyes, trying to bring the room into focus, but it only made his vision more fuzzy, as if he were seeing the room through teary eyes.

Night calmed a little now that Jack had joined her, and together they stood guard in the basement, Night occasionally barking at the workbench while Jack searched the dim, indistinct corners for movement. In the anxious process, he thought again of the woman who'd hanged herself in this very basement, poor Mrs. Scrivens, her lifeless body dangling from these rafters one night in a previous chapter of the house's story, her vacant eyes seeing no longer. Jack had frequently thought of Mrs. Scrivens since learning of her suicide, usually when he was down here in the basement, but tonight her death arrested him completely, so powerful that it felt for a moment like she was still here, hanging invisibly before him, watching.

She died down here.

Sure did, hung herself just over your shoulder, kid.

How would you know?

Because I know everything. Say, how about we get you back upstairs now, kid? Little too spooky down here this late.

Jack imagined the sound of the woman's neck snapping, and then, swiftly, the awful thump of a sunny morning came roaring back to him, Peter's bloody face storming into his head.

Night growled, barked, faced off with the workbench, but Jack was left stunned by another sound, a softer sound. There it was again, definite this time, coming from behind the workbench, muffled, as though it were emanating from behind the wall.

Mary's voice. Weakly calling his name.

By the time Night's next eruption of barks was finished, the basement was silent again, and Jack, staring blankly at the workbench, knew his embattled mind had succeeded once more in tricking him..

House of tricks.

From the depths of the woods, navigating tirelessly until they came through the basement slider windows to Jack, the howls of coyotes brought waves of nausea to his stomach.

He turned slowly to Night. "I need another drink, girl."

Chapter IX

It happened again overnight.

Jack awoke with discomfort and realized Night was standing on his back, growling with a low, eerie rage. She was facing the door as she'd done before, and when Jack stirred, mumbling and groaning, she leaped off the bed and barked, Jack rolling in time to see something moving just beyond the closed bedroom door, its shadow retreating from the crack of light visible beneath the door.

Jack's body went stiff and cold, but only for a moment.

It's all in my head, just like the shadows and sounds and Peter.

He watched the door for a while, listening to Night's continued barking. *But if I'm the crazy one, why is my dog barking?*

She always barks at night. Probably just heard a coyote.

Jack rubbed his aching stomach. He felt like he might puke, those damn tenders and fries having declared a horrible digestive war on the alcohol and ice cream. He imagined his gut as a black, roiling sea, with fifty-foot swells and lightning peeling overhead.

I wonder why she only barks in the house at night. She's always perfect during the day and on car rides.

Night eventually settled down and returned to the bed. Wary, Jack propped himself against the backboard with his pillows and stared at the thin line of hallway light beneath the door. He was sweating, tense with apprehension, his gut ache quickly sharpened to a point, until finally he forced himself to walk around the house with Night.

Only a cramp. Need to get moving a little, and five minutes later, just when the pain seemed unbearable – a sign of appendicitis? something worse? – it quickly diminished to a dull ache.

The house was dark and quiet, the clock behaving normally upon striking three and the wind chimes ringing gently outside. Guided by his nightlights and the hallway light, Jack circled the house a little while longer, brooding and rubbing his stomach. There were thoughts of Peter and his father, thoughts of Mary, thoughts of poor Mrs. Scrivens – *What could have possibly driven her to take her life?* – but mostly Jack thought about his own life and what might be wrong with him.

Convinced that this latest shadow had been yet another hallucination, he wondered if he should see a doctor (who'd invariably refer him to a shrink). The idea made him cringe. There would be tests and questions and sessions and more costly tests, only for the shrink to come back and tell him what he already knew. He suffered from PTSD – maybe even depression as well – and, when combined with a possible onset of Alzheimer's disease, the result had caused symptoms of psychosis. Medications would then be ordered for Jack, along with additional tests, and he would be forced to give up his dear old friend. Worse, he'd feel obligated to tell his sons about everything that was going on, and they'd drag him back to a retirement home for sure.

You have to keep on going, just fight through it. You don't have Alzheimer's – your memory is fine, Jackie. It's just old age, that's all. You've lost a few brain cells over the years, nothing to it.

Guilt is the main problem. I need to stop the guilt.

In spite of his ailing gut, Jack took a few more pops of J.D., then dragged himself back to his bedroom, no longer wary or alert but indifferent. Night was scratching the basement door again, but Jack walked past her without a thought toward opening it.

"Go to sleep, girl."

Chapter X

Jack awoke to a persistent ringing. The landline. Someone had been calling earlier as well, Jack ignoring it, and now they were likely trying again.

Jack, stretching in bed, too groggy to get up, listened as Oscar's voice cracked over the message machine.

"Morning, Jack, it's Oscar. I just wanted to let you know I'll be a little late this afternoon – pick you up at three-thirty, okay, pal?" A momentary pause. "I hope you're not bagging out of this thing on me, Jack. The wife ain't coming, and an old fart like me needs as many friends as he can get at these gigs. All right then, I guess you're out for a walk – see you at three-thirty. And don't go eating a big breakfast. Curt wants everybody coming to this thing hungry."

Jack let out a long, tired breath. *The wedding, that's right, the damn wedding.*

Jack and Oscar didn't even know the two people set to be married. The groom was the son of Curt Miller, one of their chess club members, and apparently the kid had done very well for himself in real estate. Curt was always talking about his son's mansion and muscle cars, but wealth had yet to buy him a happy relationship; his first two marriages had apparently produced children and little else, resulting in inevitable divorce. Today's ceremony would present him with bride number three, perhaps with tears contrived for the walk down the aisle, an event to be remembered, according to Curt, for the finest reception imaginable. After inviting the entire chess club to his son's wedding a few months back (along with plus-one tickets), Curt had explained that they were in desperate need of guests to consume all of the food that would be available. "There's gonna be so much food, people will die of overconsumption," he'd declared.

But Jack wasn't looking forward to the food. Hauling himself out of bed, his head aching mildly, he thought only of the drinks this wedding would offer.

Oscar arrived at half past three as planned, strolling up the porch steps in a tight-fitting gray suit and vest, his attire accented by a gold pocket watch and black bow tie. Tucked in his breast pocket was a folded white handkerchief.

"You look like you're ready for the red carpet," Jack said. "I would've worn something different if I'd known I was going to this thing with Sean Connery. Come in, come in, would you like something to drink?"

Looking unusually timid, Oscar remained on the porch. "Ah, I think I'm all set, thanks. We should get going, though – it's about an hour drive or so, and we might hit traffic."

Jack, briefly wondering if he was underdressed in a jacket, light blue button-down shirt, and gray slacks, looked at his friend askance. "Traffic? Oscar, we'd need to drive half a day to find somewhere with traffic."

Both men chuckled, Oscar stuffing his hands into his pockets and looking down.

What's going on with him? Jack wondered. *Is he afraid of the dog?* Night had barked halfheartedly when Oscar rang the doorbell, then returned to the sofa to sleep. If only she'd treat the empty basement as gently.

"All right, I guess we'll hit the road," Jack said, contemplating whether he should bring a few beers, maybe even the thermos. But that might lead to questions, and questions might lead to his sons finding out. If Rob called Oscar again and Oscar told him about Jack's drinking–

I'll get to the bar soon enough.

266

"This is going to be some party," Oscar said when they were on the road, Jack riding in the passenger seat of his friend's Buick Century. The car smelled of cherry cigars and gasoline, the backseat cluttered with hangered clothes, folded maps, wadded receipts, plastic grocery bags stuffed tight, and a few stray chess pieces that had escaped the travel set.

"Do you think they'll skip the vows for a guy's third marriage?" Jack said. "History hasn't exactly proven him to be the most committed guy."

Oscar adjusted his shirt collar. "Maybe his last two wives were intolerable witches."

"Yeah, sure, and he's a saint."

"Could be," Oscar laughed. "But as long as there's free food, he can be the biggest jerk on the planet. I'm still going home with a full belly."

Jack shook his head, confused. "To be honest, I'm surprised the guy doesn't have all kinds of friends he could invite to this thing. Why does he want his father's old chess buddies there?"

"It is weird," Oscar agreed. "Curt said he's a workaholic, one of those sixty-hour week guys. And the new bride doesn't have any family, I guess, which means a lot of food and not enough mouths to eat it all."

"A girl with no family?" Jack was incredulous. "Not even a half-sister or a grandma somewhere? Come on, nobody has no family whatsoever. I sure hope he got her to sign that prenup."

"What about your family?" Oscar inquired, catching Jack off guard. "You always talk so proudly about your sons and grandkids – we'd all love to meet them. Why don't you invite them to pizza night sometime?"

267

Jack looked out the passenger window, wishing Oscar hadn't taken a hard left turn on a light, amusing conversation. "They don't visit," he said flatly.

Oscar glanced over at him, expecting more, but Jack stared straight ahead at the road.

Great, now he's gonna grill me about my family.

"They don't visit?" Oscar said, acting like it was some great tragedy. "But why not?"

"They've got busy lives – they don't need to be flying out here to waste time with me in the middle of nowhere." Jack tried to keep his voice level, but his irritation with the subject was seeping inexorably through. "I fly back east on holidays and summers each year. That's more than enough."

But this summer Jack hadn't yet seen his family, a thought that dashed sprinkles of guilt into his heart. Stevie Jr. had asked during their last conversation when Jack was flying to D.C., but Jack had been half-drunk at the time and wanting very badly to continue a discussion with his old friend J.D. He'd snapped at Stevie, told him he was getting too old for flying, and Stevie had sounded sad and lonely, asking Jack if he could fly out west and they could spend a week together, maybe go fishing like they once did, maybe play some chess. No, had been Jack's firm response, and he'd proceeded to assure the kid that he would see him on Thanksgiving, no worries, that he'd be back in a blink of an eye.

Jack bit down hard on his lip, remembering how Stevie had told him he loved him and missed him. Rob and Paul and Jon had virtually echoed Stevie's words in their last conversations with Jack as well, sounding very worried about him, but J.D. had been looming over him, beckoning him to put the phone down and resume talks with his dearest friend. Hell, J.D. had practically taken the phone from his hand.

"Great weather lately, isn't it?" Oscar said, returning their discussion to a comfortable tenor.

Jack sniffed with fading perturbation, though he was still displeased with Oscar for getting personal. Ever since Rob had called him a few months back, Oscar had been a little too intcrested in Jack's affairs, asking him over to dinner with the wife and telling him he was always there if he needed a friend.

I have a friend. He comes in a bottle and he's a hell of a lot more helpful than you, Oscar. You can try, but you don't know how to help.

They were on the highway now, coming up on a furniture truck with an image of a leather sofa displayed on the back door, Jack scowling fiercely at it.

Damn Barfield and Brickley guy, why did you have to do that? WHY? WHY? WHY? And the train, those dumb old ladies in the crosswalk, too.

Jack rubbed his chin roughly. *And that stupid ass kid who got stung by the bee, Tanner What's-his-name – all Peter wanted was to help him. That's all the poor kid wanted, to just cross the street and get to the cops. Why was he wearing a suit? Maybe if he'd been wearing normal clothes like a normal kid he would have moved faster.*

He squeezed his eyes shut, craving J.D. *Peter, you were a good boy. Your parents loved you very much. Very, very much. I'm going to pay for what I did, Peter. I promise I'm going to pay.*

Then Oscar said something and he was out of it.

I could really, really use a drink.

The wedding ceremony proceeded at a painfully slow pace, Jack rocking anxiously on his heels and licking his lips and taking deep breaths. His head began to hurt, worsened by the heavy heat that oppressed them even in the shaded flower garden, a fountain splashing beyond the carpeted flagstone aisle, birds singing from their perches within the vast orchid trees.

What kind of a wedding doesn't have chairs? And what moron has a wedding in August? I should have had another beer earlier. I should have brought the thermos.

One of the guests had explained that, excluding special circumstances, the park commission didn't permit chairs at weddings (wouldn't want to crush the grass), and so everyone was required to stand during the ceremony. But Jack was getting very tired of standing. His legs were starting to cramp, and his arms felt tight and weighty.

There were gnats, too, and a crying baby…and the bride was ugly…and the reverend spoke exhaustively about the challenges of marriage and how the imminently wedded couple must face them together, hand in hand – but hadn't the reverends presiding over the last two weddings spoken similar words?

It's a sham, a fucking sham. They don't even have a damn chair, but they've got plenty of kids in suits and ties, kids who aren't going to die in a pool of their own blood today. Plenty of kids in suits. There's always gotta be a kid in a damn suit.

Why didn't I bring the thermos? No one would've been suspicious.

The couple was kissing now. People were clapping, and that meant it would be over soon, finally over, and they could all head off to the country club where the famously decadent dinner would be served. Oscar was clapping to Jack's left, Henry clapping to his right. They were all clapping – clap, clap, clap for fraud number three.

Can we wrap it up already? We all know this is gonna end with lawyers and paperwork, maybe a custody battle if the damn thing lingers long enough. Let's just get to the drinks!

As if someone had pressed the fast forward button, they were walking back to the parking lot.

Asshole people that don't appreciate marriage. Third marriage, what a joke! But I bet Peter would have been a faithful husband, such a great kid, but he didn't get the chance. Peter never had a chance.

The banquet hall at Summitview Country Club boasted chandeliers and marble flooring. From the ground to ceiling windows that comprised the north wall, guests could gaze out at the sparkling waters of the lake and, much farther, the hazy blue-gray mountains. Along the near wall, the string quartet was playing another exceedingly delicate piece. In the fray of guests, the photographer was earning every cent of his pay, his forehead slick with sweat. People were mingling and laughing at things they probably didn't find overly funny. Others were introducing themselves and trying to make themselves seem important. Like dutiful bumblebees in tireless operation, suited waiters delivered the cocktail hour foods, presenting them to each table with plastic smiles. There were grilled chicken wings and meatballs and avocado salad. There were steamed dumplings and seafood and soups. There was even pan-fried garlic bread, which Jack would have devoured on another occasion, but he wasn't thinking much about food just yet. Instead, he watched guests congregate and fill their plates from his seat at the varnished oak bar just outside the massive room – a large rectangular setup staffed by two barkeeps. To his right a little ways was the private room from which the happy couple would emerge around seven, followed by speeches and dinner.

But for now all Jack cared about was the drinks. A tumbler of Jameson in hand to get things started, he was an almost perfectly satisfied man (even though his drink was on the rocks, a minor annoyance soon to be forgotten). Later, he and J.D. would have a long discussion about that, and it wouldn't matter then if there were ice cubes or flies in his drink.

Can't believe the open bar lasts until ten. Boy, did this turn out to be a good idea. Better take it slow, though. Don't want Oscar carrying you out of here.

After finishing his drink, Jack decided he'd be well-served to get a little socializing done. This was a wedding, after all, and it seemed only fair that he should meet the people who were paying for his liquor and meal. Maybe he'd even say hello to the ugly bride later if he got the chance, wishing her and the groom a happy few weeks of marriage and pretending it wasn't the guy's third ride on the ferris wheel, the view

from the top only useful for scouting out the next woman to wear white.

Sensing a familiar flutter of comfort in his gut, smiling at the thought of getting back to the bar, Jack accepted some of that garlic bread and a bowl of steaming clam chowder. He would've gotten more food, but he didn't want a repeat of last night; he needed to save room for good conversation (not with the wedding guests but J.D.).

"Jack, there you are. We're all sitting at the same table, should be a fine time."

Jack looked over his shoulder and found Oscar, a champagne flute in hand. The sight of barely consumed golden liquid sent a little urge spiraling through Jack's heart – an urge to snatch the flute away from Oscar and down his drink.

"Oh, good," Jack said. "I was wondering where you guys were at. There's more people in here than a damn airport."

Oscar led him to a table near the windowed wall, where Henry and Charlie and a few of the other guys and their wives were eating. Larry Ramo, a three-hundred-pounder who owned a country club of his own back home, was going to town on a stack of chicken wings, his shirtsleeves pulled up and pudgy fingers crusted with crumbs and grease. Larry always brought shopping bags full of chips and cookies and other treats to their chess club meetings, munching and crunching as his opponent studied the board and tried to concentrate, the pieces inevitably smeared orange with Dorito dust or brown with chocolate remnants. He was a good guy, Larry, but he sure did eat a lot, and Jack couldn't help but think his winter would be everybody else's autumn.

Does Larry ever stop eating? I don't think I've seen him once without food.

Maybe forty minutes later the string quartet packed up and the DJ announced that – could it really be true? – cocktail hour had arrived.

What? How is that possible?
Everyone at the table was looking at each other with rumpled eyebrows and shrugging shoulders, everyone except Larry, who was devouring a bowl of meatballs. Finally Oscar asked the collective question.

"I thought this *was* the cocktail hour," the others nodding in agreement.

But then the DJ was speaking again, reading from a paper and describing the cocktail hour offerings. There would be – *Holy Shit!* – lobster claws and tails, chicken marsala, pasta, steak tips, and much more…so much food that even Larry's eyes were widening with uncertainty.

Shit, what if he can't fit back through the door?

"Lobster claws!" Oscar declared. "And pasta! Jesus, what do they have on the dinner menu if this is the cocktail hour?"

Impeccably timed, Curt Miller, father of the groom, was approaching their table with a wry smile. "I wasn't lying about this reception, people," he said, rubbing his hands together. "We won't need to eat for a week."

"I'll say," Oscar nodded. "I feel like I should have skipped dinner last night, for crying out loud."

Buffet stations were being arranged now at the edges of the room, countless innocent lobsters having been sacrificed for one wedding –

What a shame. That's life, though, right? – and Jack snuck back to the bar for a quick pop while the others were in line. It was the perfect moment to greet good old J.D., as thoughts about Peter had just begun to creep into Jack's head at the idea of the poor lobsters dying so unfairly. Such considerations of the randomness and senselessness of death always got the guilt churning and burning in his heart, memories pumping through his veins – memories of a little boy who'd died on the road in his snug suit, the hot sun beating down, "Interstate Love Song" playing on the radio, and then what? Surely the clock hadn't stopped at that moment. Time just kept marching forward, uncaring.

What song came on after Peter was gone? So much blood...and his little shoe. How did his shoe fly that far away?

Seated at the bar again, Jack gulped down his drink with little twitches of distaste. J.D. on the rocks was an undeniably different J.D., like seeing an old friend who's shaved off his longtime beard or inexplicably dyed his hair blue. This J.D. on the rocks was spurious and unfriendly – he didn't give Jack peace on the way down but instead even stranger thoughts than the ones that had driven him to the bar.

I wonder who ended up cleaning the blood off Peter's face...what a job that would be.

Jack set the ice-filled tumbler down hard on the bar, wanting to get the barkeep's attention. But the guy was taking a woman's order, oblivious to Jack glaring at him.

I said minimal rocks, you idiot. How long have you been doing this?

Jack bit his lip.

And what kind of open bar has an ice requirement for drinks? Fucking idiots.

Snuffling bitterly and shaking his head, Jack trudged back to the table and proceeded to sit through a long stretch of boring conversation, nearly falling asleep when the newlyweds and their party were stiffly introduced and the speeches progressed from tearful father of the bride to pitifully unfunny and awkward brother of the groom, all while Larry slowed but did not cease his daunting endeavor, persisting through his plate of lobster parts like a fatiguing runner who refuses to pull out of the marathon.

You're done, Larry. It's not even dinner yet. Just save some room, guy – you're making me sick.

The conversation eventually turned to chess, and Jack knew it was time to get back to the bar for a few more drinks before the real dinner. The men were discussing famous games, their wives departing in favor of other tables with similarly bored ladies. Even Jack couldn't get into the chatter about Anderssen vs. Lionel and Byrne vs. Fischer; his head was getting a little swimmy, his heart craving J.D.'s embrace (the real J.D., not the damn fake).

But he knew he couldn't just stand up and leave now. What would the others think?

A few of them will watch where I go. Probably Oscar. Yes, definitely Oscar. He'll watch me go to the bar – he'll learn the truth and tell Robert. They'll put me in a fucking home.

Jack somehow survived the remainder of cocktail hour without absconding, and then it was finally time for dinner selections, a waiter handing out menus that described entrees fit for far more sophisticated people than those gathered around this table. There was roasted duck served in plum sauce, smoked salmon gateau, bacon-wrapped filets – and Larry was looking plain overwhelmed.

He's like a kid who wants every flavor of ice cream. Or a dog who's found the kibble bag – he can't stop himself.

After ordering dinner – despite not wanting to eat much more, Jack had reluctantly settled on chicken cordon bleu – he excused himself to the restroom. Just in case anyone was watching him, he slipped into the men's room for a few moments and then doubled back to the bar, choosing to sit on the other side this time, where it would be difficult for anyone at his table to spot him with a sweeping look across the hall and into the next room. Relaxing, he ordered a J.D. from barkeep number two, and this time the ice was minimal.

But Jack didn't lift his drink, at least not right away. Scanning the crowd just seconds before the drink's arrival, he thought – no, he was almost positive – that Peter was standing in the far left corner of the hall, visible only briefly before the shuffle of guests swallowed him.

And Peter was staring straight at Jack through the maze of people, grinning again.

Chapter XI

Jack searched the banquet hall extensively, but Peter didn't reappear in his handsome, bloodstained suit, his blonde hair matted permanently red in Jack's mind, his little black-socked foot absent a shoe, a boy who would never grow up and, therefore, an image that would never change for Jack because he'd struck and killed this boy, killed him on a bright, sunny day – and all Peter had wanted was to cross the street and let the cops know his friend was in trouble.

Jack drained his tumbler of J.D. and asked for a refresh.

Damn you, Barfield and Brickley, and the train, too. And that stupid Tanner What's-his-face. If he hadn't been so weak, Peter would be alive.

And where are you now, Tanner, you little–?

A hand came down on Jack's shoulder, causing him to lurch in horror, because, without seeing its owner, that hand surely belonged to Peter Elliott. It was the cold, condemning hand of a boy whose book had been but six chapters long, morning never again to welcome him because he was dead, morning never again to welcome his father because time only moved one way but not nearly fast enough.

Jack let out a bursting exhalation when he saw Oscar Montoya. Thankfully, there was nothing accusatory in Oscar's eyes, no suspicious gleams or prying twinkles. "Ah, I see you've found the good spot," he said, and took a seat beside Jack.

As if there were eyes peeking out from the back of the barkeep's skull, he spun around and came quickly in their direction. "Can I get you something, sir?"

"Sure, son," Oscar said. "I'll have a scotch, double, on the rocks." He turned to Jack. "You'll never guess what I just heard. They're gonna have a damn dessert and breakfast buffet after dinner!"

Jack's eyes widened with incredulity. "Breakfast? How much do they think these people can take? Someone better get a few ambulances on standby."

Laughing, Oscar clapped a hand against the bar. "It's unbelievable, isn't it? How would you like your eggs after chicken wings and duck? Christ, they're gonna run out of toilet paper before they run out of food. Even Larry's getting full."

Jack broke into uncontrollable laughter. "I wonder how pancakes sit on top of wings and duck," and now there were tears in his eyes. "Did you see Larry…he was looking at the menu and–"

"It was too much food for him. I thought he was gonna cry," Oscar said between laughs, and soon neither of them could continue, a pair of friends slapping their thighs and rocking and straining their stomachs – and in that moment Jack remembered how great life could be. He hadn't felt this way in a long time, hadn't laughed this hard in years. It helped that he was half-drunk, but he was having fun, taking in the comedies life threw his way and savoring them. Cheers to old friends and new ones.

"Wings and duck and bacon and cakes," Oscar finally said, shaking his head and then exploding into laughter again. "What's next, are they gonna roll out the lunch menu at midnight? Maybe we can all have cold cuts and french fries."

"Don't forget the appetizers," Jack said. "Mozzarella sticks and nachos and popcorn – we wouldn't want anyone to go home hungry."

People were looking at them now. Jack could sense them staring and commenting, but he didn't care. This was so much fun, he didn't even need another drink.

278

Oscar sipped his scotch, still not fully recovered from the laughing spree. "Ah, good times, pal," he said after a deep sigh. "This'll be the talk of chess club for months."

Later, when Jack was much deeper in the well and the light of the day had dripped away and the inhabitants of the portraits were starting to seem like they were moving just a little, it was time for the dessert and breakfast buffet, the weary DJ announced in between sets of crazed dance music, another sheet of paper in hand. This latest extravagance would be held in the adjoining Chamberlain Room, and for the guests who somehow hadn't been bloated by the first three rounds of food, breakfast would include all of the usual staples, as well as blueberry waffles and cinnamon muffins and doughnuts. For those seeking dessert, they were offering raspberry scones, fudge brownies, carrot cake, cherry cheesecake, and pretty much every type of specialty coffee you could imagine. At these announcements there were bursts of laughter and boisterous commentaries erupting throughout the room, as well as a great deal of murmuring.

You definitely weren't lying about this reception, Curt.

With some difficulty Jack returned from the bar to his seat. Old age wasn't good for much, but at least it provided a perfectly good excuse for wobbling around a crowded room. Observers of his unsteady motion would sooner assume he suffered from arthritis than peg him as a drunk who'd taken full advantage of the open bar. They would probably think, Wow, that poor old guy should have a cane, a thought that gave Jack a quick laugh as he settled into his seat.

The others looked tired – *tired of eating* – their once bright, eager faces having dimmed. Most of them had gone dancing between dinner and breakfast/dessert, time Jack had spent more productively with J.D. Some had gone outside for a needed walk. Larry, astonishingly, was still eating, just as Jack had left him almost an hour ago.

Henry and his wife were gathering their things. "That's enough food for one night," the veterinarian said, sliding back into his jacket. "We really should get home – I've got a long day tomorrow."

There were handshakes and goodbyes, and then they were gone, Oscar checking his golden pocket watch. "What do you say, Jack, should we head out, too?" He was looking concernedly at Jack, or at least Jack perceived his expression as one of concern.

Oscar had departed the bar after only one scotch, leaving Jack to his old friend, time slipping into its unavoidable vortex, the same one that had consumed so many nights back home. He and J.D. had spent hours together on those nights, and then it had always been morning, the grandfather clock chiming the arrival of an unknown time when its nighttime silent mode expired.

Jack shrugged, feigning indifference. "You're the driver. You lead. I follow." He focused on each word, trying not to slur them. A few more drinks and it would be inescapable, as would the gradual decline of his vision. J.D. hadn't used to affect him like that, but no man could outrun his age, not with time moving relentlessly in one direction.

Oscar can't know the truth. He has to think this is a one-time thing. Everyone drinks at weddings.

Oscar checked his watch again. Looked at Jack. Studied him. "I suppose we'll stay a few more minutes." But then he said it, the dagger. "Would you like me to grab you a coffee, maybe some tea?"

Jack blinked stupidly, feeling like a slingshot pebble had just struck him square on the nose. "No…no thanks," he said, looking away from Oscar and watching the dancing frenzy.

Drunken young people were bashing into each other like bumper cars and endlessly chanting, "Table Nine, Table Nine," to acknowledge a rowdy bunch that easily eclipsed the rest. They were good people for a wedding celebration, that Table Nine – fun people – Jack thought, but he himself wasn't much for fun anymore and that made him sad.

He knows it. Cat's out of the damn bag. Way to go, Jack, you just screwed everything up. They're gonna put you in a home for sure now.

Jack stood and turned away from his friend. Gritting his teeth, rubbing his chin, craving another drink, he stared out at the dance floor, tuning the world out, a slow fade, but before it was fully gone, before the blissful half-drunken reveries stepped forth, before he could glance absently again at the portraits in which things seemed to shift and sway, he noticed a small, lonely black shoe in the middle of the marble floor. A boy's shoe. Unaware of the tripping hazard, the raving dancers hopped and angled around it, one lady seeming to step on it but failing to notice its presence.

Jack strained his eyes, took a few steps closer. *Is it really there?*

Yes, yes, it was there, a little black dress shoe, and it remained there, though no one stumbled over it. The music stopped, then a new song, an even faster song, but lifting wickedly above it was a whispered voice, one Jack knew only he could hear.

A child's voice.

"It's coming for you, Jack."

Jack searched the room frantically, not even knowing what he was looking for, trapped in a private hell beyond the detection of others – and his isolation in this terror frightened him madly, his body shuddering with nameless needs. The portraits, he dared not look at them, but yes, of course, the movement within was more pronounced now, fog rolling up to…was that a house…and what lurked there in the middle, twitching, sidling, gliding?

Jack concentrated on the portrait. Now all was still, not a house, just a mountainside lodge and a fog-cloaked lake. Nothing dark and amorphous in the middle anymore.

Need a drink. Another drink!

Jack managed only a few steps toward the bar, for now the little shoe was ten feet in front of him, puddled in blood that fanned slowly outward.

Part VI: Night

Chapter I

I'm insane, Jack thought on the way home. *Completely insane, gone off the deep end.*

How can I trust myself?

How will I live?

The night roads were quiet, sprinkled here and there with headlights but mostly left to the broad splash of moonlight. They were headed toward the highway, winding through pastures and farmland, Oscar speaking to his wife on his cell phone and driving slowly. His wife hadn't been feeling well enough for the festivities earlier, but now it was Jack whose stomach turned. The night should have come out on the better side of decent, though; even if J.D. hadn't been nearly as likable on the rocks, he should have sufficed.

Yet here Jack sat in Oscar's car, lightheaded, a water bottle clutched and crinkled tightly in hand, staring up at the moon and suffering a greater loneliness and hopelessness than he'd ever known, a massive void that overcame him. He felt as if he were trapped on a desolate island with no way out, not even a little canoe made of bamboo or a pack of chewing gum to patch up holes or two wimpy oars to assist him in steering a suicidal course through the onrushing waves. He didn't even have any food on this wretched island, and his clothes were soaked and torn, and the darkness was unleashing its wrath, and there were *things* in the interior woods that came creeping out with each morning fog, shadows that cast even taller shadows.

What if J.D. can't stop the guilt anymore?

The voice said it's coming for me. It even said my name.

What's coming for me? Peter's ghost? Has he come to finish me?

My grandfather's curse?

The magician! What did he see that day?

A while later, looking up at the moon once more…*Don't wanna go back to that house. Anywhere but there.*

Shivering, Jack rubbed his tired eyes. He wished he could shut off his brain and enter a blessed state of hibernation.

This is all too much. I'm sick, very sick, and these thoughts came to him with panicked dread because he saw no viable escape, only doors through which greater agonies lied and grinning evils waited. Doctors and family members and friends could try to help him, but he knew he was alone with this thing, truly alone. At the end of the day, when they all went home to be with their families, when the dusk became the dark, his guilt would find him anywhere, and with it would come the hallucinations, apparently made worse by the alcohol.

What will I do? What will happen to me?

Jack could medicate, of course, a popular combatant to guilt and grief, but then he'd probably turn into an obliviously numb old drip who stared agape at the retirement home TV all day, or a hyperactive nut who blabbered about the highlights of the 1956 World Series and the good old days when gas was thirty cents a gallon and his chess openings were even more rushed and thoughtless than his first time in bed. And with the wrong mix of medications, they might have to speak to him slowly and repeat things in his good ear – and even J.D. couldn't help him then because they didn't let you drink alcohol with half of those medications.

But what good are they if you can't swallow 'em down with whiskey?

Jack pictured the endless tests and syringes and nurses squeezing his arm with a blood pressure cuff. He pictured doctors with their lab coats and stethoscopes, telling him to inhale and exhale…again, please…again…again…very good, one more time now…on a scale of one to ten, how bad is the pain – but what kind of life was that? And why would he want to prolong his life when, tonight, drunk beneath the moon in Oscar's car, death appealed to him with unprecedented vigor.

Nothing. No more guilt, no more hallucinations. It could all be over, just like that. Nothing. Don't wanna go back to that house. No more memories, no more Peter in my head, nothing.

Nothing.

Jack closed his eyes, smiling at the thought.

Chapter II

Rob awoke with pestering worries a little after two the next morning. He'd been lying somnolently in bed for a time, hoping Dad would call, and then, in spite of his anxiety, he'd nodded off.

Rob grabbed his phone from the nightstand, desperate to see a message. Nothing.

"Did he call?" his wife murmured, half-asleep.

Rob tiredly scrolled through the old received calls, his eyes flashing over the numbers but not reading them. "Nope, nothing."

Rolling onto her side, she said, "He probably got home late from the wedding and fell asleep."

"Yeah, probably," he muttered, setting the phone on the stand.

A return to sleep, Rob realized, would be difficult to achieve, his worries having multiplied. Instead he lied there in the darkness, wondering if Dad had made it home okay.

***

Jack wasn't met by the usual frenzy of barks when he returned home, Oscar's car looping around the driveway circle and heading back the way it had come. There was nothing but the softly clanging wind chimes, not a single sound from within the house.

Fearing for his dog, who always put on a dazzling welcome-home display of noise, Jack staggered up the steps and into the house, fumbling for the light switches, half-expecting intruding forms to be chased away along with the darkness.

The house was quiet, far too quiet. Even the clock's ticking seemed softer than usual.

"Night, where are you, girl? Dad's home."

No sign of her.

"Night, come on – do you want a bone, old girl?"

Nothing, Jack left alone in the living room to sort through the possibilities.

Did I leave her in the back yard? No, I definitely gave her a bone in the living room before leaving.

Maybe she heard thunder and got scared.

"Night, where are you, girl?" Beginning to panic, Jack stumbled through the living room, checking behind the TV cabinet and the sofa, then moving on to the dining room and kitchen.

His stomach was aching again, and he just wanted to collapse on the bed, but where was Night, his only friend out here in the woods?

Jack jogged clumsily down the hallway, bumping into the credenza and knocking a lamp to the floor, colorful glass smashing, Jack's heart plummeting.

Shit, shit, shit! Dammit, no! Mary loved that lamp!

Jack was too worried to pick up the pieces right away. Into the bedroom, where Night was surely hiding. He searched the closet and the bathroom, bent down and looked beneath the bed, but she wasn't there.

"Night, come!" he shouted, anger joining his fear. "Come on, now!"

Next was the guest bedroom. She must be hiding in that closet, he assumed, but to Jack's astonishment there was nothing but boxes in there.

Finally, in the study, he found Night cowering in a corner, ensconced between two large cardboard boxes and a plastic bin. She looked up at Jack and wagged her tail, but she was shaking.

Jack, flooded with relief, kneeled and scratched her beneath the collar, ignoring the pain in his knees.

"Thank God you're all right, girl," he said, then realized what he'd said. But how could he have said that? He only uttered that word as a mindless reaction to anger or frustration because God didn't exist in his world.

I must be drunker than I think. Very, very drunk.

Jack whirled around, convinced he'd felt something just now, something watching him from the doorway. There hadn't been a sound to make him suspicious, just a strange instinct.

Very drunk.

"Come on, girl, time for your night-night walk," and he could only imagine what his words sounded like to his four-legged pal. Oscar had told him to sleep it off and call him in the morning – that could only mean one thing.

He knows. He really knows. The gig's up.

Chapter III

Jack spent better than a month in relative peace. The evenings came with stormy fears, but J.D. was always there to quell them, working in tandem with Night, who barked every fear down to the basement with her increasingly routine sessions, each one culminating with a stalemate between dog and workbench.

Jack had found it prudent to get family calls over with as early as possible. That way, if he swam a little too deep down the well one night, he wouldn't wake up to ten messages. He'd also discovered it was wise to bring his thermos to each chess club meeting; you never knew what kinds of thoughts those guys could get stirred up, and Jack wouldn't be attending any more weddings.

In the weeks following "the wedding", Jack had assured himself that the false J.D. had been responsible for Peter's image at the reception, as well as that of his little shoe swimming in blood-pooled marble, a hallucination whose awfulness had been matched by its vividness. Jack had feared being carted off to the nearest mental asylum that night, feared it even as he closed his eyes in bed, but momentum had swung back the other way and now things were stable.

But for how long?

The nights were getting cooler now, dusk seeming to gallop away in such a hurry, unlike summer, when light bled from the sky so slowly that you could still pick out little traces of color well after nine o'clock. But now Jack had to get himself geared up much earlier for impending darkness, the difference between twilight and full dark barely a few breaths, it seemed.

It helped to greet J.D. around sunset and get a little conversation in while the clouds were edged in orange and eventually pink; while the drivers well beyond the woods were switching on their headlights;

while the tallest trees were still squinting in the golden glare of westward light.

Way up on a mountain somewhere, with a clear view to the west, some lucky guy or gal might be basking in the late evening glow. But down here in the middle of the woods, the sun had long since dipped beneath the trees, Jack finishing a project in the garage, a bottle of J.D. on the dusty windowsill, deep shade overspreading the lawn.

Slowly, methodically, doggedly, Jack had glued Mary's lamp back together over the past month-plus, the one he'd knocked off the credenza and smashed the night of the wedding. It had taken him weeks to sort through all of the shards, figure out how they went together, and begin gluing them back into form, but Jack had mostly relished the leisurely process, like fitting together puzzle pieces and joyfully beholding the completed image. At times, he'd thought of the enslaved foreign children he'd seen in programs and movies over the years, the ones who are compelled to spend their days piecing together shredded documents, one letter, one word, one sentence at a time, until they can provide their oppressors with valuable information and earn their meager meals. On other occasions he'd thought of luckless fishermen

who wake up earlier than anyone else and buy the most expensive equipment available, only to catch nothing. A handful of times, when the stupid little glass segments were slanting or sliding out of place or otherwise discordant, Jack had considered giving up.

Overall, though, he had enjoyed the undertaking.

"Ta-da!" Jack exclaimed after clamping the last piece to the metal frame, knowing Mary would be pleased by his dedication. She would embrace him and commend his hard work, then bring her lamp back to the house and return it to the credenza; or perhaps she'd select a new place for it, a better place.

BURN, DO NOT READ!

She bought that lamp at the town fair, remember it like it was yesterday. We tried those ridiculous hamburger doughnut things, absolutely terrible.

Smiling, Jack took a triumphant pop of whiskey and folded his arms across his tattered sweatshirt. He'd been working on a beard lately; Oscar claimed it made him look like a skinny Santa Claus, but at least it was something different, a way to break the stagnation.

Mary loved going to the fair. Didn't matter which one, as long as it had a ferris wheel.

For a while Jack stared at the sticky – in places, oozing – resurrection of the shattered lamp. It didn't matter to him that the thing was a mess – what mattered was that he'd destroyed something and brought it back to life, such an important victory for a man in his condition, and now he could insert a new trio of bulbs into its candelabra-style holders.

It will light again.

He shook his head, still staring at the lamp, not quite sure this was happening. He'd fixed it, every last piece back in place (if not its original place, then at least an alternately suitable location).

I fixed it, brought it back.

Vibrations. Ringing.

Jack's cell phone was going to town in his pocket. "Who could that be?" he asked Night through the open garage doors.

The dog was licking her forepaws on the grass just beyond the garage, her tail wagging when Jack addressed her. It was quickly getting darker, the crickets chirping, the birds piping up their evening calls. Unlike past times, it was a nice, quiet, relaxing hour, the sort of hour this house was meant for, Jack thought, the sort of hour the builders might have envisioned when they'd put the boards in place and gazed up at the trees, not nearly as tall then.

Jack checked his cell phone's screen, where an unfamiliar number was flashing.

"Hello?"

"Hey, Grandpa, it's Jon. Just wanted to check in and see how you're doing. Sorry I haven't called in a while – things have been crazy with the paper."

"Jon, so nice to hear from you. I'm good, real good, pal." Jack tidied up the work table, putting the bottle of glue and spare clamps in their places. "Tell me, did you get a new phone or something?"

"No, why?"

"Oh, okay, I just didn't recognize your number. Don't have my glasses on." Except Jack did have his glasses on – he never would have been able to see the little glass pieces without them.

"Grandpa, are you sure you don't want me and Stevie to fly out there for a few days?" Jon said a while later, a question Stevie had posed yet again last week, and Jack knew he had to cut the pesky weed down once more.

"No need, not when I'm coming for Thanksgiving," he assured, shaking his head at his grandchildren's insistence. "You boys save your money – you work too hard to be blowing it on flights."

"But we miss you, Grandpa. We still haven't even seen your house."

Jack waved a hand. "It' just a house like any other, no big deal, a little one-story thing in the woods. Believe me, you'd see it and want to go home." *House of tricks.* He laughed nervously at that thought, wanting very badly to change the subject.

Can't have them out here, certainly not now. They'd talk to Oscar, and Oscar would spill the beans.

Morning does not welcome–

"It really wouldn't be that big a deal," Jon persisted. "Are you sure you don't–?"

"Positive. I'll see you boys in two months. No need to take off time from work to fly out here. That'd be foolishness. And don't go letting that little Stevie make you think I'm lonely – I've got plenty of boring old friends out here. We play chess all the time and bore the living daylights out of people."

When the phone was back in Jack's pocket, he seized the lamp by its stem, then remembered that the glue might not be fully dry.

Can't risk a piece coming loose. I'll give it a few hours, and he reluctantly closed the garage doors and snapped his fingers for Night to follow, his dog dutifully springing up from the grass and trailing him inside. The wind chimes were still tonight, even with the cool nudges that soothed the skin and reminded Jack of a comfortable bed with an extra blanket – and a few more glasses of J.D. to mark the end of another good day.

Things aren't so bad now. I just had to get my head on straight, that's all, had to nip that guilt in the bud. Couldn't let one bad night with that fake J.D. get to me.

See what happens when you trust the system, kid.

They were barely inside the house five minutes when Night began barking.

Chapter IV

Jack was jarred from sleep just before sunrise, Night once again standing on his back and unleashing fury. She didn't stay there long, hopping lightly down and scratching the door, her barks giving way to insistent little whines. Jack, groggy and bleary, felt like a dazed wasp on a cold autumn night.

There was a moment's panic, Jack's fear absolute, but soon his thoughts were rational, the strands of sleep torn away.

"You need to go out, girl?" He fumbled for the bedside lamp, finally managed to switch it on.

Night was watching him from the door, her tail offering a handful of tentative swishes. She barked once, then resumed scratching the door.

"Okay, okay, I'll let you out."

Somewhat dizzily, Jack slid into his slippers and padded down the hall after Night, realizing on his way past the credenza that he'd forgotten Mary's lamp in the garage.

Tomorrow, he thought, but then he stopped, jerked his head to the left.

What was that?

Forgetting Night, who'd dashed to the dining room door, Jack inched closer to the basement door. There it was again, that faint voice coming from below.

No, it can't be. It's in your head. It's not real, just forget it.

Still, he opened the door, wondering, but downstairs there was only darkness, silence. He flicked on the stairwell light, and now Night was beside him again, impatiently whimpering. "Hold on," he whispered, tilting an ear toward the stairwell, as if that would do anything.

The basement remained quiet, Jack thinking only for a moment he heard a distant creaking down there.

It's all in your head. Let the dog out already!

Looking down the stairs, feeling grim and heavy, Jack thought of Mrs. Scrivens and how she'd hanged herself here one dark, perhaps foggy night. She'd had enough of whatever was ailing her and decided to end her life, but why? Had she, too, heard voices in this house?

I should look. I have to make sure–

No, it's in your head! Forget it! Just let the damn dog out and go to bed!

Jack was tingling at the neck and arms, still staring down into the basement, and only at Night's continued whining did he force himself into the living room, where the clock was ticking without interest, concerned only with marking each passing second, another second that could never be redone or had back.

Hidden in fog and darkness, the woods were like a bottomless sea – unknowably deep – Jack left with his thoughts on the back deck island. Night had ventured stealthily into the woods, and she was probably at the farthest reaches of the fence line by now, chasing scents and zigzagging through the trees. Jack wished she would come inside. He was cold and tired and fraught with terrible burdens, forced to address another auditory hallucination.

For it hadn't been a stranger's voice he'd thought he heard. It had been Mary's voice rising up to him.

The basement is a very bad place.

House of tricks.

Shivering, Jack hugged himself and then blew into his fists, trying not to acknowledge the wholeness of the predawn dark. On mornings like this, winter seemed a week away, darkness always blackest – heaviest – in times of fog, but then the autumn warmth would fill the day with promise.

The sun'll come up soon. Very soon. I'll have my whiskey early if needed.

Your curse won't be mine, Grandpa!

Jack could hear Night bounding crisply through the woods, her movements betrayed by the sweep of distant leaves. There were no coyotes howling this morning, the only accompaniment for the crickets that of an owl hooting blandly in the depths of the woods, where…

…A man got lost and died out there. He lived in this house.

A house of tricks.

Night eventually tired of scent-hunting and trotted into the house, stopping briefly at her bowl for water and a few licks of dinner's remains before heading back to Jack's room. The clock, dark and dignified in the corner, served its continual reminders, never fatiguing or forgetting, each second recorded and announced. Soon its hourly greetings would return, another night complete.

It'll be ticking long after I'm dead. It won't care, the damn thing.

Jack came to the hallway, his eyes cast sidelong upon the basement door, his ears fixed upon the clock's whispers. He walked very slowly toward his room, delaying so that he might have a chance to hear Mary's voice again, a part of him craving the hallucination because his wife was gone and her voice sounded terribly real and he only had so many years left, himself. Then he'd be gone, too, and there'd be no more memories of them together, time only moving one way.

Time runs out for everyone.

Jack stopped a little ways past the basement door, then returned and pressed his ear against it. He knew he was acting crazily again and didn't care. A drink of water, he decided, would give him a few extra moments to hear her voice again, if it had ever been there, but what if Mary's voice didn't come? What would he do then? The thought disturbed him even more than that of hallucinations.

How can I keep going without Mary?

A glass of water in hand, he went back to the basement door.

And opened it. Listened for a while. Thought at length about Mrs. Scrivens and what could have gone so horribly awry. Still faceless in his mind, he imagined how her eyes might have looked in those final moments; the sounds that had stormed through the basement as her body wrenched and twisted; the panic and fear of one last realization.

I wonder who cut her down from the rafters. The smell, it must've been awful.

There was a noise just then, a little sliver of sound squirming up from the basement, scarcely a creak but…something. Gripping the handrail, Jack descended the staircase halfway, hyper-aware of every component of this absurd hour – the distantly ticking clock, the soft groans of stair treads beneath his shifting weight, the clatters of his restive heart.

There's something down there, I know it, he thought with tingles returning to his neck. His chest felt as if it had been zapped with bursts of electricity.

People have died in this house, and there's something down there. I'm not crazy. There really is something down there!

Night barked from the bedroom, and suddenly, breathlessly, there it was again – Mary's voice, as thin as silk, a gossamer voice no higher

than a whisper, emanating, it seemed, from a place very, very far away, a place where the sun didn't shine and even the clocks didn't tick, not the basement but somewhere farther, too far, frighteningly far.

"Help me, Jack. Help me."

Jack blundered down the remaining stairs, tripping on the penultimate tread and careening around the corner…and now he was facing the workbench, hearing Mary's voice again. It was louder – coming from behind the bench? – a voice with volume and strength.

"Help me, Jack. Help me. I need you, Jack. You're the strongest person I know."

But there was something about the voice Jack despised. It was wheedling and deplorable, a voice that coaxed spuriously in his head.

It's not real. She's dead. It's not her voice. It can't be!

Jack was backing away, but the voice grew louder, more desperate.

"Help me, Jackie! Help me!"

Another sound behind him, thudding heavily down the stairs. Jack whirled around to find a shadow bustling toward him. Night. She pulled up beside Jack with a growl, her attention fixed upon the workbench.

"Help me, Jackie!" Mary shouted, and Jack watched his dog, trying to tell if she could hear it, too. The voice was so loud – how could she not hear it?

Night remained still, her face set and angry.

298

Jack, stupefied, came to the bench and groped at its contents – ratchets, wrenches, hammers, boxes of nails, a ruler, a measuring tape, a tire iron from another decade – until finally he clutched with shaking hands a flashlight he'd forgotten down here one of those times Night had torn

into the basement. Its light was weak but sufficient, Jack shining it below the workbench with frantic sweeps, then spreading it over the

shelves of boxes and tools. There were shadows leaping and cavorting in the little interstices between items, but Jack feared they weren't all harmless; surely something sinister lurked among the ludic creations of a dim flashlight.

Something's in there. It's been there all along. It's causing all of this.

Jack went down to a knee, spraying the light over the same boxes at a different angle, then beaming it slowly across the wall behind the bench. Night stayed quiet, watching Jack with worried anticipation.

"What am I doing?" he muttered after a while, trying to work himself through the madness. He knew his mind was like a flickering light bulb and that he should return to bed, but something deep and abstruse kept him at it, waving his flashlight and studying the shadows, at times zipping the light back to a previous destination because he thought he'd seen something.

Finally the upheaval passed – *I'm literally chasing shadows* – and the flashlight went still in his hand. He was kneeling, the light fixed upon the wall past the workbench, and if he hadn't been looking from that precise angle, he never would have noticed the crumbling concrete just beyond one of the rear vertical supports for the bench. The support and the wall itself were mere inches apart, rendering the damage to the concrete nearly invisible without a light source.

But a closer look revealed not only crumbling concrete but thin cracks running the length of the wall. Years earlier, he might have overlooked them as water damage during a more thorough review of the wall, or maybe he hadn't noticed them before. He couldn't remember.

With a hammer Jack reached through the workbench shelves and began striking the concrete at the weak points, several chunks easily breaking free and landing on the floor with delicate clinks. Inspired, he whacked

the wall with greater force and quickly opened up a fist-size hole, then a cabbage-size hole – and Mary's voice was whispering through it.

Yes, yes, it's coming from in there! I found it!

"Help me, Jackie."

Then, like a tsunami of sound, her screams sent Jack sprawling backward.

"HELP ME, JACKIE!!!"

Beside him Night snarled and barked, keeping her distance from the opening. Jack, feverish with desperation, ripped the bench free of its anchors with surprising strength, forming a large enough gap for him to work in, boxes and tools sliding and spilling onto the floor. He wondered even as the frenzied crash endured if he'd completely lost it, the ball of yarn in his head fully unraveled, but he didn't care.

I'll rip this place apart until the voices stop!

Jack took up a sledgehammer from the far corner and stumbled over the mess to the wall, where he swung wildly at the little hole he'd made. In seconds it expanded to the size of a basketball, chunks of concrete hurtling through the dusty air, and then, with a sound that reminded Jack of downed bowling pins, the whole section of compromised wall collapsed in on itself, uncovering a two-foot recess.

Within that alcove was a black wooden door nailed frenetically shut, and behind the thin door rose a swift and steady pounding.

300

The door rattled in its frame. Then silence.

Night stopped barking, came to the door, sniffed interestedly, then growled. After a while she receded, but Jack didn't move, staring disbelievingly at the door and thinking, thinking, thinking.

People died in this house, and now Mary's calling. She's calling for help, but she can't be. Mary's dead. How can she be calling?
He flattened a hand against the cold door, felt a little jostling bump from the other side, but now he was getting dizzy, too dizzy, his vision

going blurry. He staggered, tried to keep his balance, Night's latest barks sounding as distant as the howls of coyotes in the foggy forest.

His chest hurt. His legs trembled. His breaths became labored. The sledgehammer fell to the floor.

Music.

Somewhere there was music, but it wasn't a random song. "No, please, no!" Jack cried with abject realization, falling to his knees, but still he heard it, heard it and suddenly knew. All this time he'd been thinking yet thoughtless, seeing yet sightless, oblivious to that which had always been there.

The house.

A house of tricks.

Upstairs, from the radio, the volume turned up high, came the easy, fluid opening to "Interstate Love Song."

Chapter V

Jack awoke disoriented, unable to tell if it had all been a nightmare.

"No," he whispered, sitting up and glimpsing the open door.

He really had torn out the nails and–

With broadening panic he became aware of what flanked him – two empty bottles of Jack Daniels.

***

Stephen Gibson's gaze roamed across the shady late morning lawn to the manor hall, a decidedly dreary old building that had been repurposed years ago to accommodate the admissions offices. To his right, the sprawling facility that housed the gymnasium, arena, and natatorium gleamed brightly with its golden dome and facade of dark reflective glass. Millions of dollars had gone into that building, and today Steve's latest gift to the school would help fund the construction of a new dormitory hall. Maybe they would name one of these structures after him one day, he pondered (Gibson Hall – it had a nice ring to it).

"As I mentioned on the phone," said Headmaster Melvin Bishop, "your son has returned this semester a different boy. He's only had two tardies in as many months, and not a single transgression otherwise. What's your secret, Senator – ah, Steve – how on earth did you manage it?"

They'd been ambling about the campus center, discussing Steve's generous contribution and the dinner they would attend with the trustees that night. Steve couldn't seem to stay focused, though, his mind wandering mischievously back to last night, specifically a foxy little thing named Jessie. Jackie? No, it had been Jessie. Hadn't it?

Anyway, the wrath of marriage had become a lot easier for Steve to endure when the girls kept him young at heart.

"It wasn't a big deal," Steve said with a dismissive wave. "When you work in Washington, you become a specialist in getting stubborn punks to do what you want."

The headmaster laughed a little uneasily, his seemingly endless chatter finally taking a momentary break, long enough for Steve to check his latest text messages. One of them was from Rob – it had come in around eleven o'clock.

Call me when you can. I'd like to talk about flying to see dad sometime.

Steve rolled his eyes. Another idiotic idea from his brother. Visiting Dad's house was pointless; eventually, hopefully very soon, Dad would be leaving that place and returning east, where he could be monitored and kept under control. If Steve was serious about a presidential bid, Dad was a loose end that needed to be quickly tied. Steve certainly couldn't afford another dead kid in the road, his father behind the wheel.

No need, Steve texted back. *Dad's coming for Thanksgiving and we need to get serious with him this time about a retirement comm.*

Chapter VI

I check my watch. It's 11:52, five minutes from 11:57, the time at which all clocks in this house stop.

For now the place is at peace again. Stevie is sleeping, still on his stomach. Night is calm now that the house is almost fully lit, even Grandpa's dusty electric globe. The hallway light, the one that went out and sent me into panic, remains dark - a dead bulb, that was all - but the rest of the house is brightly illuminated.

11:53.

I saw it and it saw me.

How did Grandpa's door inch open?

I try to think rationally. The wind. Yes, a draft from the wind. A dead bulb and the wind.

But what about the candle? The wind and the bulb and the candle, all within a few seconds?

BURN, DO NOT READ!

The book. BURN, DO NOT READ!

It's just a book, I tell myself. I'm a grown man afraid of a book? No, this won't work. No way.

I scramble down to the basement, searching for the room Grandpa described, anticipating, dreading, pulling every light string...but there is no room, at least not that I can see. Grandpa might have sealed it up like every other room in the house, but definitely not with duct tape.

11:56.

Back upstairs. Back to the guest room, a calm, yawning Night behind me.

The book waits on the bed, but I want to outlast it until midnight, proving to myself that the house won't spontaneously explode or cave in at 11:57. It's a senseless urge, I know, but sense has been in remarkably short supply tonight.

I check my watch. The minute hand has climbed even closer to 12, past that terrible equidistant place.

At last the hands meet. Feeling a little better (and yet still very childish), I climb back into bed and pull up the covers.

305

The book. I continue flipping through it, seeing one blank page after another.

Then another and another. For some reason I think about my watch. It tends to run fast.

There is a lost man wandering the fog – and a suited boy upon the sofa, the book eventually reads, and my initial terrors are quelled by the next line:

Peter died in his little suit, died in the middle of the road.

Grandpa was talking about Peter Elliott, I realize with a sigh, the boy he'd killed in the accident six years ago, not Stevie, who'd earlier been wearing a suit and is now sleeping on the sofa.

I read on despite wanting to stop, and it's like rolling down a steep hill without brakes. More blank pages, dozens of them, nothing all the way to the last page. No, this isn't the last page. It's stuck to the last page. I pull them apart, the smell of paint leaping out at me.

The red, streaky, somewhat smeared paint in the middle of this final page looks fresh, so fresh it might not be fully dry.

DON'T LOOK UP. IT'S ABOVE YOU.

Night bursts into snarling, bristling rage. But this time she's looking up at the ceiling directly above me, a wild, ruthless glint in her eyes.

I look up.

Chapter VII

Stevie Gibson, Jr., who, since becoming a teenager, had tried unavailingly to go by Steve Jr. at family events, was on the verge of sleep again when he sensed someone in the room. He'd turned onto his back. He'd remembered his times with Grandpa. He'd let those memories carry him high above his grief.

Now sleep was close, advancing tide-like to take him. But beyond his closed eyelids Stevie perceived brief movement – approaching and retreating and swaying – and then it was as if he were sunbathing and someone was hovering over him, eclipsing the sun.

There was a whispery exhalation to accompany the eclipse, passing coolly over his face like autumn night air.

Stevie's eyes shot open. He sat up, scanned the room. He was pretty sure Jon had turned on many of the lights during Night's last barking episode, but now only the candles daggered the dark, one up on the mantelpiece, another on the bookcase – yet still the living room was mostly black.

The creepy grandfather clock ticked in the corner.

It was raining heavily outside, the wind leaning stiffly into the house.

For a few wary moments, Stevie studied the darkened room without clarity now that he'd removed his contact lenses for the night. His head nestled comfortably in the hood of his sweatshirt, he should have been warm with the blankets pulled up tight – but a deep cold had trickled down to his bones.

Stevie didn't like this place, not even a little. Above all else, he didn't like what the house had done to Grandpa. He'd lost his mind here. He'd gone insane.

With a pang of guilt, thinking of Grandpa, Stevie remembered he'd forgotten to pray before bed. When he was alone he prayed aloud, though he was always too embarrassed to pray in his roommate's presence at the school or, in this case, with his cousin down the hall. But tonight he would at least pray silently, his mother having taught him to always thank God for daily blessings.

Our Father, who art in–

There was a creaking noise directly behind Stevie. It sounded very much like a single footstep.

Irrational fears skittered through him, conflicting with the shame of admitting fear. Still, Stevie was wholly and atavistically averse to turning around. He didn't want to look over his shoulder, just wanted to close his eyes and hide in the blankets, and that elicited an inner mortification. He was almost an adult – he had to look. His cell phone was right there on the table. He would click on the light and check the room.

But the dread was too sharp and heavy. For a moment he couldn't move.

More footsteps. They were coming from the hall. A shadow slid into view, the clock seeming to tick even louder, Stevie's heart jolting in his chest, a sick feeling in his gut.

"Couldn't sleep with all those lights on, huh?" came Jon's voice, and the living room light switched on, but as it did, with the millisecond transition from dark to light, Stevie thought he glimpsed something on the floor, a bulge thinning on Grandpa's mattress, the blankets flattening. Further back, the clock in that suspended moment was hooded, robed, razored, reaching.

Stevie leaped off the sofa, stared at the mattress, Jon's words gone from his head.

The mattress was empty, of course, the clock normal as well.

But perhaps Stevie really had seen something twining and withering amidst those blankets. Perhaps, for an obscene brevity, the clock really had become something else, for Jon was holding a book – and he looked even more frightened than Stevie felt.
"You'll never guess what I found," Jon said.

Chapter VIII

At the heart of the cold, dark forest lied a clearing. And at the center of that clearing stood a house, its lights burning bright as rain prevailed upon its roof. There wasn't another light for miles, the nearest neighbor far across a stretch of wilderness routinely patrolled by fog and beasts.

No one could hear Jon Gibson reading aloud to his cousin at that late hour, the rain and the wind and the clock equally persistent as Jon read, "Don't look up. It's above you."

"Holy shit!" Stevie glanced frantically about the room and up to the ceiling. His eyes wide and searching, contact lenses having been reinserted when Jon began reading, he sprang up from the sofa as he'd done a handful of times already, whenever his cousin had read something particularly disturbing.

"I was in bed when I read that," Jon said, still feeling a little shivery inside. "You wouldn't believe what happened. As soon as I read it, Night started growling and looking at the ceiling right above me."

Night was relatively calm for the moment, lying on Grandpa's mattress and keeping nervous watch of the room. She often looked behind her toward the hallway, then immediately up to the living room ceiling, then into the dining room, a repeating pattern, as though she were watching an invisible menace flit through the house.

Stevie grabbed his cell phone. "We need to get out of here. Now. This place freaks me out, Jon."

"No cell service tonight," Jon reminded, regretting having shown the book to Stevie. "Just relax, this is all a crazy coincidence. We're tired, it's a weird house, and Night's going nuts cuz she misses Grandpa. You saw shadows cuz your contacts were out. And the book's just making it all worse."

Stevie was pacing now, looking ridiculous in his boxers and black socks that stretched up to his knees, the hood of his sweatshirt pulled tightly over his head, his eyes red from the contacts being taken out and put back in place. Jon, in spite of his apprehension, nearly laughed at the sight of his cousin, but he knew he wouldn't be able to find humor much longer with the rain beating down and the clock ticking in the corner…and the book in their possession.

Still, Jon's fear had descended considerably from the apex, especially now that he was in the same room with Stevie and Night – and yet he wondered if everything really had been a series of coincidences. The power had gone out and there'd been strange sounds and the clock had started up again. Grandpa's door had clicked open. The hallway light had failed – *just a dead bulb* – and then the candle near Stevie had seen its flame go to smoke, all while Night barked and growled in the very house Grandpa had written those outrageous things, the very house whose windows he'd covered and doors he'd sealed.

Don't look up. It's above you.

"This place is haunted," Stevie said, almost in a whisper, his complexion losing its color. "Grandpa wasn't crazy – he wouldn't have written all of this unless it was true. Clearly this book was meant to warn us. Jon, we have to get out of here," and now his voice was pleading. He started toward the landline. "I'm calling my dad to come get us."

"Wait, let's just take a second and think," Jon said, trying to convince himself as much as Stevie, realizing just how ridiculous it would be for Uncle Steve to have to drive back over here because they were too afraid of a house in the woods.

For a moment Jon eyed the closed book, which sat arrogantly on the coffee table with its carved and painted front cover, demanding to be read again.

The paint on the last page smelled so fresh, Jon thought. *It's like the place came to life once we got here.*

"Suppose everything in this book is true," Jon continued. "Why wouldn't Grandpa just call the police, or at the very least let my Dad know about it during one of their calls?"

"Maybe It wouldn't let him," Stevie said, speaking softly, peeking over his shoulder and above him. "He said It wouldn't let him leave – maybe It wouldn't let him call either. There's something in here, Jon, I swear to God. I saw it!"

"But you're practically blind without your contacts."

"I know what I saw, okay? I saw it pass over me, then I heard something behind me. And you heard a noise earlier – face it, man, this place is fucked. We need to get out. *Now.*"

Panic flooding into his eyes, Stevie dug through his travel bag and found a pair of jeans. He jumped into them, then put on his sneakers. "I'll walk to the motel if I have to. I'm not spending another minute here."

"Okay, okay, call your dad. If you don't get him, I'll call my parents to come pick us up."

"*It comes in the darkness,*" Stevie repeated, his hands unsteady as he zipped up the bag.

He turned to Jon then with an awful torment in his eyes, a flickering color well beyond the black and gray of guilt and grief, beyond the bleary red irritation his contacts had caused, reflecting a deep burden

that could seemingly never be lifted. "Jon," he said flatly, "I think whatever's in this house killed Grandpa."

Jon pulled Stevie into a hug, his cousin's words scaring him even worse than the book. "It's okay, it's fine – we're gonna get out of here. Don't let that book get to you. Grandpa was drinking again and I think he kind of lost it. Now we're the ones losing it. This place isn't haunted, at least not literally."

BURN, DO NOT READ!

Chapter IX

The call to Uncle Steve went to voicemail, but Robert Gibson answered after a few rings.

Rob, alarmed by Jon's brief descriptions of the book, agreed to drive to the house and pick them up.

"My dad's coming right now," Jon told Stevie, who grinned as though he'd won the lottery. The night had softened him, worn him down, and now he looked exceedingly young and vulnerable and afraid. "I'm gonna go pack up my stuff."

As Jon had expected, he found himself followed to the guest room not only by Night but Stevie as well. There were no thumps elsewhere in the house now, no strange noises or lights turning out, and Jon, separated even further from his once brimming fear, found the whole thing to be almost laughable. Grandpa, it turned out, had been drinking again – and if he'd been routinely getting drunk, there was no telling what could've popped into his head. Certainly the guilt from killing Peter Elliott had been prominent in his mind, for the boy's name had made it into the book, as had Grandma's name. Perhaps the entire thing had just been a drunken, guilt-induced debacle of a project, a senseless piece that, under the wrong circumstances, could engender profound levels of terror within its readers.

It comes in the darkness, for example, would be frightening in any lonely hotel room or beside a forest campfire, but they were just words, just scary words written by an isolated, regretful, likely drunk man in his house in the middle of the woods, a man remembering the little boy he'd killed and the wife he'd lost, a man with too much time on his hands and not nearly enough support from his loved ones. But he'd pushed everyone away, even his friends who'd dropped by to check on him – he'd pushed them all away and written warnings to be interpreted in any number of ways by those who found them. Then he'd spread

315

newspapers across the windows and taped up the doors, Jon beginning to think Grandpa's mind had been like a pool of water cupped within two palms; eventually, for a man living in such conditions, the water

had been destined to leak out, Grandpa's demons overwhelming him, their conquest paved with every can of beer.

Had Jon known about his grandfather's own grandfather's fate, he would have arrived at an even firmer conclusion. But instead…

Don't look up. It's above you. What the hell was that all about? And Night, sweet, loving Night – she'd exacerbated the entire thing tonight, glancing up to the ceiling and growling precisely when Jon had been shaken by those words. But they were just words, figurative representations of Grandpa's problems and weaknesses, "It" no more than a metaphor for the consuming guilt and addiction. The longer Jon thought about the contents of the book, the more sense his theory made. *I let it out, and I fear it will eventually kill me* – what a powerful symbol for alcohol. And, *It comes in the darkness* seemed like the perfect way to describe his guilt. The entire thing had been a desperate alcohol-driven compulsion, Jon imagined, Grandpa's deepest troubles flowing out onto the paper, sometimes with ink and other times with paint.

Jon felt better now, ready to move past the house and its darkness. As he put on tomorrow's clothes and made the bed he wouldn't be sleeping in tonight, Stevie rummaged through the boxes in the closet, where Jon had told him he'd found the book.

"There's another one!" he gasped, his head buried in a box. "Jon, it's another book!"

Night barked sharply, looking out into the hallway, Jon recoiling at the suddenness of it all.

"Another book?" Jon said unhappily. He started toward his kneeling cousin, who was trying to wrench the book free of the box, a battle he

316

won with some difficulty, extracting a book identical in size and color to the other one, though the front cover was smooth, unblemished. "It doesn't have a title," Stevie said, a curious yet apprehensive tone to his voice. He rotated on his knees to face Jon. "Should we read it?"

Night whimpered, then walked between them and sniffed the book. There was a strange moment of anticipation, Night regarding both of them worriedly, as if she might open her mouth and tell them to throw the book away. Eventually she shook her head forcefully enough to snap her ears, hopped up to the bed, and sighed, her head lowered to her forepaws.

"I guess we have to read it," Jon said. "If we don't, my Dad will."

Stevie, who'd seemed emboldened ever since learning that Jon's father was coming to their rescue, said, "If it's creepy, I'm stopping and waiting till we're at the motel. Wait a sec." The book tucked beneath his arm, he went to the door and shut it, then slid the latch in place. "Okay," he said, exhaling, and began…

"I have seen this house for what it is now, seen it for just a second of perfect clarity, but that was all it took."

Stevie stopped, bit his lip, looked at Jon as though to make sure he was still there, and Jon launched into his ideas pertaining to symbols and metaphors, Stevie nodding but not seeming to buy any of it. "You read," he said, and handed the book to Jon.

The writing undoubtedly belonged to Grandpa, the same hurried scrawls that had filled the other book, but a quick flip-through revealed no red paint or extended stretches of blank pages.

Jon went back to the beginning, resuming where Stevie had left off.

"There's something dark in these foggy woods tonight. There's darkness in the house too. A man gave me fair warning, you know. He said it was a house of tricks."

"*What?*" Stevie interrupted. "A house of *tricks?*"

"That's what Grandpa wrote. What's the big deal?"

"I heard a guy say that after the funeral," Stevie said, remembering. "At the country club – he said house of tricks when I went by. I didn't know he was talking about Grandpa's house."

"Which guy was that?"

"I dunno, an old guy. They were all old guys."

Jon shrugged. "Grandpa probably filled their heads with this stuff."

Stevie was looking at the book. "Keep going."

Jon nodded, found his place. Outside, the rain was relenting.

"I've seen Mrs. Scrivens hanging in the basement. She was there but then she wasn't. That's what this house does to you, messes with your head. You don't realize what's happening until it's too late, but It's always there. It might have even chosen me, and soon it will have me but only the body, never the soul. I finally found God last night."

Jon had to repeat the line, wondering if he'd misread. Yes, Grandpa had really written that. "I finally found God last Night. Peter showed me the way. I was so afraid, so resistant. Peter has always lurked in my darkest thoughts, but last night he came to me in his bloody suit and there was light. He still hasn't found his other shoe and his face is a mess, but that's just the body, he told me, not the soul. That's just the temporary life, the imperfect life, he said, not the eternal life. It is how I will always remember Peter, but it is not him, not anymore. I wanted to run, wanted to find somewhere to hide, but Peter extended his hand to me, the man who killed him, and still he reached out his little hand to me. I was scared out of my senses, but then I thought what Mary would do, what Mary would want me to do."

Night stormed into a barking rage. She was staring with darting eyes up at the ceiling, following the path of some unseen object. "Holy shit, it's here. *It's* here!" Stevie panicked. "We need to get out, Jon!"

Again Jon felt danger peeking in on him, Night's rage still fixed upon the ceiling. *She's just barking at the rain on the roof,* he thought, but the sustained madness of the night had led to psychological attrition. He'd thought the answers had come definitively to him, ending the seemingly insoluble puzzle of Grandpa's final weeks, but now he didn't know what to think.

"Let's get out of here," he agreed.

Jon slid the latch back.

Opened the door.

Poked his head into the hallway.

Felt very much like a child.

Heard the ticking clock.

The hallway was empty, Jon suddenly swallowed by fear. The house felt completely different somehow, yet absolutely nothing had changed – and that was the most frightening part. The clock was still ticking. The lights remained lit (excluding the hallway light). There was nothing out of place as they hurried to the front door, Jon leading the way, but the house felt infinitely heavier than before, threatening, a guillotine blade about to fall.

Jon opened the front door and stared out into the black, rainy night. The wind chimes were calling gently, the storm slowly moving away, and together they leaped off the porch as if chased by flames and jogged to the driveway, Night right there with them.

Stevie was panting lightly, not from exertion. "Are we far enough away, you think? Should we go to the road?"

Night growled at the house, hackles raised.

Jon, ignoring the cold rain on his face, stared through the lighted windows…and he thought he saw something in there, something black

and angling. "My dad will be here soon," he said, turning away. "Let's just wait – there's nothing in the house, Stevie. It's just our imaginations."

"And Night's too? The place is haunted, I'm telling you. *It* is real, Jon."

That two-letter word made Jon crawl with something unpleasant. His stomach felt a little queasy. "It's not haunted," he said without conviction.

They waited, looking guardedly at the house. Night didn't lose interest and roam the yard, didn't even take a pee break, watching the house closely and the woods as well. Protecting them.

Minutes passed slowly, Jon at times thinking he heard noises above the rain – which had lightened almost to a drizzle – rustling in the woods, scraping on the roof, thudding from within the house. Sometimes he thought he heard noises behind them, footsteps crunching down the driveway.

But each time he searched there was only the rainy dark to be found, and a house, a weird house in the middle of the woods, a house where Jack Gibson had been found dead of a heart attack, a house where a book had waited to be read, a book titled, Burn, Do Not Read!

Another noise behind them, a hollow snap, and Jon spun around to the sight of approaching headlights. Though he would never admit to the relief that surged through him in that moment, it was as absolute as the darkness.

Chapter X

Now that Robert Gibson was there, they found the strength to reenter the house. When Stevie elaborated on everything they'd read and their reactions to it, Jon's father looked at him like he was insane.

But Jon backed his cousin up. "It's pretty crazy, Dad. Wait till you read it – Grandpa was a lot more messed up than any of us thought."

Robert tiredly rubbed his eyes. "You don't need a book to tell you that. Just look at what he did with the house."

"He was drinking again, too," Jon said. "We found beers in the fridge."

"Yeah, Paul and I saw those, too. He said he'd get rid of them but apparently forgot," Robert confessed with a noisy sigh. "Look, guys, there's no other way to put this. Your grandfather obviously got into a real bad way in this house. In hindsight, I should have just dropped everything and flown out here when the calls started getting weird."

They stood in a tight circle in the living room, listening to the clock's unflagging fulfillment of obligation. In a moment Jon retrieved the books and handed them to his father, who began reading the second book. It wasn't long before he reread certain lines and made incredulous comments.

Finally Robert reached the part they hadn't gotten to, both Jon and Stevie shifting with anticipation.

"I want you all to know I took Peter's hand and found the way to God," Robert read slowly, his finger tracing each line as if he were struggling through a book written in another language. "Now you must do the same. It's the only way to survive this house. Disregard my instructions in the previous book. God is the only way out."

"Jesus Christ," Robert muttered. "There's more, too."

"What's it say?" Stevie said eagerly. In the foyer, remaining by the front door, Night was blinking unhappily at them.

Robert continued, "I saw it and it saw me, and it told me I'm too far out this time, can't get back to shore. I'm coming for you, Jackie, don't look behind you, it said, I'm everywhere, Jackie, and then it was dragging me toward the basement, couldn't get away, and I already knew the pain of forever. I could feel myself starting to burn, it's like slowly bringing your hand down over a candle until you can't take it anymore, but then it stopped, disappeared."

Eyes wide, Robert went quiet, reading along on his own.

"Keep reading!" Stevie implored, and Robert, as if he'd been so captivated by Grandpa's words that he'd forgotten he had an audience, glanced confusedly at them. "Right, sorry, guys," he said.

"I looked up and Peter was there. He was smiling. He told me morning does welcome those who die – it's just a different kind of morning. He told me there's a place where time doesn't exist. He told me I'll see Mary again if I just believe, just believe now, and I took his hand. It was so cold, his little hand, and the blood won't leave his face, and his sock, forever separated from the shoe, such a terrible fate. But it's just the body, not the soul, it's just the haunt of memory, not how things really are – and even a man consumed by darkness can find the light, he said. I know I must find the light, for it still watches me from down the hallway. I can see it, just barely, and I can feel how close it came to ending me. Even now, it's waiting for me to make the wrong move again, to fall back into the darkness. If you look hard enough, you can probably see it too, but it can't hurt you, not if you believe. I've been blind all these years, miserably blind, but the light has been waiting for me to come around, just like Mary wanted, so I can embrace a life where time is not marked by the ticking clock."

Robert licked his finger, turned the page. "There's only one more line, guys. It says, Morning DOES welcome those who die."

Robert Gibson could tolerate nothing further from his father's writings, at least not tonight. "Let's get back to the motel."

"But what about the other book?" Stevie said. "Aren't you gonna read it?"

"Tomorrow," Rob groaned, his eyes drifting loathingly about the living room. "I'm exhausted, guys. Let's all just try to get some sleep."

Both books in hand, Rob led them outside, into the cold dark. The rain had stopped, residual spatters rising up from the woods. Without a word the three of them slid into Rob's rental car, Night taking the back seat beside Stevie, who began rereading the first book as he scratched Grandpa's dog beneath the collar.

"Tell you what, guys, how about we keep these books between us for now?" Rob said, slowly easing the car around the driveway loop, and now they were headed out, away from the house. "Grandpa wouldn't want everyone reading his private thoughts – there's a lot of personal material in those books. As you both know, he was very disturbed. I don't think he ever recovered from killing that poor kid, and writing seems to have been a sort of release for him."

"That's what I was thinking," Jon said, looking back to the house as they came to the curve at the edge of the black pond.

Though Jon was positive they hadn't turned off all of the lights, not a single bulb was burning back there, the place completely dark, one with the woods.

***

The next morning there was no fog, the woods limned with glinting sunlight and cascading shadows. It was a better day already. Checking his watch, Stephen Gibson counted the hours until his flight that evening. He could hardly wait to depart this dreary town and get to the airport, where he would board a plane and get back to his life.

The others were busying themselves again as they had yesterday, packing and cleaning in what seemed to be an interminable process. But what did any of it matter? *Just burn the damn house and be done with it*, Steve thought as he stood on the porch, smoking and brooding and staring out across the lawn. *You should have listened to me, Dad. You should have gone to that retirement community.*

Steve was shaking his head, a victorious wisp of a smile playing across his lips at the realization that a very sharp thorn had been extracted from his foot, the road to the presidency cleared of an obstacle. Now there would be no more worrying about what Dad might do if he fell off the wagon, no more fearing another call about some dead kid in the road, no drunken skeletons for the media to pull out of the closet.

The past will just fade away now. One less thing to manage.

The door opened behind him, footsteps coming up quietly on Steve. A hand on his shoulder. "We were thinking you might like to have the grandfather clock," his wife said, smiling pityingly.

Steve sneered. He couldn't recall the last time his wife had wanted sex, and yet here she was acting like she still cared about him, acting like there was a single meaningful shred left in their marriage, besides the fact that it was still intact, which of course helped preserve the image that needed to be presented to facilitate progression in the game.

Steve waved a hand, flicked his cigarette onto the soaked ground below the porch. "Why would I want the stupid clock?"

Flinching, she said, "Don't you want a few things to remember your dad by? It's such a beautiful clock, Steve – your mom loved that clock. Rob said it's yours if you want it. You really ought to be more involved in this process."

"Why? This place is dead to me," Steve said curtly, crossing his arms and lifting his chin. "Nothing here justifies the cost to ship it across the country."

"You should have the clock, Steve," his wife insisted. "I think in time you'll be glad you took it."

"Fine, fine, we'll take the clock if it's so goddamn important," and he turned from her, exiting the porch from the other end, wanting only to be left alone with his developing headache, but now it was Stevie seeking his attention.

"Hey, Dad, Uncle Rob wants you to come in and look at Grandma's old jewelry," his son said from the doorway. "He said I could have a few of her crucifixes."

Steve blew out a frustrated breath. He'd almost made it out of sight. Almost, but now he had to hear from his unfathomably religious son, a kid who actually liked going to church and wore a stupid cross around his neck but couldn't behave to save his life at school. At least this semester he'd been better...so far. "Why would you want those?" Steve said, and Stevie's smile wilted.

"Stephen!" his wife scolded. "How could you say something like that?"

Steve shrugged. "Go for it, kid. Take all the little Jesus and Mary figurines while you're at it. Maybe they'll give you some sense next time you're about to make a dumbass decision."

***

Later, while the others were eating grinders and pizza they'd ordered for lunch, Rob quietly summoned Jon and Stevie into the basement.

"I've read both books three times now," Rob told them, "and I'm not sure I'll ever make sense of everything Grandpa wrote. A lot of that stuff...it's just bizarre. Anyway, I did a little searching down here and" – he was leading them toward the workbench at the far end of the basement – "I found the room your grandfather was talking about."

Jon and Stevie exchanged nervous glances as Rob removed tall stacks of boxes from the workbench, then dragged the bench forward – and there it was, a thin, splintered wooden door inset shallowly in the

concrete wall. It was black and grim, about two feet wide, with dozens of tiny circular wounds indicating where nails had gone recklessly in and subsequently found themselves ripped out. The lower half of the door had been occluded by the workbench, the upper half blocked from view by the tower of boxes stacked atop it.

"I found it this morning," Rob said. "I had to put the bench back in place and pile all the boxes up like they were so no one would see it. Last thing I want is to get everyone riled up with speculation."

Stevie flattened a palm against the door, traced his fingers across the nail holes. His hand drifted to the rusty knob, lingered there momentarily, then snapped away. "Have you looked inside?" he asked Rob.

Nodding, Jon's father pulled open the door, its hinges creaking in protest, Jon and Stevie peering curiously into a square, windowless room not in excess of five-by-five.

Stevie took a cautious step into the room, looking back at them as if asking permission to enter. "Go ahead," Rob said. "There's nothing in there."

"This is the room where Grandpa found *It*," Stevie commented once they were inside, but Rob quickly dismissed the idea.

"This is the room," Rob corrected, "where your grandfather *thought* he heard voices after having a few too many beers. The rest was just his imagination, Stevie. I know the books were scary – even for me – but all of it was your grandfather's imagination."

Jon wanted to expand on his father's remarks, but Stevie spoke first. "Those books were messed up," he said quietly, his eyes wandering up and down the room's uneven brick walls. There were no closets or alcoves, just a square of brick, the raftered ceiling thick with cobwebs.

They were about to leave when Stevie, always observant, kneeled down and squinted at the base of the door. "There's names here," he noticed, blowing dust away and coughing. "Scratched into the wood."
Rob, eyebrows raised, retrieved a thin flashlight from his jeans pocket and beamed it upon the door. "Mary," he read. "Peter. Jack. Tommy. Janine. Richie." He looked up at them. "It has most of our names, too. Looks like Grandpa carved them into the door with a pocketknife or something – took him a long time to get them this legible."

Stevie glanced at Jon with great consternation in his green eyes, not the eyes of a teenager who'd downed his grandfather's beer last night but the eyes of a frightened boy. "What if it wasn't Grandpa who did that? And who are Tommy, Janine, and Richie?"

"Could be Peter's family," I said.

"Maybe," Rob added. "Grandpa connected with them after Peter's death, but those names aren't familiar."

Stevie grimaced in dismay. "But why would he come all the way down here and carve everyone's name into the bottom of a door?"

"For the same reason he covered up all the windows and taped the doors," Rob said. Underscoring his words, he pulled loose a section of bricks along the far wall a moment later and revealed a little stash of liquor (mostly Jack Daniels).

Stevie said nothing further. He examined the names once more, then, with a shrug, left the basement and did not return. Later, when he and Jon reconvened out back, Stevie said, "Guess we'll never know what really happened, but at least Grandpa's away from this house. He's in a better place now."

Having grabbed a bottle of J.D. down in the basement, Jon poured each of them a shot in a pair of plastic cups. "To Grandpa. May he rest in peace."

"To Grandpa. Amen to that."

***

The next chess club meeting, at Oscar Montoya's request, began with a moment of silence to honor the life of Jack Gibson. The nine of them sat there in silence, a few of them holding hands – Larry pulling his hand free of the Doritos bag to do so – until Oscar finally told them it was time to get the games on.

There would be an odd man out for the foreseeable future, now that their group had been reduced from ten to nine, and Oscar knew they had to begin searching for a new member. But not too soon. Oscar was adamant about that – Jack's seat at the table would remain unfilled for a time, because sometimes in life things needed to be as they ought to be, even if they were strange or uncomfortable.

"I feel terrible about missing the funeral. Absolutely terrible," Oscar said. At the moment he was the odd man out, watching a game between Henry Howard and Charlie Andersen.

Charlie's brother Patrick had pulled up a chair beside Oscar. On nights when Patrick had nothing better to do, he enjoyed stopping by the chess club and ragging on his brother's poor moves. Perhaps, if they were unlucky enough, he would eventually become the tenth member.

"Don't beat yourself up, Oscar," Henry said. "Everyone knows you wanted to be there. What you just did with that moment of silence would mean more to Jack than anything they said at the funeral."

The others nodded, and after a while Patrick murmured, "It's the house that got him. That house is bad news, real bad news."

A leaden silence loomed, broken only by the sound of Larry's hand delving into the Doritos bag.

"It's not the house," Oscar said at last, unable to let the comment go. "Let's not open up that can of worms, Pat. Jack certainly wasn't the healthiest guy." Last night, on the phone, Oscar had informed Robert Gibson about his father's drinking, specifically his wild night at the wedding. And Robert had proceeded to tell Oscar about Jack's alcoholism, a revelation like a punch to the stomach.
Now Oscar was left cold and convinced that he could have done more to help Jack, or at least recognize where the signs were pointing.

"It was a heart attack, plain and simple – had nothing to do with the house," Henry said, scowling coldly at Pat.

No one really cared for Pat all that much; he rarely even played games when he came around because he thought he was too good for everyone (*I can spank you people with one eye and no queen*). And if you dared to give him a little dose of his own ribbing, he would become pouty and self-pitying, saying things like, *Sure, go ahead, kick a guy when he's down,* or, *Real nice, beat up the cripple some more, why dontcha?*

For Oscar, Pat's tireless rumors were even more annoying than his insults and pomposity.

"You fellows can think what you'd like, but I know that house is big trouble," Pat maintained. "Real big trouble. Kills everyone who owns it. Who knows, maybe it kills everyone who steps inside it."

"It didn't kill Tommy Talbot," Henry retorted, and Oscar had to look away. None of them knew about Tommy, that he'd died almost a year ago in a freak accident, falling off a ladder while helping to renovate his new church. The only reason Oscar had learned of his death was because his wife had been close with Tommy's wife, Janine.

Pat was refreshingly silent for a while, his stubborn mind like a spinning tire in the snow, desperate to crank out a response. Then, in his odd way, he said, "I'll never forget that bit of writing Tommy's boy, Richie, turned in about the house writing its own story. Strangest thing, really. I've always had a nose for plagiarism, and I wonder from time to time if he really wrote that piece, or if he found it somewhere…else."

***

Robert ended up caring for Night over a brief period. No one else, besides Stevie and Jon, had expressed a willingness to adopt the dog, but Stevie was at boarding school and knew he couldn't take on the responsibility of a pet. And Jon was living in a no-pets-allowed apartment, leaving Rob as guardian by process of elimination.

But Rob had never been a pet person, and so he wound up giving Night to his neighbor, Mrs. Hutton, who'd owned dogs for most of her life. Her husband had died a year ago, as had one of her golden retrievers, and it just so happened that Night fit in great with her other two dogs, an aging golden and a lab mix puppy. Additionally, there was plenty of room for Night to hunt and run on Mrs. Hutton's fenced, two-acre property, and Rob knew he was doing right by his father's dog.

Up in Heaven, Dad would certainly approve.

***

Eight years later, Stephen Gibson was staring absently at the grandfather clock, the one his wife had insisted he take from Dad's old place. Steve didn't mind the clock so much. Its hourly chimes reminded him that, for a man in his lofty position, time was on his side.

Steve had risen quickly to the top of the party. Soon he would embark on a run for the presidency, at which time he would reluctantly cease his weekly sessions with young women disguised as meetings with constituents and backers. The scrutiny of a presidential run was fierce, far too intense to get away with the tricks of a senator.

But for now he could still indulge in the tight, youthful pleasures that helped him forget his fattening wife and a personal life from which he often felt the need to abscond. He could feel young again, young and wanted, all while maintaining his elevated position in the game.

"I've got a meeting tonight," Steve told his wife on the phone a few hours later, while making little spins in his office chair. He'd found that such conversations were easier conducted from afar, when she couldn't search his eyes, though in recent years she hadn't been nearly as suspicious of his nighttime rendezvous.

"Okay," she said flatly, getting Steve to thinking once again that she, too, had something cooking on the side. If so, he could only hope she employed the same cautions as he to avoid getting caught. It didn't matter to Steve if they only spoke to each other at public functions when he was president – as long as they looked the part, they didn't even have to make eye contact in private.

But looking the part, of course, meant his wife would need to commence a regimented weight loss program – a topic imminent for discussion.

"I'll see you when I get home then," Steve said, glancing out his window and imagining a far more impressive office.

"Have a good day, Steve."

Stephen Gibson never made it home that night. At sunset, his vehicle veered off the road into a tree, and he wasn't wearing a seatbelt. Later, a jogger who'd witnessed the one-vehicle crash would tell police he'd seen someone dash out into the middle of the road, forcing the driver of the wrecked sedan to swerve.

"It all happened so fast," the jogger reported. "I was facing west, looking into the sun, so I can't be sure how old the person was, but judging by the height it looked like a kid. Just ran out into the road, then disappeared."

***

Robert Gibson and his wife enjoyed a full life together, Rob eventually leaving the firm to pursue a career in what became his true passion: teaching. He spent eight years teaching high school history, then finished his working life as an adjunct professor at a rural college, discussing politics every Tuesday and law every Thursday. His

students, always engaged and dedicated, made it a joy to come to class, and Rob didn't retire until he was nearly eighty years young.

Jon Gibson, as his grandfather had predicted, wound up reporting for the New York Times, beginning his coverage in the political arena and shifting his focus after five years to Wall Street news. He rarely thought of the night he'd spent with Stevie at his grandfather's house, but sometimes, when things were quiet and he didn't have much to do, he remembered everything that had happened and wondered, *What if...?*

Stevie Gibson relied heavily on faith to find the strength to balance his medical school and work responsibilities in the wake of his father's death. He hadn't wanted to take up politics as many people close to him suggested – hadn't wanted to follow in his father's footsteps – instead forging his own path. And his tenacious commitment eventually earned him residency as a surgeon at a leading program in Massachusetts. He'd been only fifteen that night at his grandfather's house, and so it had faded to the depths of his mind as youthful memories often do, returning to him very sporadically, usually at family get-togethers when there was talk of Grandpa and Grandma and things long past. In time that night left him altogether. He worked long hours at the hospital, saving countless lives as a trauma surgeon, and the hours he wasn't working were devoted to his wife and daughters. There was no time to dwell on the past, not with such a bright present to warm him.

Night lived a long, happy life under the care of Mrs. Hutton, barking only when strangers came to the door or a skunk's odor slipped through the windows. She never fully relinquished hope that her old masters would one day come back for her, wagging her tail in the car whenever she spotted someone on the sidewalk who resembled Jack or Mary, the source of her spontaneous joy unknown to Mrs. Hutton. But Night's hopes slowly dwindled with the years, her old and new lives synthesizing.

She died comfortably on Mrs. Hutton's bed just before her sixteenth birthday.

Jack Gibson's books – Burn, Do Not Read! and its untitled sibling – inhabited the same box of **DAD'S THINGS** for decades, a duct-taped, nondescript box in Robert's attic, sitting unassumingly among a stack of other boxes. Rob didn't open the box again until he was a very old man, with three great-grandchildren and two legs that barely got him around anymore.

On Thanksgiving weekend, guided by a strange nostalgic impulse to look through his old things, Rob had asked his grandsons to retrieve a few of the boxes from the attic. Now, having uncovered the untitled leather-bound book, Rob gathered his reading glasses with shaking hands. A nervous flitter cooled his gut. He couldn't remember what this book had contained all those years ago, but pangs of dusty, unpleasant memory fired up when he pulled open the cover.

"Oh, yes, that's right," he said. "What a strange place that was."

Rob read interestedly through the book, though at first the words sprawling across the pages were mostly foreign to him. It even took him a few moments to remember who Peter Elliott was, but what else could be expected after so many years?

"That was a bad house for you, Dad," he muttered at last, closing the book and looking down at its sibling, his eyes wandering across the faded marks and colors of, Burn, Do Not Read!

And, as would almost every sound-minded, reasonable person in his position, Rob Gibson opened the book and read.

Sitting in his study, reading his father's book by the early evening light, memories drifted back to Rob with each passing page. But on the very last page (which had been stuck nearly to the point of ripping its precursor), the writing took an unfamiliar journey after MORNING DOES NOT WELCOME THOSE WHO DIE, Rob convinced he'd never read these next lines before. Surely he would have remembered…

I have heard this is a house of tricks, a house that writes its own story, but it cannot alter my story. I wish that final night could be erased and rewritten, but time, it moves backwards for no man.

Mary. Mary, my sweet, beautiful wife, I failed you. I'll never know if you needed me on your last night because I wasn't there, sweetheart, I wasn't there for you. Can you ever forgive me? You're in a beautiful place, Mary, and I'm still here, wishing I could go back and change that night.

Peter tells me you're waiting for me. He tells me not to beat myself up, but I was drunk that night and I have to get it off my chest. I must confess my sins and find peace with myself. I led you to believe I'd fully recovered, but I was drinking in the basement that night, Mary, and it wasn't the first time I left you and fell asleep down there. I remember watching the clock around midnight, thinking I would come up soon, and then I just nodded off. Peter was on my mind, of course he was, but that's no excuse. I failed you again, let you sleep all alone. I came up very late, didn't even kiss you goodnight, just slid into bed, afraid you might smell the stuff, God forgive me, and in the morning you were gone because ~~morning~~ well, Peter says morning does welcome those who die. He says he would make the sacrifice again, for all that was really lost that day was the temporary. His death was not in vain, he says, for with it the saving of a soul was set into motion.

I love you, Mary, and I hope to see you very soon. Please find it in your heart to forgive me. It's been a terrible weight to carry all these years, so much guilt thinking you might have suffered before you died. Did you call out to me for help? Could I have done something for you that night, maybe gotten you to a doctor? I'll never know how you were feeling because I wasn't there.

Peter tells me to let it go, just let it go. It will all be different soon, he promises, because this is only the imperfect life. I pray we will be together again.

Rob closed the book and smiled, glad to know Dad had found a little peace at the very end. Growing sleepy, Rob returned the books to the darkened annals of possessions accumulated and forgotten, wondering oddly if the pages just might allow themselves to go blank now that the story was conveyed, its author at eternal rest.

In another place, having been carefully restored, the grandfather clock continued its diligent observation of that which can never be recovered or outrun or even delayed, at least not in this life.

Many hours later, when morning finally came around with its welcoming light, the grandfather clock's chiming song heralded the arrival of a new day. Children would sit restlessly in churches. Travelers would begin their journeys. The expected and the unexpected would accept their assignments without question.

And a new family would move into a little house in the middle of the big woods, its story not yet told.

MEET THE AUTHOR

A lifelong resident of Massachusetts, Kevin Flanders has written over ten novels and multiple short stories. In 2010, he graduated from Franklin Pierce University with a degree in mass communications, then served as a reporter for several newspapers.

When he isn't writing, Flanders enjoys spending time with his family and two dogs, playing ice hockey, and traveling to a new baseball stadium with his father each summer. He also takes part in several functions and mentors student writers, currently serving as a guest instructor at David Prouty High School in Spencer, MA.

But no matter where Flanders travels or who he meets along the way, he's always searching for inspiration for the next project.

The author resides in Monson, MA.

For more information about upcoming works, visit
www.kmflanders.wordpress.com.

UP NEXT

WELCOME TO HARROW HALL
Jan. 2016

…Through the burning cymbal crashes of pain he searched for Vicky, though there was nothing but falling snow beyond the wall now, falling, falling, falling relentlessly, as though Vicky had never been there, only the snow and a dream of her hand in his, a dream destined not for recollection because magic wasn't real.

INSIDE THE ORANGE GLOW
Feb. 2016

… He had to get inside, had to find a way to keep from crumbling. But as he started toward the house, a presentiment whisked a deep chill through his bones. He thought of the groaning tree and the fleeing birds, and somehow – impossibly yet unmistakably – he sensed the evil that was coming for him.

Made in the USA
Columbia, SC
03 September 2019